Copyright 2023 Cal Clement
All Rights Reserved

*The characters and events portrayed within are fictitious.
Any similarities to real persons, alive or dead, is coincidental and not intended by the author.*

No part of this book may be reproduced or stored in a retrieval system or transmitted in any form or by any means, electronic, mechanical, photocopying, recording or otherwise without express written permission of the author.

ISBN-978-1-7376655-6-4

Cover Artist: Juan Padron
Printed in the United States of America

This one is for Jerry

Smooth seas don't make skilled sailors.

UNDER THE BLACK FLAG

by Cal Clement

PART ONE
"Hoist the Colors"

1

'H.M.S North Wind'
12 May 1809
17 degrees 43' N, 76 Degrees 25' W

A crack of lightning split the sky. It sent a flash of light through the storm cloud darkened sky and brought into clear focus an image that sent a chill through Lieutenant William Pike's veins. He was facing three enemy vessels amid a furious storm. One of those ships he had already watched sink below the waves in a cove along the Haitian coast. Another of the ships was sporting red sails, an ominous sign. The third ship seemed to sail in a more haphazard fashion than the other two, like her crew wasn't well seasoned to sailing in foul weather. The roar of cannons intermixed with rolling thunder and sent a screaming whistle through the wind and rain. He braced himself for the impact and opened his mouth to scream at the rest of the crew to take cover. Before his voice could form the words impacts tore into North Wind and threw him down onto the deck. Wood cracked and splintered. A hail of debris flew. Lines snapped and recoiled like deadly serpents over the deck of the ship. They had gotten the drop on him. He was outnumbered and positioned at a disadvantage. A thought crossed his mind as he lay on the rain soaked and windswept deck of North Wind, a memory of Captain Grimes and the Valor. Lieutenant Pike forced himself to his knees. A fresh gale blew droplets of rain into his face. The Maiden was sailing close to the ship with red sails while the third had made a clumsy tack and was struggling to right her course and remain with the others.

"Master at arms, prepare a boarding party." Lieutenant Pike called out across the deck, "Quartermaster, give them a broadside and then come about on that separated ship."

"Aye, aye!" the response seemed to come all at once from both men.

North Wind deck shifted with a tremble as her helmsman brought the starboard side battery to bear down onto the pair of reeling pirate vessels. Lieutenant Pike could see the flurry of activity on their decks. They were making ready to fire again while also dealing with the howling wind and waves. In this, he had a significant advantage. North Wind was a massive vessel and much better suited to slugging through the foul weather. He also had an overwhelming number of guns. Each broadside from North Wind would overpower the total number of guns from both vessels. Lightning split through the sky again as North Wind's broadside aligned to the Drowned Maiden and the ship with red sails. The cry rose on deck and was repeated below an instant before cannons began firing in a deadly droll that drowned away the thunder and sent a plume of smoke into the storm whipped air.

Lieutenant Pike fixed his stare onto the two vessels and watched for the effect of North Wind's broadside. To his delight a scatter of impacts scored hits onto the Drowned Maiden hitting her railing and hull in several places. The vessel with red sails did not escape unscathed either, a flurry of wooden planks and shards of debris could be seen flying through the air. The lieutenant narrowed his eyes and waited for the report that his batteries were reloaded. He glanced over at the third vessel which had drifted away from the first two. The plan Lieutenant Pike had formed was coming together, though it was a slippery thing, the smallest change could throw it off.

"They are turning to, sir! Looks like they've had enough!" a voice shouted from the starboard stern up to where Lieutenant Pike was standing.

"Very well, come about on our target. Let her taste the larboard battery and bring us up into pistol range!" the lieutenant shouted back. "Master at arms have your men ready to board!"

"Aye, sir!" the master at arms replied in a grizzled voice.

North Wind's decks shifted hard as the helmsman brought her around to bear down on the third vessel.

Lieutenant Pike stole fleeting glances as the Maiden and the red sailed ship. They had turned back with the wind to limp away and deal with their damage and wounded.

"Larboard batteries, ready!" a voice echoed up from the gun decks.

Lieutenant Pike turned and nodded to the quartermaster as the ship came into alignment with the remaining enemy vessel. Whoever was sailing it was unaccustomed to foul weather, her turns were dogged and sloppy, her sail handling looked as if it were being performed by amateurs.

"Fire!" a voice screamed out from the gun decks.

The roar of reports blended in a near simultaneous volley that trembled through the deck boards of North Wind and sent another billow of gun smoke whirling into the air. The sound of impacts followed. Wood split and shattered from a series of hits while several plumes of seawater rose high into the air from misses. Voices cried out from the deck of the enemy vessel in tones of pain and panic.

"Hard a-starboard!" A shout rang up from the quarterdeck.

Lieutenant Pike could feel the blood in his veins go cold. A series of shouts floated over the washing waves between North Wind and the enemy vessel. Panicked cries mixed with screams of the wounded as the sound of cracking wood split through the storm. Men jumped from the enemy vessel into the sea as the main mast wavered and shuddered. The splintering sound of cracking and twisting wood announced the doom of the ship as her main mast tipped and came crashing down into the storm-tossed waves. A shout of celebration rose from the deck of North Wind and Lieutenant Pike felt the chill in his blood boil away.

"Hold your cheers!" He shouted over the men, "The job is not done! Hold your cheers! We will board her and take the ship and whatever prisoners we can. Do no harm to anyone who surrenders."

North Wind's decks shifted again as the helmsman steered her onto a course to come alongside the wounded enemy ship. Sailors and marines gathered on the larboard rail with weapons in hand and tucked into their waistlines. Looks of fear and excitement were exchanged as they drew closer to the wounded ship. Lieutenant Pike stepped to the railing with a brisk pace and put one hand on the shoulder of a marine who stood ready to board.

"Take the ship quickly, men!" He shouted over the wind and rain. "Those other two ships could come about at any time. Let's not be caught with our trousers around our ankles."

A ripple of laughter made its way through the hands assembled at the rail. The enemy ship bobbled and tossed in the storm battered sea as grapple hooks were tossed onto its deck. The lines were hauled tight and the hooks bit into wood while North Wind pulled alongside the floundering vessel. In an instant, a gangplank flopped across decks and the boarding party crossed over to take their prize.

Lieutenant Pike watched as the lead element of the boarding party fanned out across the deck with their weapons held at the ready. Wind howled in his ears and drove rain down like needles against his neck. A chill worked its way through his spine and into his ribs. Something was wrong. He could feel it, deep in his bones. The scars he carried on his back from being keelhauled tingled as if they were still healing. His fingertips felt hot while the rest of his hands ached from the chill of the wind and the rain. A wooden clunk reverberated through the air. Lieutenant Pike snapped his gaze back toward the enemy ship's quarterdeck just in time to see a tall, broad-shouldered man emerge from below deck with a cutlass in one hand. His black skin glistened as the rain soaked him and his arm rose high as he prepared to attack.

"There!" a shout rang into the storm from the boarding party. Several musket shots roared and sent little clouds of gun smoke into the wind. The charging man toppled to the deck, sword stilled gripped in his hand as the musket balls ripped into his flesh and spilled his blood to the deck. As if cued by the sound of the gunfire, the deck of the crippled ship erupted into a scene of pure bedlam. Men and women poured from the weather hatch and cabin onto the deck. Pistols roared. Swords clashed. Blood from both crews spilled onto the deck of the storm-tossed ship. For a moment, it was all Lieutenant Pike could do to watch as the chaos unfolded before him. Sailors locked into combat, blade to blade with the enemy crew. For the briefest instant, he held hope that the struggle would turn and come to a quick and decisive end. Then she came up on deck. A sword in one hand and a pistol in the other,

her silky black hair twisted in the wind. Lieutenant Pike's heart jumped into his throat. Her skin was lighter than Lilith's, it couldn't be her. But she fought like someone possessed by a devil. Her sword slashed at a marine and sent a spurt of blood into the wind. She raised her pistol and leveled it at a sailor before firing into his chest at point blank range. With a fluid motion, she tossed the pistol into the air and seized the barrel in her hand to use as a bludgeon. The dark-haired girl clubbed a sailor over the crown of his head before driving the point of her sword into the chest of another. Lightning ripped through the sky. Her eyes settled across the gangplank onto Lieutenant Pike before quickly turning back to the fight raging on deck all around her.

The lieutenant couldn't believe what he was seeing. His boarding party was being cut to ribbons by a crew of Africans and a young girl who had barely been able to sail their vessel in the storm. He turned aft and found Lieutenant Thatcher staring with an open mouth and wide eyes.

"More men," Lieutenant Pike shouted with an edge of panic creeping into his voice, "call up more men! I will lead them across myself. We must finish this now!"

With a deep breath, Lieutenant Pike drew his sword and stepped up onto the gangplank. The fight was pitched. Bodies of fallen sailors and marines littered the deck in between those of the slain enemy. Pistols and muskets boomed their reports and steel clattered against steel. A cry went up from the deck of North

Wind and Lieutenant Pike charged across the gangplank with a score of sailors and marines at his back. He slashed down at a thin man who wielded a severed line with a sharp grapple hook attached to it. The blade bit the man's skin and opened his chest from shoulder to sternum. In an instant, the lieutenant was engaged by two men, one held a musket with a bayonet that had been discarded by a royal marine, the other had a short sword in one hand and a rail pin in the other. He blocked a thrust from the bayonet and countered with a stabbing lunge into the attacker's chest. With only a beat of time to spare, Lieutenant Pike withdrew his blade and managed to parry an attack from the second man's sword before wheeling his blade around and slashing across the second attacker's arms.

A series of shots thundered, and a cloud of smoke mixed with the haze of rain and wind. As the haze cleared, the lieutenant could see that he had turned the tide of the fight. The deck was nearly clear, with only a few enemy holdouts still pressing their counterattack.

"Enough!" he shouted as the smoke cleared away in a gust of rain laden wind.

The dark-haired girl stood with sword in hand, blood spattered across her face and seeping from a cut wound high on her arm. She raised her blade and twisted the point downward in her grip. A defeated scowl snarled from her lips as she drove the point of her weapon down into the wooden deck and raised her hands above her head.

"Bind their hands and lead them below," Lieutenant

Pike ordered. "The ship is too damaged to salvage as a prize." He looked over at the surrendering pirates before letting his gaze lock onto the dark-haired girl. With narrowed eyes, he called out to the marines that began securing their prisoners, "Burn it."

'Drowned Maiden'
12 May 1809
17 degrees 43' N, 76 Degrees 25' W

The joy of firing first faded as quickly as it had come. It was replaced by terror. Terror and anger. Lilith watched as the massive line ship turned to and ran out three decks of gun batteries. Hopelessness reached up out of the sea and wrapped its chilling fingers around her throat until she struggled for breath. The Maiden couldn't stand against this behemoth, not in open water. Her fears came to fruition as the ugly snout of cannons roared and spit fire and smoke behind whizzing balls of iron. Impacts tore into the ship beneath her boots. Fragments of wood sliced through the air as wind and rain continued in gusts and torrents. On impact, Lilith was knocked from her feet. She slid across the rain-soaked deck and slammed into the opposite rail of the Drowned Maiden. Screams rose through the storm. She fought her way to her feet. The wind seemed to gust all the harder as she ran back to face the damage that had been inflicted on her ship.

"Captain!" a voice shouted through the wind and rain, "Captain! We need to turn to! That's the same ship that did us in the last time!"

Lilith turned and looked out over the gap of rolling gray waves. Clouds of gun smoke wisped away in the wind while the massive ship lurched into a hard turn. It was the same ship, or at least it was just as big as the ship that had sunk the Maiden before. She looked toward the bow of the lumbering vessel and watched as the last of the stern of Havana's Mistress disappeared behind an enormous wave. Panic filled her. Havana's Mistress was on course to run right into the navy ship's broadside.

"Captain!" Chibs cried out from across the Maiden's deck. "They blew a hole in our hull! We're taking on water! We need to turn to and get out of here!"

Lilith turned toward Chibs; a reply formed in her mind just as the thundering report of a broadside of cannons filled the air. Her heart sank. A chill squeezed her ribs and refused to let her take in a breath. Just off the Maiden's bow, she could see Batard De Mur adjusting sail and reeling as it turned with the wind. She was paralyzed. Men and women hurried across the deck; blood dripped from their wounds. Several bodies were scattered along the starboard side, casualties of yet again being outmatched. Her plan had been to slip into Kingston harbor and set fire to the ship that had sunk her before. She had failed, and more of her people had died for it.

The sound of splitting wood cut through the storm and a cheer rose from the deck of the large navy ship. Lilith gripped a stay line and heaved herself up onto a section of the starboard rail that had survived the volley. Havana's Mistress had been de-masted, and the navy vessel was turning to come alongside her. Emelia and dozens of others were on that vessel.

"Chibs!" Lilith shouted as she found purchase with her lungs again, "Come about and ready at the guns!"

Chibs dashed from the quarterdeck to the rail where she was standing. "Cap'n, we've already taken some serious hits! Another volley like the last one could do us in! We can't raise her from the depths out here!"

He was right. Lilith hesitated for a heartbeat. The sound of battle echoed through the storm as the navy ship began boarding Havana's Mistress. The Drowned Maiden couldn't stand toe to toe with this enemy. She was already wounded, and the advantage of multiple ships had slipped through her fingers with Havana's Mistress being taken and Batard De Mur already turned with the wind. Pressing their attack would be suicide.

"Heave her about, Chibs. Turn with the wind and run out every scrap of sail we have. This is a fight for another day."

Chibs nodded his approval. "Aye, Cap'n. A bitter taste for today, but we'll go on living to fight again."

Lilith stepped off the railing, her eyes still locked on the towering navy vessel. A shift in the deck announced that the Drowned Maiden was making her turn.

"Bring the wounded to me!" Dr.LeMeux's voice carried through the wind from where he was kneeling near the quarterdeck. "Chest and belly wounds first, and anything that is bleeding profusely."

Chibs sauntered to the helm where Omibwe was

struggling to handle the ship's wheel. "Here, lad. I'll help you hold her steady. She is going to be a bitch to hold on course in this gale. Good job for two good men, but I suppose we will have to do."

Batard De Mur had begun to make their run southward, ahead of the wind flying mains, tops and gallants. Her red sails billowed and snapped tight as they filled with wind. Her prow rode high on the sea, splitting through the murky gray waves and sending a bow wake out from her wooden hull. As Drowned Maiden came about, and her sails adjusted to fill with wind a shudder coursed through her decks. She was listing on the starboard side. Lilith wrapped her icy fingers around the pommel of her cutlass and glared back across the growing gap between her and her enemy. Havana's Mistress was in the hands of the enemy now. Emilia, and so many others were either dead, or being fit with shackles. Lilith cringed inwardly. Her blood seemed to curdle in her veins. Chibs was right. Staying to fight the navy ship would be suicide. But it didn't sit well with her. She felt like she was abandoning her mother all over again. Tears welled in her eyes and blurred her vision.

"We're taking on water through a damned hole in our starboard side. It sits just above the waterline when we are cresting waves, but if she keeps listing much more than she already is, I'm afraid it'll be the end for us. We won't be able to bilge her out quick enough." Chibs huffed as he made his way topside from the gun decks and holds, "We need to stop her up to get us out of this weather and into calmer seas, then we can repair it proper."

"Do whatever needs to be done, Chibs. Take as many hands as you need. We can't afford to lose her again."

"No, we can't, Cap'n," Chibs replied with a shake of his head, "no we can't."

With that, the salty quartermaster motioned toward two of the hands-on deck and disappeared below to work on the breach in the Maiden's hull.

Lilith moved along the deck and helped the crew with lines that had been severed during the exchange of fire. The starboard railing was blown away in several places, and there was a rift in the deck where a cannonball had torn through wooden planks before becoming lodged. Luckily, the masts had all escaped unscathed, but judging by the condition of the sails, just barely. Lilith found two holes in the mainsail that were close to the mainmast and three holes in the top sail that were even closer. An arm's length. If any of those shots had been just an arm's length closer, they would have lost their sails.

"Renly!" she called across the deck to one of her crewmen that had been a royal marine before turning pirate. "Did any of our shots land?"

Renly shook his head as he was coiling a length of line to replace some that had been severed. "A few, captain. But nothing that would cause any serious damage."

"When I first came aboard the Maiden, Captain James taught me that de-masting a vessel was the surest way to take her." She looked at Renly and narrowed her remaining eye. "But I'm not trying to take that vessel. We couldn't crew her even if we did. I want to sink her."

"It's a tall order, captain, sinking a line ship. I suppose it is doable, given the right circumstances, but it would be a bloody business going toe to toe with a ship like that." Renly took the rope he had been coiling and handed it to a crewman that was waiting on the ratlines. "There's no guarantee we could ever sink her. Those line ships are built with thick hulls that don't penetrate easily. Even if we managed to blow a hole in her, nothing above the waterline would do us a damn bit of good. Not unless we landed a shot into her powder magazine. But those big line ships usually keep their powder deep in the hold, well below the waterline. They're made to line up against an enemy fleet and slug it out, exchanging broadside after broadside until one side either burns or sinks beneath the waves."

"Wouldn't that be a sight?" Lilith said looking back over her shoulder as waves rolled out behind them. The distance between the Maiden and her foe was growing, but rather than take comfort, Lilith only felt a nagging sense of failure. "They will take their prisoners to Kingston, right?"

Renly nodded, "Aye, there's a fort there and a stockade."

"I had intended to sail Havana's Mistress into the harbor at Kingston. I had thought that if I could somehow set that ship on fire…"

"You wouldn't get within a half mile of her, captain.

They keep a watch on her, even at port. Plus, there are the fort guns to contend with. A ship arriving under the cover of dark will be assumed to be hostile. No, the only way to get to her is to sneak your way close enough to climb aboard. Even then, you'd have to fight through a score of sailors on watch, maybe more."

Lilith turned forward and took in the sight of the Maiden's new cohort and her blood-red sails. She wondered how steadfast her newfound friends would be. They had sailed right alongside her, faced the warship, and fired their cannons right along with hers. But, they had turned away while Havana's Mistress was taken. It left a nagging feeling in her gut.

To the south, the storm clouds were giving way to open skies where golden beams of sunlight broke through and shone down onto rolling blue waves. The Maiden pitched and rolled in the waves as the storm winds from the north filled her sails and propelled her southward, leaving the lightning and dark clouds to fall away behind her.

"Cap'n!" Chibs' voice announced his presence as the grizzled sailor came up on deck. He looked like a drowned rat, soaked from head to heel with water dripping from his beard. "It's not a permanent fix, Cap'n, but it will hold until we can get it fixed proper."

"Very well, Chibs," Lilith replied. "We will put in somewhere as soon as we can and make repairs."

"Where do you plan to sail, Cap'n?" Chibs wiped away seawater from his face as the rains died to a drizzle under the breaking storm clouds.

Lilith looked back at the Batard De Mur as a column

of sunlight washed over her red sails. "See if we can coax some more speed from her, Chibs, and follow our new friends."

'U.S.S United States'
12 May 1809
35 degrees 59' N, 74 Degrees 25' W

"All hands! To braces!" The order rang loud and clear through the wind and waves as U.S.S United States crested over a roller and pitched forward to slide into a trough between rising seas. "Reef gallants and tops, ready on the capstan!" Responses from the hands on deck chimed, and footfalls clattered on wooden deck planks as the sailors readied the vessel for their maneuver. Captain Roger Woodhaven watched from the quarterdeck as his second lieutenant prepared for the next set of orders. The seas were running higher than normal, though it was nothing the United States couldn't handle with ease. Winds were steady out of the east and the skies were clear and bright. It was a glorious day for sailing, and any day at sea is a perfect opportunity to train. "Ready on jibs and stays!" The captain clenched his jaw as he watched his ship's second lieutenant hesitate. He stood fast, waiting for what seemed like hours, while he could feel his heartbeat throbbing up into his throat. *A performance like this, in my youth, would have gotten me thrown into the sea. This boy has no business issuing commands on a ship if he cannot act decisively.* Another moment passed. The captain folded his arms across his chest and shot a glaring look at Mr. Folson, the United States's sailing master.

"Oh, get on with it! I could have tacked over twice already," Captain Woodhaven growled across the quarterdeck, drawing every eye toward him.

"Turn to!" the voice of the second lieutenant cried out in response to the captain's prodding. "Loose tops and gallants and hold course."

Captain Woodhaven shook his head and rapped his knuckles against the wooden railing at his side. "If that were an evasive maneuver, we would be shot all full of holes before the helm even had a chance to turn. Mr. Pickett, this is not the first time you have been coached on such maneuvers, nor is it the first time I have given you leave to make a run at it while we are under sail. Do you think it is no small matter to waste the crew's time and efforts?"

"No, sir," the lieutenant replied, "I was trying to avoid the mistake I made last time by ordering the course correction too early, captain."

Captain Woodhaven softened at hearing this. As stern as he had been with the lieutenant today, he had been much firmer on the day that the young man was referring to. "I understand, young man. Tacking over before the sails are properly rigged is dangerous, but the purpose for us to do the maneuver is to maintain speed while making the course correction. If we lose momentum, we are dead in the water. You held it this time. Barely. Like I said before, if we were evading another ship, or maneuvering to gain advantage, we would have lost. I expect a better performance next time." He strode closer to the young lieutenant and gestured aloft. "Watch the top men, you will be able to see when they are ready to reef and when they are ready to re-set their sails." He gestured down toward the seas over the windward rail. "Keep an eye on the swells. It's best to make your tack when the ship is in between sets if the seas are running high, such as they are today."

"Aye, sir." The lieutenant replied.

"Very well. That will be all for maneuvers today. Set your course southward, the Carolinas await. I will be in my quarters if you need anything." He turned to his first lieutenant. "Mr. Smith, you have the ship."

The captain left the glorious sunshine and retreated below deck and into his cabin. The fresh air above had been enjoyable enough, but he had logs to look over and charts to review. Below decks, fresh air was a luxury. He could open the portholes and get some in if he so desired, but even then, there was little relief from the smell. A mix of unwashed bodies, ripe from labor, the scent of the stock animals they carried on board and the smell of timbers. It was a pungent smell, and not always so unpleasant. When the crew had a chance to bathe, it brought relief for several days. On particularly long voyages, or in especially warm climates, the smell below deck could be unbearable. His quarters were sequestered enough to spare him the brunt of it, as were the lieutenant's and midshipmen in their mess. The main body of the crew however, generally slept and lived in shared quarters. Cleanliness was a part of good order and discipline, but no amount of saltwater splashed over sweaty, grimy bodies could wash off the smell once U.S.S United States ventured southward into the heat of the Caribbean.

In his cabin, Captain Woodhaven found a moment of solitude and reflected on his situation. He was sailing one of the American Navy's proudest new ships. A frigate in the same class as the U.S.S Constitution and the U.S.S Chesapeake. It was no secret that the British regarded these ships as a legitimate threat to their superiority at sea. It seemed the war for independence was not such a distant memory and already there was saber rattling for a renewed conflict. British warships had been pressing American sailors from military and civilian vessels into their service, and now there was word of a conspiracy within the ranks of the British Navy that involved American co-conspirators. The legislative bodies from both nations had outlawed the transport of slaves from Africa and Brazil onto their shores, and somehow there were still slaves being imported. To add to these woes, a fresh wave of piracy problems was plaguing southern trade routes. Captain Woodhaven had a list of missing ships to be on the lookout for. It was enough to make his head throb. The latest reports, which he had just received, also indicated that the U.S.S Constitution had sighted a first-rate line ship sailing toward the Caribbean. A line ship in the Caribbean, one hundred and twenty guns. Captain Woodhaven was a confident man, bold even by some people's standards. He wondered about his odds if he were to face down a ship that size on the open sea. U.S.S United States had a hull nearly two and a half feet thick. It was made of hard white oak that regularly took the brunt of a cannon shot and sent the projectile harmlessly careening away into the sea. In terms of frigates, their British counterparts simply could not match them. They were shallower on the draft, more maneuverable, faster running broad reach or before the wind, and almost impervious to the effects of nine-pound guns. A ship of the line, however, carried as many guns on one side as an entire frigate. Nine pounders would make up the bulk of their deck array, and most of the upper gun deck, but the lower decks would be outfitted with heavier ordinance, a whole battery of twelve pounders. United States was fast, and agile, somewhere deep in his bones he thought it could be enough. He hoped it would.

The early afternoon was spent reviewing logs. Watch officer logs, the purser's log, galley inventory, officer's mess inventory, all needed his approval. He scoured over each entry and rectified it with the corresponding tallies he had been keeping for himself. Everything seemed well in order. The ship was well-provisioned for their cruise. Fresh water stocks would last them nearly three weeks. If he dropped rations, it could last four. Their food would last them a minimum of five weeks. If that were rationed lower, he could make it last seven weeks. The Caribbean was a tricky beast to sail in, shoals and reefs that were ever changing, ports and harbors that had fouled more vessels than they served, and a pirate problem that seemed to rival the eastern coast of Africa. Two to three ships going missing in a year was nothing sailors would note. Foul weather regularly caused the demise of lesser captains and their crews. A half a dozen ships. Now that would raise some eyebrows. Especially within the time span of a year. Eight ships going missing while reports of pirate activity circulated. That was news. That was enough for certain senators in Washington to ask pointed questions. His orders to sail for the Caribbean had been dispatched promptly after the senate drafted a memorandum of concern over the issue. Boston, to Washington, Virginia, the Carolinas and then off to patrol the quagmire of small islands and vexing winds and weather patterns of the notorious Caribbean. Crystal blue waters and lush green islands did little to dissuade Captain Woodhaven of the trouble that could be found in those southern stretches. He hated the hot weather, and he loathed how unreliable charts could be in seas that changed as much in a year as some did over decades. There wasn't a single port south of the Carolinas that he felt comfortable with. Too many Brits, too many French, always too many Spaniards. If he had been given his choice of seas to patrol, he would choose the coast along Maine stretching down toward Boston and New York. Those were ripe targets for the Brits, should conflict break out. He and his crew could eat far better up there also, cod, salmon, crabs, lobster, and when they put into port, fresh beef, not all the salted stuff they had sitting in barrels down in the hold. But what he wanted counted for little in the service.

"Captain," a knock came at the door of Captain

Woodhaven's cabin.

"Enter," the captain replied without looking up from a paper detailing the contents of his ship's magazine.

A fresh-faced midshipman entered the cabin with rigid movements and stood at attention to report. "Mr. Smith sends his respects and requests your presence on the quarterdeck. Sails have been spotted off our larboard beam, sir."

"What colors?" the captain asked in a flat monotone.

"Pardon, sir?" the midshipman replied with a confused frown crossing his brow.

Captain Woodhaven looked up from his paperwork and raised his brow. "What colors?"

The midshipman nodded and replied dutifully. "The sails. Yes. They are white, sir."

"No, not the sails you buffoon. What colors are they flying? Their flag? What nation is the damned ship affiliated with?"

The midshipman's face blushed beet red as he recognized the elementary nature of his folly. "Yes, sir. Of course. Their colors are not visible. Mr. Smith is trying to determine their origin by the make of their ship, but he is having a difficult time of it."

"Ah, I see. That makes much more sense, now doesn't it?" Captain Woodhaven stood from his chair and moved around his desk. "I will come out on deck presently. See that the stewards get some coffee going. It may turn into a long afternoon."

"Aye, sir." The midshipman made an abrupt about face and retreated out onto the deck.

Captain Woodhaven smiled at the young man's

error. As silly as it was, there was some humor to be found in it. White sails. Of course, they were white. The days of pirates sporting red sails had gone the way of Blackbeard since, well, Blackbeard. There were ships of the Spanish navy who still sailed with royal crests emblazoned on their sails, but those were holdovers, aged ships from a time when Spanish power in the west was something to truly be feared. He opened his wooden sea chest and retrieved the collapsing telescope he had purchased when he was a young midshipman. It wasn't as impressive as some others he had seen, but it had always served him well enough while spotting vessels out on the open sea or skylarking at the moon from high in the rigging. Clutching the instrument of brass and glass he made his way out onto the deck.

The sails were hard to miss. Even as U.S.S United States slipped off the crest of a wave and slogged through a trough between rollers, the white spot on the eastern horizon remained visible. They were still quite distant; it would be awhile before they would be close enough to spot a banner. But, to the experienced eye, the make of the ship would reveal her country of origin. Mast heights, hull shape, rigging, all these details could give subtle hints of who made her, and most of the time, whoever built the ship would be the ones sailing it. The captain moved to the larboard rail and extended his telescope for a study. Her sails were big, judging by the distance and how tall they stood above the horizon. As his eye focused, a few more details came into view. What to the naked eye looked like a spot of white turned out to be a cluster of white. Multiple sails, from multiple ships. His chest tightened. The Constitution was in the Mediterranean, Chesapeake was restocking in Virginia and would be for the next week. The likelihood of sails that size being friendly was almost nonexistent. They could be French, but it was doubtful, France was having enough trouble with Britain in the channel and elsewhere. The captain removed his telescope and examined the spot of white on the horizon with his naked eye.

"Shall we turn to intercept, sir?" a voice asked over his shoulder.

The captain turned and found Mr. Smith, his first lieutenant. "No, Mr. Smith. It was well spotted. Stay on course. If they continue on their current heading, we will intercept them."

U.S. Capital Building
12 May 1809
Washington City

Bird songs greeted John Gaillard as he made his way up the steps of the Capitol building. The morning was cool and calm, and a heavy dew had settled over everything. Under his arm, he carried a leather case filled with documents and letters sent to him from his constituents in South Carolina. The letters ranged from angry complaints to tears stained pleas all centered on one significant issue that had become one of the fiercest topics debated within the newly constructed halls of the American Capital. Once inside, John was swarmed with the sounds of footsteps on granite and voices echoing through the chambers and corridors of the building. It seemed everywhere he turned there were conversations, quiet whispers and tense debates between colleagues. He moved with purpose, but managed to pick up bits and pieces of chatter as he made his way toward his office.

"… the U.S.S Constitution came across a British fleet making sail for the Caribbean…"

"This is the third report I have gotten, this month, about men being pressed into the service of the British navy!"

"What can we do about it?"

Snippets and bits of conversation worked their way into John's ears. He caught a spectrum of looks as he walked through the corridors, sour stares from pro-war representatives who had favored taking drastic, solemn looks from colleagues who understood the implications of another war with the British Empire, and warm smiles and friendly nods from those who he had known for years.

John turned a corner and opened his office door. It was dark but for columns of morning light slanting in through the windows. He gently slid his leather case onto his desk and removed his coat. It would be a long day, a day he had dreaded for months. Circumstances were piling up, tempers were flaring, and the strange visit he had endured in his office almost a year ago was still weighing heavily on his mind. All signs pointed toward war.

The office door sounded with a pair of firm but

polite knocks.

"Enter," John said while leaning back in his chair. He smiled when he saw William Crawford, a gentleman senator from his neighboring state of Georgia. "Will, how are you?"

"I am as good as can be expected, John. Tired. But, then again, I suppose we are all afflicted with that malady as of late."

John crowned and cocked his head. "Have you not been sleeping well, my friend?"

Will's smile faded and he shook his head. "No. I'm afraid I have not been sleeping well, there is something that has been gnawing at me, something I need to tell you."

John held up a hand. "I know your troubles, Will. I am hearing the same things from my people at home as well…"

"It's more than that, John," Will interrupted, his face grew a dark shade of red as if he were angry or embarrassed about something. "Several months ago, while I was at home tending to my affairs, I received a visit from a stranger."

John's veins chilled as he heard his friend speak of a similar visit to what he had received right in his office. "What stranger?"

Will shook his head. "He never gave me his name. He was a younger gentleman, perhaps early in his thirties, he was well dressed and well mannered. But, he delivered a demand that I should have told someone about right away."

"What was it Will?" John asked.

Will eased himself down into a chair opposite John's desk and let out a forlorn sigh. "He said that when the time came and the congress should vote whether to levy war against the British, that I should vote in favor of the declaration."

John nodded and broke a half smile. "Will, it is no secret that you have favored war since these troubles first began."

Will grimaced a little and scrunched his nose. "And it is no secret that you have been staunchly against it."

John tapped the leather case on his desk with one finger. "I was, until I received this latest batch of letters and reports from home." He leaned back into his chair and folded his hands across his midsection. "Do you know what they are saying?"

"I imagine they are similar to the complaints and letters I have been getting," Will replied.

John nodded. "Over a dozen documented cases of the British Royal Navy forcefully boarding merchant vessels bearing the stars and stripes with over thirty men taken and forced into their service. That's not to mention the complete disappearance of a number of vessels, all under very suspicious circumstances."

"You mean they were smuggling slaves," Will interjected.

John softened his tone. "I received an unwelcome visit from a stranger myself, Will."

Will shriveled his nose and furrowed his brow. "When?"

"It was near a year ago," John cast a suspicious glance toward the door and then continued, "but it was the same message. And he made it clear that there are many interested parties that would like to see this confrontation boil over. Both in England and here at home, as well as in other places in Europe."

Will raised and hand and rubbed at his jaw. "What do you propose to do?"

John shook his head. "There isn't much we can do. If tempers rise much more, our hand will be forced. I intend on retaining my office, and the overwhelming consensus I am getting from my constituents is that the abuses of the crown must be answered."

"That is something we can agree on, on both counts, John." Will said with a smile.

"You are missing the overarching point here, Will." John said with a sigh.

Will leaned forward in his chair, his face growing long in the dim light of John's office. "And what point is it that I am missing? We have cause, damn it."

"Obviously," John said, "but, what if all of this has been engineered? What if this has been arranged to manipulate us into doing someone else's bidding? We could be blundering into some great trap. A war with Britain will most definitely be a war fought largely on the sea, and they still have the most powerful navy in the world. Thousands will die. Do you want that on your conscience?"

2

Governor's Mansion
13 May 1809
Kingston, Jamaica

Golden columns of light streaked in between the breaking storm clouds overhead as Admiral Torren looked out over the sprawl of Kingston. The beams of sunlight landed on a scatter of green foliage, wooden shake roofs and the blue-green water of the harbor. He took in the sight from the balcony of the governor's mansion, a space he was occupying now that the fort had been retaken and order was being reestablished in the province. The clatter of carpenter's hammers rattled within the house as repairs were being made to bring the residence up to standard. Kingston was slowly beginning to resemble an orderly and productive colony again. Buildings were being repaired, the harbor was being cleared and the fort was undergoing a complete overhaul. Every wooden structure within the stone walls was being rebuilt while a new barracks of brick and mortar was being built from the ground up. The progress was satisfying, but in Admiral Torren's eye it was just the beginning. He intended to have the shipyard revamped once the harbor had been cleared. Soon, Kingston would be able to service and refit every manner of king's ship from a sloop to the heavy frigates or line ships. He intended to have a palisade wall erected around the perimeter of Kingston's outskirts. There would be manned gatehouses at every entrance to the city. With a clear harbor and a secure city, trade would flourish once again, and Kingston would become the jewel of the Caribbean that it was meant to be.

"Pardon the interruption, sir," a voice from behind the admiral said.

Admiral Torren turned to find Sergeant Dodd, a marine from North Wind who had stayed in Kingston to help with securing and rebuilding. "Nonsense. The only thing you are interrupting is some brooding."

Sergeant Dodd dared a grin for a heartbeat before resuming his rigid manner. "I delivered your letters to the next outbound ships. A trade sloop bound for Barbados, a galley sailing to Trinidad and a brig headed for St. Kitts."

Admiral Torren nodded. "And the letter intended for Nassau?"

"That was a little more difficult," Sergeant Dodd replied, "There were no ships who intended to sail for Nassau. I had to contract a fishing vessel to carry your letter, along with some other mail from the men. It took quite a sum to convince the fishing captain, sir."

Admiral Torren offered the sergeant a grin. "A short-term measure, Sergeant Dodd. Once my letters reach their intended recipients, I expect things will come along nicely as far as our infrastructure is concerned. Additional troops and supplies, material support and renewed trade. In a few months, I expect Kingston will burst at the seams."

Sergeant Dodd's grin faded, and he held out a rolled parchment. "I also have the report you requested, sir. A summary from the garrison commander's logs. Well, the ones we could find."

A chill gripped Admiral Torren despite the warmth of the Jamaican afternoon. "I'll read the report, sergeant. Give me a summary."

Sergeant Dodd's eyes dropped to the balcony floor for a heartbeat before he spoke. "Much of it is as we expected; entries outlining the raiding activity on nearby settlements, comings and goings from the harbor, disciplinary proceedings within the garrison and supply inventories."

Admiral Torren furrowed his brow. "None of which explain your hesitancy. On with it, sergeant."

"Well, sir. There are some entries of a rather vague nature. Curious operations ordered by the governor himself. It seems the garrison was assisting some of the local gentry in putting down slave revolts, but the entries give very little detail, and they are too infrequent to be responses to a widespread action like a slave revolt." Sergeant Dodd said as the admiral took the rolled parchment from his hand. "We all know that the governor was involved in something. It almost seems as if he was using the garrison to whatever ends he was in pursuit of."

"I suspect that was the case, though I have had very little evidence to base that suspicion on. Whatever the case, the garrison and its commander likely knew very few details, if any. I doubt they would have been complicit if they had." Admiral Torren looked back out over balcony rail and drew a deep breath. Residents of the colony were hard at work on the streets below him, rebuilding their shops and homes after months of lawlessness. "Whatever schemes Governor Alton was involved in, it is obvious to me that the garrison was ordered to limit their patrol activity throughout the island. The bandit problem would never have gotten this out of hand otherwise. Once we have sufficient reinforcements, we will need to see about correcting that."

"I can organize some patrols of the immediate area surrounding Kingston, sir. Beyond that, I agree, it would be better to wait until reinforcements arrive," sergeant Dodd replied.

Admiral Torren smiled without turning away from his view of Kingston. "That will do, sergeant. Close patrols will serve as a deterrent. But don't go on the hunt. We can't afford to lose any of the men we currently have."

Sergeant Dodd replied, "Aye, sir. I will see to it this afternoon."

"Very well, sergeant. That will be all." Admiral Torren turned and faced the marine sergeant to dismiss him. He returned the crisp salute in quick fashion and walked through the balcony doors into a large room that he had decided would serve as his office. The space was still barren but for a desk he had brought up from the ground floor. Governor Alton had a massive collection of books, though most of them had been scattered onto the floor and a few were stained by spilled liquids. The bookshelves had been battered, but would serve for a time until he could have them refinished or replaced. The admiral wanted to make the space comfortable and functional for a time, he knew this likely would not be a permanent situation. Britain's king would assign one of his favored lords. Kingston was a prestigious posting, and there would be no shortage of lords petitioning for assignment. But, that was a problem for a different day. For now, he would do his duty and restore Kingston to the glory and prosperity it had once been renown for.

For now, there was no shortage of food in the markets. Fish, meat, livestock and fruit filled the stands of vendors lining the streets. Timber, cotton and tobacco were plentiful enough, but in their raw form. Of trade goods, however, there was precious little. There was a significant lack of spices and finished goods that typically arrived by merchant vessels. Among the shortages, and perhaps most troubling of all, was a lack of coin from the exchange of goods and services. The news of Kingston's state had spread far and wide throughout the Caribbean. What had once been a hotbed of trade and traffic was all but a deserted port with a harbor impassable to all but the smallest of vessels. All but the hardiest of residents had left for colonies with more promising futures. There was a shortage of skilled craftsmen, and a high demand for the work that required them. A pair of blacksmiths remained, and their shops were filled with the racket of hammer and bellows from early morning until late in the night. There were few carpenters, and those that remained were well tasked with the restorations of the fort and the governor's mansion. The shipyard was in desperate need of both skilled shipwrights and the laborers they needed to complete their work. Refits and overhauls were out of the question for the time being, until there was adequate manpower the shipyard would be limited to minor repairs.

The series of letters Sergeant Dodd had referred to were pleas for aid. St. Kitts, Barbados, Trinidad and Nassau would all send men, ships and supplies. From Nassau, his message would be forwarded to both Bermuda and London, though it would take some time, he expected even more support and supplies would follow. In a matter of months, he would recover the colony. For now, he was limited by a lack of manpower and supplies. He hoped Lieutenant Pike was faring well on his patrol, so much rested on the young officer's shoulders. It was unheard of for a lieutenant to take the command of a line ship. North Wind's captain was currently serving as an interim governor in the colony of Nassau after the governor there had been assassinated by the same band of rogues that was currently terrorizing the Caribbean. Though the lieutenant was guilty of falling in with them, it had been a means of survival. The young man had proved himself to be loyal to both the crown and the admiral himself by taking up against a mutiny attempt spurred by an American prisoner. Admiral Torren was as perplexed by the series of events as anyone. Never before had he heard of such vexing circumstances. By all rights, the young man should have been hung. It brought a hesitant smile to the admiral's face as he looked over the scene of Kingston and contemplated the young man's promotion to captain. He was certainly capable. Even after the admiral had him keelhauled, he had taken up arms and defended him when doing so was an almost certain death sentence.

"I could do with more officers like him," the admiral said to himself as he looked over the barren walls of his office. "A portrait of the old man, Lord Horatio Nelson, right there opposite the desk. I will have to acquire one so I may have it displayed." He wondered what the grizzled legend of the royal navy would think of the circumstances unfolding in the Caribbean.

Pangs of pain struck the admiral in his legs. Arthritis, gout, old age and a lifetime of use were weighing against his joints. He decided a walk to stretch his legs was in order. Motion helped to shake the pain from his knees and ankles. He donned his hat and officer's coat and plucked the ornate cane he carried everywhere with him off of his desk. He would see to the progress being made at the fort and let himself be seen throughout the streets of Kingston. A curved stairwell leading down to the foyer of the mansion was his first obstacle. The first few steps were murderous, but he forced himself to continue. By the time his feet touched onto the marble floor of the foyer Admiral Torren could feel the burning ache intensifying in his knees and ankles. He grumbled to himself, "Nothing for it but to keep moving."

The heels of his shoes clattered against the rough cobblestones of Kingston's streets. He passed a street with a row of homes that had seemed to fare well through much of the chaos that had ensued over the previous months. There was a bookshop with its windows shuddered. Planks had been nailed across the shudders and the door to help secure the property from the lawlessness that had ravaged Kingston. Admiral Torren smiled when he saw it. Crooks don't read. The proprietor might as well have left his wares out for the world to see, they would have been safe enough. He passed the storefronts of jewelers, clockmakers, tailors, butchers, coopers and a gunsmith, all of them boarded up or appearing vacant. Closer to the harbor there was still some activity. Merchants had opened stands to peddle their wares. A baker had his shop open, and the smell of fresh baked bread wafted out into the street and lingered with the aroma of a smokehouse that was curing meats from nearby swine farms. He nodded to passing residents as he made his way down the hill and to the waterfront. The road curved between shops and stands, inns, taverns and stables. It seemed as he got closer to the harbor, the more alive Kingston became. As he reached the edge of the docks the road curved and snaked its way back uphill and toward Fort Charles. Its walls stood stark against the lush green of the surrounding countryside. He could see the forms of dutiful sentries standing their posts along the battlements and the ugly snouts of cannons protruding from the crenelations along the tops of the walls. With a deep breath, Admiral Torren continued his way up the hill toward the fort as a sense of pride nestled in his chest. He had good men with him. Duty bound men with zeal for king and country. They could overcome the challenges before them, and any others the Caribbean thought to throw their way.

'Drowned Maiden'
12 May 1809
16 degrees 4' N, 76 Degrees 20' W

A shadow from Batard De Mur's red sails stretched over the deck of the Drowned Maiden as she slipped through gently rolling seas and came abreast of the smaller vessel. Lilith stood near the helm and awaited the sight of the French pirate captain that she and her crew had just recently found themselves aligned with. It seemed odd, that a chance encounter on the high seas would result in the reunification of old friends half a world away. But, Dr.LeMeux had recognized the grizzled pirate almost immediately. It was as if fate had stretched out its hand and delivered exactly what the Maiden had needed, and though Lilith had not known it at the time, exactly when she needed it.

"Two against one with a line ship," Chibs said as the Maiden slid through gradually calming waves as they left the storm behind them. "There isn't much advantage there, considering their firepower. But three against one. That is the only reason we escaped with our lives and the Maiden intact."

Lilith stared up at the taut red sails of her new cohort. "Emilia and the Mistress probably don't see it that way."

Chibs paused for a long moment, letting the sound of wind and waves fill the gap in conversation. "It is an awful thing, Cap'n. I won't deny it."

"I can't help but think, Chibs. This is all my fault. If I had listened to you, we would have been sailing somewhere else." Lilith paused as a wave broke and the Maiden slid further ahead in the sea pulling abreast of Batard De Mur. "Havana's Mistress would still be whole. She would still be with us."

Chibs took in a deep breath and let his good hand fall to rest on Captain Lilith's shoulder. "What is done is done Cap'n. There is no use staring over the stern."

Lilith let her hands rest on the hilt of her cutlass. "I want to send that ship to the bottom, Chibs. I know it sounds like madness. We cannot stand against her at sea. That much has been made clear to me."

"No, we cannot," Chibs replied. "But, there is a weapon we possess that they can't match."

Lilith narrowed her eye and turned to her salty quartermaster. "And what is that, Chibs?"

"Our wits, Cap'n," He said with a smile, "we will defeat her using out wits. Same as we did when we sank the other navy ships. We didn't outmatch them in guns or sailing prowess, we used our brains and ran them into the reef or blew a hole in their hull by towing a barrel full of powder. That is how the Maiden wins her fights, that is always how the Maiden has won against the Royal Navy. Even Captain James, when he ordered the Maiden to sail circuit around that little spit of land. Those navy boys thought they had us on the run right until they sailed around the bend and there he was, standing on the beach with a pair of cannonades and a bonfire blazing away. He used his wits then, Cap'n, and we should do the same."

Lilith stared out over the seas ahead of them. The clouds overhead were breaking away and sunlight poured down onto the open water. "It's not over, Chibs."

"Not by a long shot, Cap'n."

On the deck of Batard De Mur, Lilith could see the French pirate captain make his way to his larboard rail. He cupped his hands around the sides of his mouth and bellowed a shout, "We run southward, away from that behemoth!"

Lilith looked at Chibs for a moment. The old sailor shrugged an agreement. She turned back toward the other captain and shouted in reply, "Where are we bound?"

Batard De Mur's captain called back, "Spanish port, Maracaibo."

Lilith turned toward Chibs to see his reaction. The old sailor's brow furrowed into a deep frown.

"What is the matter, Chibs?" Lilith asked.

Chibs shook his head before returning her gaze. "Maracaibo is a big port, Cap'n. Every bit as big as

Kingston, maybe even bigger. Big ports aren't good places for pirates to make sail." He took a deep breath and ran his hand over his beard. "If you think that navy ship was a big one, you should see some of the war galleys the Spaniards sail. It's enough to make your blood run cold even on the hottest days."

"Is it wise for us to follow them, Chibs?" Lilith asked with an edge of apprehension building in her voice.

Chibs shrugged. "When is anything we do wise? Wisdom would be sailing us west and finding a deserted stretch of coastline to live out our days on. Wisdom would mean us all scattering to the winds and casting off our calling to disrupt the slave trade. That would be wisdom, Cap'n. It would also have the foul taste of cowardice, by my thinking." He paused and stepped toward the rail under the shadow of Batard De Mur's red sails. "Aye, follow them where they lead. If this fellow knows more about the slavers, he may well be our hope of cutting them off at the knees."

Lilith nodded and remained silent for a long while. The wind whipped at her hair and brushed her skin. She thought long and hard about why she had chosen to take up with these pirates in the first place. Her mother, Captain James, Trina. Faces visited her mind as she stared out over gently swelling seas. The big navy ship had blown her crew to ribbons in their first encounter without so much as a warning. Trina had died in the aftermath of their relentless volleys of cannon fire. But, the Maiden had been hunting slavers since before she had come aboard. It had been Captain James's mission. It was what he gave his life for.

"Chibs, do we have any charts of the southern Caribbean?" Lilith asked without moving her glare from the open seas in front of her.

"Aye, Cap'n. I believe we do." Chibs replied.

Lilith stepped toward the helm and gave Omibwe a nod as the young African boy held steady on their southerly course. "Fetch them. We will need to familiarize ourselves. If we run into another big warship, I want to have a plan."

"Aye, Cap'n!" Chibs answered before making his way below deck.

Lilith smiled and turned to Omibwe. "Keep us on this course, Omi. If our friends change their heading, have someone come get me. Chibs and I will be below deck looking over the charts."

Omibwe nodded to the captain, chancing a quick look away from the sails just long enough to answer. "Aye, captain. Holding our course."

Lilith paced the railing forward and took in a close observation of Batard De Mur. While the Maiden had suffered several direct hits, the pirate ship with crimson sails had come through the ordeal with relatively little damage. A bit of shot away railing, a few holes in her sails and some damage to the deck. The Maiden had not fared so well. Her railing had been shot away in several places, two of those wounds bordered deep impacts to the deck where gouges of crushed and splintered wood remained. The main and top main had three and four holes in them, respectively, and there were three shot holes blasted in her hull, one of which was dangerously close to the waterline. Carpenters were already hard at work to make what repairs they could while teams of hands took turns at the bilges below deck. It wasn't as severe as the cove attack, but if the big navy ship had swung around and leveled another broadside at them, it certainly could have been. The Maiden needed an out of the way anchorage where permanent repairs could be made. Another glance across to her newfound companions revealed the French pirate captain, standing proudly by the helm of his ship. Lilith let her stare linger. He looked like a hard man, someone who had seen plenty of action at sea. The scars on his face and the black leather eye covering were evidence of that, but there was something else that made Lilith take a pause. His crew. They scurried about the deck and scrambled through rigging like any crew at sea. The men looked as grizzled and hard as their captain, some even more so. She noted several men who were working despite missing a limb and the captain wasn't the only man sporting leather over one eye. More than any of that, Lilith took particular notice of three of the pirate crew, one on the deck and two up in the rigging. Their skin was a dark shade of mahogany, darker even than Lilith's. She continued her walk along her own ship until she was even with the helm of Batard De Mur. The captain looked over and held his stare on Lilith while the wind flustered a plume of red feathers extending from his hat. He gave Lilith a slight nod and then resumed his stony stare out over the deck of his ship and the seas beyond.

Below deck, Lilith made her way into her cabin. She

was pleasantly surprised to see that aside from the few belongings she owned being scattered across the cabin floor, there was no damage. She stepped into the room and close the door behind her. The chest that had been in the cabin when she first became the captain of the Drowned Maiden was laying on its side. There was a white shirt laying on the deck with a leather wrapped brass telescope and a pair of cutlasses lying on top of it. Lilith stared at the stained white shirt for a long moment as a wave of memories and emotions rolled over her. A night spent with Captain James on the deck of the Maiden as he explained the constellations and regaled her with the mythic tales associated with them.

A knock at the cabin door snapped Lilith back into her present surroundings. She drew a deep breath and wiped away tears that had been welling in her eyes.

"Enter," she said.

"Beggin your pardon, Cap'n, but I have the charts you were asking about." Chibs entered with a smile and a fistful of rolled paper charts.

Lilith averted her eyes toward the stern window array. "Very well, Chibs. Let's have a look at them." She hurried to return the white shirt and her other belongings into the sea chest and then moved to the table that served as her desk at the rear of the cabin.

"What exactly are you hoping to find, Cap'n?" Chibs asked as he spread the charts out onto the table one at a time.

Lilith looked over the outline depicting the northern coast of South America. "Anything that can help us. Our new friend wants to sail for Maracaibo, those are unfamiliar waters. It would be nice to have a plan, in case things don't go as we expect."

"What do we expect, Cap'n?" Chibs looked up from the charts with a frown.

Lilith sighed and met his gaze. "I'm not even sure I know anymore, Chibs. It seems that Dr.LeMeux's friend has an ax to grind with the slavers. Perhaps, he wants to take some of their ships. Or, maybe, our trip to Maracaibo will yield us some valuable information. From the sound of it, it is a big port, in Spanish waters. So far, the Maiden has only engaged with British and American ships. Maybe the southern stretches will be safer for us."

Chibs arched one eyebrow and fumbled in the leather pouch at his hip for his pipe. "A chance to repair our damage and take on supplies. Aye, that'll do Cap'n. We could use some fresh blood too; things are getting a bit thin out on deck."

Lilith smiled and returned her gaze onto the sprawling miles of coastline. "Aye, Chibs. I was thinking the same thing."

'U.S.S *United States*'
12 May 1809
35 degrees 59' N, 74 Degrees 25' W

Afternoon wore long into evening as the U.S.S United States continued her southerly course while maintaining a close watch on the sails that had appeared off her leeward beam. The shadow of United States stretched out over rolling gray waves as the sunk sank low toward the horizon and it began to appear to Captain Woodhaven that he may not intercept the mystery ship before nightfall. It had been a maddening afternoon with far too few developments. The unidentified ship would angle windward and run on for a bit before turning to and running back out of visual range. Half a dozen times at least, Captain Woodhaven had made up his mind that United States would turn with the wind and close distance on the ship only to have her appear on a windward course running close haul. If the ship was hostile and he surrendered the wind gauge for fault of his lack of patience, he would be the subject of lessons for every American naval officer for the next hundred years. He held his commands and continued his course southward while scouring the horizon for every detail he could find. He was convinced the ship belonged to some hostile foreign power, with the way she was behaving by sneaking closer only to turn back out to sea. Every time she tacked over, he inspected closely in hopes of catching a sight of her colors, to no avail. Both the senior midshipmen and the lieutenants alike were giving their most junior member a full ration for reporting to the captain the color of the unidentified ship's sails. It had become a running joke on deck. "She's sighted again, sir. Still flying white sails." It proved to offer levity to the afternoon, though not nearly enough to elevate Captain Woodhaven's mood. After hours of the exercise, he had enough. He retired to his cabin after leaving strict instructions for the watch to come and get him if there were any developments. Within the confines of his cabin, Captain Woodhaven commenced brooding. He stared out the fantail windows while his steward delivered his dinner, a plate of sliced pork with a heavily peppered gravy dribbled over the top, a baked potato, and a bowl of steaming carrots and peas. The captain acknowledged his steward and resumed staring out the fantail window array. He grumbled to himself, "Off to the damned Caribbean to chase away pirates while the Brits are stomping their feet at our doorstep," he let out a resigned sigh and muttered, "madness." The smell of his dinner was finally able to draw his eyes off of the horizon to the north.

Captain Woodhaven turned to his plate and took up his fork and knife, he cut into the sliced pork before realizing his food had gone cold while he had been staring out over the ocean. Forcing himself to eat, he took a bite of the well-seasoned meat and began to chew. It wasn't bad fare, especially for having gone cold. He took another bite and thought hard over the ship currently sailing just out of reach off of his leeward beam. Turning inward and then back. What sense does that make? If she were hostile, wouldn't she just make her course to intercept or turn tail and run? He chewed over another forkful of pork before spearing more and mopping up a dollop of gravy. Why would their captain make such frivolous advances toward them? It was almost as if he were taunting them, daring them to come closer. Captain Woodhaven stabbed at another piece of pork and shoveled it into his mouth as he thought about the odd maneuvers of the vessel. Why would they feign coming closer and then turn back out to sea? He swallowed and dropped his fork on his plate, thoroughly maddened by the list of unanswered questions. Then, as if struck by lightning, another question dawned on him. He felt a chill running through his veins. What if, instead of making the maneuvers to taunt the United States, the maneuvers had nothing to do with him and his ship at all? He pulled his cloth napkin off of the desk that had been serving as his dinner table and wiped his mouth before casting another long stare out of the window array behind him. The zig-zag pattern made no sense for a ship off of his beam. But, it made perfect sense for a ship that was trying to evade fire from a ship of similar class. The captain would run close haul and force his pursuer to do the same, this would force them to change the angles of their gunnery and make sail adjustments in order to maintain pursuit. Then, once he had put his pursuer through that maneuver, he would then change course and run with the wind at his quarter and open a gap between him and his pursuer. United States' lookouts had not reported cannon fire, but at such an extreme range and with the stiff winds, it would be impossible to hear.

The captain threw down his napkin and shoved back his chair so suddenly that it toppled over backward. He edged around the desk and swung his cabin door open before plunging out and racing up the ladder well and onto the weather deck. In his haste he had forgotten to don both his officer's coat and his hat, but that was the furthest thing from his mind as he plotted his course up the deck and to the helm where his watch officer was dutifully standing by.

"Officer of the watch, call the lookouts to scan the horizon again," Captain Woodhaven ordered.

Mr. Smith, the first lieutenant of U.S.S United States walked up alongside the captain with a deep frown shrouding his eyes. "Sir, this is highly irregular. Is everything alright?"

Captain Woodhaven turned to his first lieutenant and shook his head. "No, Mr. Smith. I'm afraid I missed something when we first spotted that ship."

From up in the rigging one of the lookouts called down, "She's still out there, sir. White sails and all!"

A ripple of laughter worked its way through the crew on deck, but Captain Woodhaven paid it no mind. He cupped his hands around his mouth and shouted up to the lookout, "Look off of her stern, as far as you can see. Is there anything else?"

A long moment passed as the lookout scanned the horizon with a brass telescope raised to one eye. Captain Woodhaven could feel the stares of his crew and officers as the seconds dragged into minutes. Mr. Smith pulled one of the midshipmen off to the rail and gave him some hushed instructions before walking back over to the captain's side. "Sir, if I may? With respects. Could you enlighten me?"

"Sail ho!" the lookout shouted down.

Captain Woodhaven locked his stare up onto his crewman in the rigging. He cupped his hands around his mouth and shouted up to him, "Where away?"

"Off the stern of that other ship, I put him two, no, three points off our larboard stern!"

Captain Woodhaven clapped his hands together and squeezed them as if he were trying to wring out a cloth. "Damn! This entire time, and now it is near dark." He turned to his first lieutenant. "Mr. Smith, come about with the wind. Hard a-larboard until we are bearing down on that ship's current position. Lookouts remain posted, an extra ration of tobacco for the first man to spot their colors."

"Aye, aye, captain." Mr. Smith touched his brow and turned to disseminate his orders.

Captain Woodhaven studied the heavens as shades of evening began to paint the western horizon. He had scant few hours of daylight remaining, but if the winds held as they were he just might be able to identify both the fleeing vessel and the one giving chase. The deck of United States shifted beneath his feet in a hard larboard turn that swung her bow around to the east. Sailors scurried through the ratlines and across yards as they set their sails to the optimum configuration for running before the wind.

"Hands to the stays! Make ready with fore tops and gallants!" Lieutenant Smith called through his mouth trumpet as sailors finished their tasks and prepared for the next phase. "Loose fore tops and gallants! Haul slack from sheets and tie down smartly!" A sudden burst of propulsion sped United States along on her new course while Lieutenant Smith beamed a broad smile and made his way back to the quarterdeck. Without a breath of hesitation, he continued.

"Quartermaster, let's run the line. I'd like to see what kind of speed we are making."

"Aye, sir," the quartermaster touched his hat and turned to his mates to begin the process of checking their speed.

Captain Woodhaven nodded his approval to his first lieutenant and moved forward toward the bow with his telescope in hand. He watched the horizon carefully as he strode the length of the ship. The first sighted vessel was still far off in the distance. He judged that if United States could sustain her current speed, he would be within cannon range just before nightfall.

"We're making twelve knots on this heading captain," Lieutenant Smith announced, "that should put us in between both ships within the hour, maybe just a little over."

Captain Woodhaven nodded his approval and peered toward the horizon with his telescope. "Very good, Mr. Smith. But I think we can coax a couple more knots out of her. See what the sailing master thinks about running out stunsails, I want every scrap of sail catching wind."

"Aye, aye captain," Lieutenant Smith replied before turning to walk back to the quarterdeck.

"Captain! The southern vessel! She's an American!" a lookout's voice rang clear from high in the rigging, "I can see her hull now, sir! Looks like she's listing onto her larboard side!"

Captain Woodhaven snapped his telescope shut. He gripped the brass instrument in his fist so tight that he thought he may dent the metal tube. "Damn!"

Lieutenant Smith stopped in his tracks just forward of the foremast. "Is everything alright, sir?"

The captain shook his head. "No, Mr. Smith. But, I'll bet you my share of our next prize that the ship in pursuit of them is a damned Brit." He paused for a moment before re-opening his telescope and aiming it toward the northern horizon. A haze of gray and blue danced in the distance as he panned across the distance. Hues of pink and orange were mixing into the blue sky as the sun signaled its descent into night. He found a stacked set of white squares. Sails filled with the wind. The captain studied them until his eye began to strain with the distorted image from his telescope. "Two masts that I can see, with mains, tops, gallants and royals flying. She could be a brig, she could be a frigate. Damn the luck." He turned to Lieutenant Smith. "Come about to the north, Mr. Smith. I want all guns loaded, but don't run them out just yet. Have a pair of gun crews come up on deck and get the chase guns ready as well."

"Aye, captain!" Lieutenant Smith replied with a touch of his hat.

Captain Woodhaven pulled his telescope back to his eye and continued studying the approaching vessel. "Mr. Smith."

The lieutenant paused mid step and turned back to his commander. "Yes, sir?"

"Beat to quarters."

3

'U.S.S United States'
12 May 1809
36 degrees 4' N, 74 Degrees 5' W

The sharp staccato of a rattling drum echoed over the deck of U.S.S United States as her hull slid through the sea. Hands scrambled to their battle stations, their footfalls drummed over timber and creaked on taut rope. On the gun deck, commands bellowed through tight spaces as men prepped and loaded their cannons. Captain Woodhaven stood on the bow, scouring the outline of the vessel that United States was closing with. Her sails remained, her course unaltered as the two ships drew nearer and nearer. The winds had held and United States was moving along nicely with every stitch of canvas flying from the tops of her masts all the way down to the main sails which were bordered on each side by a set of stunsails. The last reading had her clipping along just over thirteen knots. The captain knew he could coax out another knot or two by sailing with the wind at his quarter, but he wanted to close with the unknown vessel and remain upwind of her. The unknown ship had been giving chase to a vessel his crew had found to be flying American colors. Whoever it was, Captain Woodhaven was duty bound to intercede.

As U.S.S United States forged northward through calm seas, the captain kept a close eye on the vessel ahead of him. At first, he believed they would turn to and run at the sight of a warship sailing their way. They didn't. Their sails remained set and their course stayed steady even as the distance closed, and Captain Woodhaven knew they would easily be able to identify United States as a man of war. He studied the vessel through his telescope until the slight distortion of the glass strained his eye and threatened to make him sick. She was a fully rigged ship, with two masts that he could see through the distance and possibly a third over her stern. Her size was enough to set tension in his stomach. She wasn't a line ship by any means, but she was too big to be a sloop. The remaining classes of ship were still within United States' depth, the heavy frigate was among a class of ships designed and built in American shipyards to check British power at sea. So far, the ships had proved themselves to be formidable. The U.S.S Constitution was already something of legend among seafarers with tales circulating about cannonballs bouncing off of her oaken timbers. United States had yet to be in such a confrontation, though, Captain Woodhaven hoped his ship would prove equally formidable.

"Any idea who it could be sir?" Lieutenant Smith said over the captain's shoulder as he continued to stare through his telescope.

Captain Woodhaven withdrew the instrument from his eye and gave his first lieutenant an exasperated look. "I am quite tired of the guessing game today, lieutenant. Her build looks Brit to my eye, though I have been wrong before. My guess is she is a king's ship."

"What would they be doing chasing a merchant ship bearing American colors, sir?"

Captain Woodhaven chewed at his lower lip. He shifted his gaze back to the ship on the horizon. "The Brits have been boarding American vessels and pressing our countrymen into the service of their king, against their will. Most often at gunpoint. Not much a merchant sailor or fisherman can do when he is faced down by a wall of royal marines with muskets and bayonets trained on him. I suspect this is exactly what we have stumbled into, Mr. Smith. We've caught them with their hand in the cookie jar, so to speak."

"Time we take them to the woodshed, sir?" Lieutenant Smith said with a broad grin.

Captain Woodhaven narrowed his eyes and fought off a chuckle. "Aye, Mr. Smith. It is time someone takes them to the woodshed. See to it Captain Coburn has his sharpshooters up in the tops straight away. If we engage, I don't want to be outmatched in marksmen."

"Aye, captain." Lieutenant Smith briskly touched the brim of his hat and marched off to deliver the captain's orders.

Alone again, the captain raised his telescope to study his approaching adversary. The distance had shrunk considerably. He turned to a midshipman. "Pass the word for Mr. Dailey, smartly."

"Aye, aye captain." The midshipman touched his brow and hurried off to retrieve the ship's gunner.

It wasn't but a few minutes and the ship's gunner, a warrant officer named Tiller Dailey, arrived at the captain's side. "Reporting as ordered, sir."

"Yes," the captain replied, "Mr. Dailey, would you suppose that ship is within range of our bow chasers yet?"

The gunner looked over the sea gap and grinned. "Oh, yes sir. She sure is."

Captain Woodhaven nodded his approval. "Fire one of the long nines in front of her bow. Let her know we are here, and we mean business."

Mr. Dailey grinned all the wider. "Aye, captain!" he turned to one of his mates and started spitting orders as fast as his mouth would move. "Hurry now, boys. The captain wants a shot off of her bow. Get those muzzle caps off and let's get powder rammed and primed. Round shot will do, don't use my canisters until we are within musket range."

Captain Woodhaven raised his telescope to his eye and inspected the approaching ship. They were drawing rapidly closer, and he could see far more detail than even just moments before. On her prow rode a carved figurine, the ship's lady. She was definitely a warship. On her decks, Captain Woodhaven could see the crew was scurrying about to make ready. He clenched his jaw and looked up into the rigging. The yards held a line of sailors ready to make adjustments on a moment's notice. Captain Woodhaven inspected the rigging closer and found a pair of men in red coats climbing the ratlines with muskets slung over their shoulders. "They mean to have at it then, so be it." He pulled his eye away from the telescope and cast a glare at his chase gun crews. "Mr. Dailey, are we ready on those guns yet?"

"In a heartbeat, captain. I'm adjusting elevation now." Mr. Dailey replied in a growl as he focused on the elevation screw with one eye squinted shut. "That'll about do her, ready when you are captain!"

Captain Woodhaven took a half breath before replying, "Fire at will, Mr. Dailey."

The report of the nine-pounder cannon thundered over the sea in front of U.S.S United States and a cloud of smoke belched forth before washing away in the wind. Captain Woodhaven silently counted the second until he saw the impact. A geyser of water shot high into the air just a few yards off of the approaching ship's bow. Captain Woodhaven could feel his ribs tighten with excitement as he saw the water spew upward. The shot was right on, a follow up would definitely find its target.

"Well done, Mr. Dailey. I believe you may have gotten some of their deckhands wet with spray." Captain Woodhaven said as he continued to watch the ship through his telescope. He analyzed every detail, every movement on board that he could see. Seconds dragged out for what felt like an eternity. Nothing. No sail changes. No shift in course or additional movement on deck. He could see a pair of officers standing near the bow, one in a bicorne hat with a telescope raised to his eye and another extending an arm outboard in the direction of Captain Woodhaven. "Mr. Dailey, it seems they either didn't understand our message or they aren't taking it seriously. Let's land a few into her hull and see what they do, eh?"

"Aye, captain!" Mr. Dailey replied.

The captain looked over one shoulder and focused aloft. The winds were holding steady out of the west and slight southwest. If he timed it right, he could execute a hard larboard turn and launch a broadside before turning back with the wind. If it worked, he would be able to get a volley off and then readjust to continue closing, and without losing the weather gauge. The roar of another nine-pounder cannon echoed into the late evening. Captain Woodhaven scoured the enemy ship with his telescope and silently mouthed his countdown to impact. Much quicker than before, the shot hit home sending a cloud of dust and debris scattering over the deck. A smile threatened to cross his face as he watched the two officers reappear on deck from where they had taken cover. One of the men shook his fist defiantly before turning and shouting some orders back over the deck of his vessel. The captain watched for another heartbeat until he saw the hull of the enemy ship begin to turn with the wind.

"All hands! Hard a-larboard! Fire the guns as they bear and take cover!" Captain Woodhaven shouted as loud as he could.

The echo of distant cannon reports sounded. Soft booms that blew clouds of smoke from the side of the enemy ship. United States reeled in a hard turn and her guns thundered their response as the enemy came within view. One by one the cannons blasted out clouds of thick smoke as their projectiles took flight. The shriek of incoming fire came in the midst of United States' cannons thundering their shots. Part of the starboard railing exploded into a storm of wooden shards, a brace line snapped and recoiled through the air as a third impact slammed high on the hull. The deck of United States had become a frenzy. Sailors rushed to aid their wounded brothers while others scrambled to correct the ship back onto their original course. Below deck, the air was thick with cannon smoke and shouted orders as the gun crews raced to make their guns ready to fire again.

"Mr. Smith," Captain Woodhaven shouted.

"Aye captain," Mr. Smith called back as he dragged himself to his feet and began to make his way across the deck.

"Bring us about with the wind on our larboard beam, have the gun crews ready to fire as her stern presents." The captain shouted as he made his way along the starboard rail while helping a pair of crewmen to their feet.

"Aye, aye, captain." Mr. Smith turned and ran for the quarterdeck to pass along the captain's orders.

The light of evening was fading fast. Captain Woodhaven knew he had to press his advantage now, once the sun set, his enemy could slip away under the cover of darkness. He extended his telescope again and raised it to his eye. The ship had turned and exposed her side to launch a salvo of cannon fire. She was a frigate. Captain Woodhaven felt his ribs tighten as he scanned the side of his adversary. United States had landed some shots on her, a section of railing was blown away and there were two-gun ports that had ragged holes blown next to them. He shifted his telescope and looked over the vessel's stern. His jaw clenched tight with anger as he saw the Union Jack billowing in the wind.

"Damn," he collapsed his telescope and turned inboard to face the deck of his own ship. His crew had recovered from the impacts and were making the course correction he had ordered. If he timed everything correctly, United States would be able to make a hard starboard turn and bring her battery to bear on the Brit's stern.

"Captain!" Lieutenant Smith shouted from the quarterdeck, "Starboard battery is ready to fire!"

"Very well, Mr. Smith," Captain Woodhaven replied, he shifted on his feet and looked out at the British frigate. They were reloading their guns as well. "Hard to starboard. Gun crews may fire as the stern presents to them."

"Aye, aye captain!" Lieutenant Smith replied before running to relay the orders down the ladder well.

The deck of the U.S.S United States shifted hard as her helmsman heaved the ship's wheel for all his worth. Captain Woodhaven could feel his pulse pounding up into his throat as the British frigate's quarter presented. His gun crews held their fire, waiting for the target he had ordered. United States slid through her turn and the quartermaster ordered the helmsman to return course to bear straight away. Captain Woodhaven paced his way up the starboard railing before pausing by the mainmast to extend his telescope. He lifted the instrument to his eye and gave a hard look at the Brit's stern.

He growled under his breath as he read the ship's name. "H.M.S Cutlass, never hear of you before…" His words were drowned out by the roar of cannons firing from the gun deck below him.

Fort Charles
13 May 1809
Kingston, Jamaica

The cold kiss of iron on his wrists kept Tim Sladen in a near constant state of pain. His cell was cramped and cold, even when he could feel the heat of day coming in through the iron barred window that looked out onto the harbor below. The dungeon cells beneath Fort Charles were a vast improvement from being locked away in the belly of a ship. There wasn't a constant slosh of water on the floor, though condensation did gather on the stone walls in the early morning hours. Unlike being on ship, Fort Charles remained still. Tim had hated the constant sensation of movement on ship. Incessant pitching and heaving, back and forth, side to side. It never ended. Even when the big vessel was sailing in calm shallow waters near the port, there was a constant sense of rocking. His cell, on the other hand, remained unchanging. Its stone walls were unyielding. The iron grate that fronted his cell allowed a draft of cool, humid air to wash through his cell while the window looking out into the world brought little relief even during the heat of the day. His bed was a pair of thick timber planks braced together by iron banding and suspended from the wall with a pair of chains. There was a bucket to relieve himself and a bucket for water. Several times he had dipped his face into the water bucket only to find that the guards had gotten the buckets mixed up when they were refilling his water and dumping his waste. The foul taste would linger in his mouth and nose for days. Just as his water would begin to taste clean, then the guards would do it again. Tim loathed them. The British marines who stood guard over the fort took particular delight in making sure he was miserable. He spent most days listening to the ongoing construction in the fort echo through the cavernous stone tunnels of the dungeon. When the sounds of hammering from the fort ceased serenading him, he drew particular ire in listening to the repetitive clank, ting, clank, ting, coming from the blacksmith shop just downhill from the fort. The repetitive song of construction was interrupted by footfalls of leather soled boots on stone floor and the clanking of iron keys. Tim lay sprawled on his suspended bed of planks as a guard kicked the iron grate that made up the front wall of his cell.

"On your feet, yank. You have a visitor," the marine guard ordered in a growl.

Tim pushed himself up from the plank bed. "How many times must I tell you, I am not a Yankee. I am from the south."

The marine shrugged his shoulders as he sorted through the keys in his hand. "All the same to me."

There was a rattle of iron keys and a metallic click as the guard opened the grated iron cell door. Tim rose to his feet and moved to the rear of the cell as he always did when the sentries came in to remove his waste and refill his water. He faced the back wall and stared out of his barred window. Storm clouds lingered on the southern horizon, but the rest of the skies were clear and bright blue while the harbor was a deeper shade of blue green. It struck him how clear the water was. He could see the outlines of the wreckage his men had caused. Even as he marveled at the sunken warships a pair of merchant brigantines were working to clear the wreckage from the harbor.

"Admiring your handiwork?" a voice asked stiffly.

Tim turned and found the aging admiral he had first met aboard H.M.S North Wind, Admiral Torren. "Quite remarkable progress going on. Judging by the sound of things, the fort should be reconstructed within a matter of days. At least, I hope they will finish. I am beyond sick of listening to the incessant hammering."

Admiral Torren tapped his cane onto the stone floor and tightened his lips before replying, "I wouldn't worry too much about listening to the construction much longer, once the essential elements are completed, I have ordered for a gallows to be erected."

Tim couldn't help but smile. "Admiral, you could have killed me a dozen times over by now. You could have had me shot aboard your ship. You could have hung me from the yards, you could have had my hands bound and tossed me overboard for the sharks. But that lieutenant was right, wasn't he? You want something from me."

Admiral Torren stood with unchanging demeanor. He tapped his cane on the stone floor of the cell and stared at Tim from beneath hooded eyes. "Right you are, Mr. Sladen. Right you are. My visit to you today is not a social call. I am here to learn every bit of information I can about the illicit slave trade going on in my area of responsibility. I want to know who is involved, who is funding the endeavor and who is going to take the helm now that you are incarcerated."

Tim leaned against the stone wall at his back. Weeks of deprivation had left him weakened, and the tainted water had only made his condition worse. "Why would I do anything to help you admiral? You said so yourself. You plan to hang me as soon as your gallows are completed."

Admiral Torren drew a deep breath and traced the floor with his eyes. He tapped his cane on the floor so aggressively that Tim thought it may very well break in half. "I am prepared to offer you your life in exchange for your full cooperation." He let out a deep sigh before continuing, "If you will freely give me the information I desire to know, I will personally sail you to Charleston and turn you over to your American brethren."

Tim shifted on his feet. His head spun with the possibility of not only having his death sentence revoked, but the possibility of having his freedom restored. He had long surrendered to the fate of living out the rest of his days as a prisoner before feeling the bite of a hangman's noose. A rush of emotions overcame him, but he was careful not to let it show in front of the admiral.

"You expect me to believe that?" He asked.

Admiral Torren tapped his cane again and stared hard at him. "It makes little difference to me what you believe. I came here to present you with an option. I believe you know information that could spare lives that will otherwise be lost in this conflict. That is the only reason I am willing to offer you such a barter. Tell me everything you know, and I will let you live, otherwise, I will take exceptional pleasure in watching you hang, as will a good many of my men. Admiral Sharpe was well loved among the fleet, and a very dear friend of mine."

Tim slunk back onto the chain suspended planks that served as his bed. "What do you wish to know?"

The admiral turned and nodded toward one of the marine sentries waiting in the corridor. "Get me a chair, and coffee and something to eat for the both of us. We will be here for some time."

"Aye, sir." The marine replied before marching off to relay the admiral's wishes.

"I would like to know the exact nature of your affiliation with the Lord Governor Geor Alton, and any other governors who were actively cooperating with your scheme. I want to know who you answer to, and I want to know if the threat against Kingston is still active." Admiral Torren took in a deep breath. Tim could see he was clenching and flexing the fist he held his cane with. "I want to know who was cooperating with you in the admiralty office, and don't bother denying it, I know someone was working toward your ends on that side of the Atlantic."

Tim could not fight the smile that threatened to cross his face any longer. He leaned back against the cold hard stone of the fort's foundation. "Admiral, you wouldn't believe me if I told you."

Admiral Torren craned his neck forward, thrusting his jaw toward Tim. "Try me."

"You have no idea who you have crossed, admiral. It would be very wise for you to hang me, bury me, and ask no further questions." Tim sneered as he felt the chill of the stone wall creeping into the flesh of his back.

The admiral took a sidestep as a marine sentry carried in a wooden ladder-back chair and a steward brought in a short table and another a tray loaded with a pot of coffee, a pair of mugs and a platter with bread, butter and a fruit jam. "I'm waiting for my answers Mr. Sladen." He tapped his cane onto the stone floor before lowering himself down into the wooden chair.

"Very well then, admiral," Tim said with a sigh. "The current plot involves using whatever means necessary to feed the demand for slave labor in the United States. Your Governor Alton was my selection. He was weak, easily manipulated, and Jamaica has plenty of coastline. It was a bit out of the way, but I figured at some point the southern coasts of Mississippi and Louisiana would become my preferred delivery to market. Things were falling into line quite nicely. Sure, your Admiral Sharpe was sniffing around, but I figured at some point I was going to have to deal with him anyway. My hope was that the next admiral that was sent would be the same breed as your oaf of a governor." Tim cast a look at the coffee pot as Admiral Torren poured the rich, dark liquid into each of the two cups. "The governor of Nassau, he was sort of an alternate plan. I made sure he was as informed as he needed to be. He and his garrison commander were compensated well so that if the need should arise, they would be cooperative."

The admiral offered Tim a steaming cup of coffee with an extended arm. "The garrison commander?"

Tim smiled as he took the cup, it was warm, and the brew smelled strong and delicious. "Oh yes, admiral. I had to have full cooperation, should the need arise. I didn't want to deal with the same issues twice. East India ships would bring the slaves from the African coast, cross the Atlantic and unload them here in Jamaica. Some of the slaves would be sold here to support the sugar and cotton plantations, while the rest would be cross loaded into American vessels for the last leg of the journey."

"Can't have a company ship sailing into an American port, eh?"

"No, no, admiral, that would draw far too much attention." Tim replied before drawing a sip of his coffee. The warm liquid flooded his taste buds and beat back the chill that had been gripping his bones.

"Just the two governors, then?" Admiral Torren asked as he lifted a slice of bread from the tray and smeared it with butter and then a healthy dollop of red fruit preserve.

Tim nodded as he swallowed a mouthful of coffee. "Just the two governors, and the garrison commander in Nassau. The commander here was awful to work with, I had to have Geor draw up orders for him every time I needed something from his men. It was a massive inconvenience."

"Good," Admiral Torren smiled and handed a piece of dressed bread to Tim, "that means he was doing his duty." He leaned back into his chair and took a bite of his own slice of bread. He chewed for a long moment while casting a stern glare Tim's way. "That answers two of my questions."

Tim swallowed down more of the hot coffee and wiped his mouth with the back of his hand. "Right. The admiralty. Being honest, admiral, I don't rightly know exactly who The Order has within those hallowed walls. But I do know they have someone. They have their fingers everywhere."

"They," Admiral Torren's voice had a hard edge to it, "you keep saying they, they, they. Who is they?"

Tim set his coffee down on the planks next to him. He brushed crumbs from the slice of bread off of his trousers and closed his eyes in a grimace. The Order would kill him for revealing anything about their construct to an outsider, but, then again, so would the admiral if he didn't. He supposed he could feed the old Brit half-truths and see if that would suffice, but what had they ever done for him?

"They, admiral, are the masters of Europe. They have masterminded plots beyond reckoning. The slave trade is just the most recent, and that is because they see it as a means to fund their other endeavors. These men mean to exert their control over the world at large."

'Drowned Maiden'
16 May 1809
14 degrees 33' N, 73 Degrees 15' W

"We've done about all we can for the damage to her hull, Cap'n. We'll need to anchor up somewhere to make proper repairs, but for now, she should hold just fine. There's about two feet of water in the hold, but the pumps are keeping up well enough, so long as we keep them manned, we should be fine." Chibs reported in his growly voice as he struggled to handle his pipe with one hand. "Any ideas where this rogue is leading us to?"

Lilith shook her head. "There are too many Spanish towns along the coast to be sure, though I can't see why he would want to sail for a port, especially flying those red sails."

"Might be he has some connections with the Spaniards, Cap'n. He wouldn't be the first pirate to get cozy with them."

"He is a Frenchman, Chibs," Lilith replied.

"Aye, and my mother was a Scot," Chibs snorted with a chuckle, "That doesn't mean I can't fancy a buxom English girl when I'm in port. Where he's from has little to do with it, Cap'n. He could have friends down there, and let's hope he does, for all of our sake. If you think that line ship was a scary sight, wait until you see a war galley up close and personal like. It's enough to make your hair fall out."

Lilith stared over the starboard rail as sun glittered off the surface of the sea. Steady winds from the east were propelling them along nicely. When she had gone over the chart with Chibs, they had found a plethora of small coves and inlets that would work perfectly to repair the damage to the Maiden and put crew ashore to find supplies to replenish their dwindling stocks. Fresh water would be the first order. The seawater that had invaded the Maiden's hold had spoiled half a dozen barrels, which put them in a precarious position. Fresh water was always a problem at sea. Fresh water and food.

"We'll follow her until we see the coastlines. Another day, maybe two, wouldn't you say Chibs?"

Chibs nodded as he finally wrangled his pipe stem in between his teeth and set to stealing some flame from a nearby lantern. "Aye, two days is a fair reckoning, Cap'n, so long as we don't run into any more weather."

Lilith shook her head and muttered, "Let's pray we don't."

Clunking footsteps announced the presence of someone else at the starboard rail. Lilith and Chibs both turned to see Dr.LeMeux approaching with a piece of folded paper in one hand.

"Doctor. How do our wounded fare?" Lilith asked before Chibs could admonish the pale Frenchman.

Dr.LeMeux shook his head. His hand quivered as he extended the piece of paper in his hand. "Not well, captain. We've lost more than I care to admit."

Chibs growled, "What's the matter? Cutting off their hands not working?"

Lilith shot a glare at her quartermaster before snatching the paper out of Dr.LeMeux's trembling fingers. "What is this?"

The doctor stuttered for a moment before spitting out his reply. W-w-we need supplies, captain. Medicines, bandages and such. I need silk thread for stitching, laudanum, th-th-things of that nature. I thought it prudent to let you know in case we have the opportunity to get some."

Chibs spread his arms open wide. "What? Out here? Are you as dumb as I first thought?"

Dr.LeMeux shook his head. "No, Chibs. In fact, I am quite well educated. I know we won't just find these things floating around out at sea, that is why I need to inform you both, we should put into shore at the first opportunity so that we may acquire these items. It, it won't matter for some of our wounded. Their days are numbered no matter what we do. But it will make a difference for a few."

Lilith opened the scrap of paper and looked over the scribblings. She nodded and handed the paper to Chibs. "Aye, doctor. We'll do what we can. I believe we will be making anchor within a day or two. Supplies will follow shortly after."

Chibs growled deep in his throat and gave the doctor a sideways glare. "A day or two. Can you manage until then?"

Dr.LeMeux nodded and flicked a fleeting look between the captain and her quartermaster. "Y-yes, I suppose w-we can. Though it may mean a few of our more seriously injured may not recover."

Lilith watched Chibs chew at the stem of his pipe and bellow forth a cloud of bluish smoke. She knew he had never been fast friends with the French doctor, a relationship that only became more tense after the amputation of his hand and part of his arm. "We are already short of crew, Chibs. We can't afford to lose the ones we have." She paused for a moment and stared out over the sea gap between the Maiden and the red sailed Batard De Mur. "I don't suppose your friend would be willing to share any of his supplies with us, would he doctor?"

Dr.LeMeux cleared his throat and shifted on his feet in a nervous gesture. "If he has the supplies we need, it would certainly be helpful. I could ask him, if we were to come up abreast of his ship close enough for me to shout across."

Lilith turned to Chibs in time to catch his scowl before it disappeared from his face. "See if we can coax some more speed from her, Chibs. If our new friends can help, we owe it to our crew to try."

Chibs looked aloft and blew a cloud of pipe smoke into the wind. "Aye, Cap'n. I think we can get a few more knots from her." He gave her a quick nod and walked for the helm to order some adjustments.

Lilith stared at her quartermaster for a beat before turning to the doctor. "Doctor, you surprised us all. I didn't expect that you would be an old acquaintance with a pirate of repute."

Dr.LeMeux braced his hands along a section of wooden railing and shook his head. "Nobody is more surprised than I, captain. I had not seen Laurent for years, since we were both young men. We were inseparable in our youth."

"Is he someone we can trust?" Lilith asked.

Dr.LeMeux stared out over the water sweeping by the Maiden's hull. "I think so, captain. But time changes people. The young man I knew, I would trust him absolutely. The man who captains a pirate vessel flying red sails and a red flag. I'm not sure."

Lilith let out a sigh. It was not the answer she had been hoping for. Captain Fontaine had expressed a desire to exact vengeance against the Order for altering the trajectory of his fate. But could he really be trusted? He could be an agent of the Order, luring the Maiden, the first real challenge to their power, into a trap. Her vision traced along the fabric of Batard De Mur's red sails as the Maiden began to pull closer with Chibs' sail changes. Her crew had already suffered enough death and torment. She thought of the onslaught from the British warship. Volley after volley of cannon fire had slammed into the Maiden. She didn't stand a chance. Silently, she admonished herself for her revenge plot. It was selfish and silly. But, somehow, deep inside, there was a part of her that could not let it go. She pictured Trina, the last time they had spoken, the endless fencing practice and all those lessons on sails and lines and ship handling. Her stomach burned with a cold rage. There had to be a way.

The seas rolled with little waves that gently washed along the Maiden's hull. In less than an hour they had sailed close enough to Batard De Mur for Dr.LeMeux and Captain Laurent Fontaine to exchange shouted greetings and for some of the necessary supplies to be passed between ships in a barrel strung onto a line. The supplies proved to be just what the doctor needed. Silk thread, laudanum, a disinfecting ointment and clean bandage material. The captain also sent over herbs he claimed helped to fight off fever. Dr.LeMeux seemed pleased with the supplies and disappeared below deck to continue tending to his patients. Afternoon wore on into evening and soon the Maiden was sailing beneath a clear night sky dotted everywhere by thousands upon thousands of twinkling stars. Fair winds held, and the cool of night was a welcome relief from the sun's burning rays. Batard De Mur pressed southward with the Maiden sailing close on her stern quarter. Calm seas helped to boost the morale of both crews and as the cool of evening set in the smell of cooking food soon lingered in the night air between both ships. Lilith remained on deck long into the night, while memories of her early days aboard the Maiden came over her in waves. She looked to the quarterdeck under the glittering light of the stars and could see her first stint behind the helm with Chibs close at hand to help guide her in her new task. She looked aloft and found that she could see herself clinging to ratlines high in the rigging as Trina pointed out the various sails and stays. She remembered how frightening the heights had been to her and how the movement of the ship almost seemed to paralyze her legs.

"One hand for the ship, girly, and one hand for yourself. Never more than one limb moves at a time. One missed step up in the rigging could cost you your life." Trina's voice played through her mind. She could see her mentor's face just as plain as the day they had that conversation.

The big navy line ship had stolen so much from them. From her. Lilith tried to push down the image of the Maiden's masts toppling over as her decks exploded into a hailstorm of wooden shards. The billowing cloud of dark smoke that had poured from her hull. They had been lucky that the powder magazine hadn't caught fire. The powder magazine. That brought another image into Lilith's mind. She could see herself throwing a ship's lantern into a compact wooden room loaded with barrels and barrels of gunpowder. The explosion would surely take her own life. Chibs would never allow it. If only there was a way to set fire to the magazine without being on the warship itself. Lilith's mind burned with the question as she stared out over the Maiden's stern and watched the sea slip by in a wash of rolling waves. She recalled the last time she had seen Lieutenant Pike as he was rowing toward Nassau. Her gut burned with regret. She had sent both of those men to their deaths on her quest to destroy the network set up by the slave smugglers. If that hadn't been enough to stop them, where would it end? Could she deal a deadly enough blow to stop them? Under her command, the Maiden and her crew had raided plantations, sunk slavers and freed men and women from their oppressors. To her best recollection, Lilith could count half a dozen ships they had taken by force. At least two hundred slaves freed. But, still, the Order continued. Lilith traced her eyes along the dark horizon where only the absence of stars showed the border of the sky and the sea. Batard De Mur's dark outline stood stark on the sea south of her, their red sails billowed black in the night. Perhaps they were her answer. Cool night air whispered past her ears as the breeze caressed her skin. It felt good. Her skin felt a chill while her insides burned with questions and possibilities. Silently, she resolved to see her mission through to its end, even if that meant hers as well.

'H.M.S North Wind'
16 May 1809
17 degrees 6' N, 76 Degrees 13' W

The tea had long gone cold as Lieutenant William Pike stared out the aft array of windows in the captain's cabin. Rolling blue gray waves washed over one another and crested in white caps as they were battered by shifting winds. The lieutenant remained lost in his thoughts as North Wind sailed her course back toward Kingston. He had been tasked with finding and confronting enemy pirates in the Caribbean, and he had done so. The pirate pirates he had encountered, however were in the company of a ship he had watched surrender to the sea in a cove on the coast of Haiti. North Wind had a handful of prisoners from the ship they had managed to overwhelm during the brief engagement, one of which was an especially combative young woman. Lieutenant Pike intended to question her sharply before their arrival in Kingston, though he was unsure if he would gain any reliable information from her. He did not recognize her from his time spent aboard the Drowned Maiden, although she did remind him of Captain Lilith. Seeing the ship again had been a shock. He had seen it succumb to an overwhelming mass of fire from North Wind's own gun batteries. Her hull had been smashed open; her masts had toppled over in violent crashes that sent plumes of water rising all around. The cove had been a scene of smoke and wreckage. When he first witnessed it, he had assumed nobody could have possibly survived. A small plate with cold sliced meat, soft white cheese and a cup of cold tea greeted him as he finally turned inboard and realized he had been adrift in his thoughts. He had tasks awaiting his attention, unpleasant as they may be, he could put them off no longer.

"Mr.Tallun," the lieutenant said in a voice loud enough for him to be heard through the thick cabin door.

"Yes, sir?" the response came from a marine sentry as the cabin door opened slightly.

"See to it that the Spanish girl is brought to my quarters in irons, for questioning," Lieutenant Pike said with a wave of his hand, "and pass the word for Gareth not to worry about supper, I have not touched the food he brought in earlier, but I would like some coffee. My tea has gone cold."

The marine sentry nodded and knuckled his forehead. "Aye, sir."

Lieutenant Pike pulled at the thinly sliced meat and took a bite. The flavor of tangy smoke and salt invaded his senses as he chewed on a mouthful before dabbing some into the soft cheese and taking another bite. He hadn't realized how long it had been since he had last eaten. Hunger pangs dug at his stomach as he wolfed down another bite of meat and cheese while waiting for his coffee.

A knock at the cabin door notified him that his marine sentry had arrived with the prisoner.

"Enter," he said as he set the emptied plate to the side of his cabin desk and stood from his seat.

The cabin door opened and a dark-haired girl with copper toned skin was escorted in with a sentry at each shoulder. "The prisoner you requested, sir," one of the sentries reported.

Lieutenant Pike motioned to a chair on the opposite side of his desk. "Thank you, gentlemen. You may leave us." He looked the young woman in her eyes and found a cold fury that made his blood chill. "Have a seat."

"Vete el diablo!" the young woman snarled without moving from the spot the sentries had left her.

Lieutenant Pike stood for a moment and surveyed the young woman. She was beautiful, with curls of long dark hair that fell across her shoulders. Her eyes were a deep brown with long eyelashes, high cheekbones framed her angular face over a proud jawline. Her lips were full and thick. The lieutenant found himself at a loss for words, dumbstruck by her beauty and fiery intensity. She stared at him with a burning hatred. If there were a weapon within reach, he knew that she would attempt to use it.

"I have called you in here to ask a few questions of you. Please, sit, there is no reason we cannot behave in a civilized manner."

Her eyes shifted from one side of the room to the other, searching for something she didn't find, but she did not move. "This is the ship that opened fire and sank the Drowned Maiden."

Lieutenant Pike nodded. "It is."

"So, you are the enemy of my friends. Why would I help you?" the girl asked as she let her gaze fall back onto him.

Lieutenant Pike did his best to meet her stare. "The Maiden is after slavers in the Caribbean, is she not?"

"Among other things, yes," the girl replied with an edge in her voice.

"It was not I, who ordered the batteries to open fire on the Maiden and her crew. In fact, at one point, I sailed aboard her."

The girl deflected her face toward one side of the cabin and pursed her lips. "Lies."

"Not at all, young lady. In fact, I probably know

more of her crew than you think. Lilith, Chibs, Omibwe and his mother Jilhal. I rescued Trina after her ship was sunk by a slaver and she was left adrift at sea. I have no reason to want them dead. In fact, the Royal Navy shares part of Captain Lilith's mission."

The young woman turned back and stared at the lieutenant. "What is that?"

"Parliament has abolished the slave trade. It is the duty of the Royal Navy to enforce the rule of law on the high seas for vessels bearing our colors. If there are British ships continuing to smuggle slaves, we are duty bound to stop it and bring their captains and crews to justice."

The girl shrugged. "It seems to me you are more concerned with sinking ships and taking prisoners of your own."

Lieutenant Pike laid his hands flat on the desk, he leaned some of his weight forward onto his wrists and carefully considered his next words. "I was not in command of this vessel when she opened fire on the Maiden. Piracy is a crime, however, and I am duty bound to bring Captain Lilith and all of those who sail beneath a black flag to justice."

"What do you want from me?" the girl asked.

Lieutenant Pike pulled in a slow breath through his nose. If she was scared, she was skilled at hiding it. "In time, I would like to know where the Maiden is sailing to next. It may be that you don't know. If that is the case, fine. You were aboard a vessel sailing in concert with the Maiden, a known pirate crew responsible for the taking or sinking of at least five vessels. You will be brought before a representative of the king and stand trial for piracy. Given that you are a woman, and your age, I imagine you will be spared the gallows, but it is nonetheless a serious charge." He paused to see if his words would have any effect on her. They didn't. She stood firm in front of his desk with her chin held high as the iron shackles binding her wrists creaked with the motion of the ship. "There are considerations we can make, for you and for those who still sail with Captain Lilith. Given the nature of her past, and the motivation behind her crimes, she may even be offered a pardon. But much depends on the manner of her surrender."

The girl's eyes narrowed. "I have not spent much time with her, but I doubt she will give surrendering much consideration."

He shook his head. "I think you are probably right. But it is not too late for you. Tell me. How did you come to be in the company of the Drowned Maiden?"

Silence hung in the air and Lieutenant Pike found himself sipping at his coffee to break the tension. "There was a man, my father and I found him unconscious in a ditch next to the road south of our villa. He was wounded. His hands, arms, knees and feet were all torn to shreds like he had been hacked to ribbons by a dozen swords. He had deep cuts in his face and along his side. My father said that if we did not help him, he would die before the day was gone. We took him to our home. I cleaned and bandaged his wounds, and we watched over him until he woke up several days later. It took many weeks, but slowly his strength began to return to him. He said that he was aboard a ship that was attacked by pirates. He described a nearby cove where he said they had made their anchorage. My father tried to convince him to move forward with his life, to find peace with the wrongs he had suffered and to forgive those who had wronged him. He ate from our table and slept beneath our roof. We clothed him and nursed him back to health. He lived with us for months.

"Eventually, my father let him help with chores around the house. When he was strong enough, he started to help with the lumber for the shipwright. I believe my papa was planning to help him get his own tools and introduce him to one of the craftsmen in Tortuga where he could work under a master and learn a trade." The girl's voice faded as she spoke, its hard, defiant edge softened. "He murdered my father and fled from me before I could take my vengeance."

Lieutenant Pike stared at the girl for a long time while her words sunk in. North Wind shifted beneath his feet. Bells rang and the clatter of footfalls sounded as the watch changed. Her face remained unchanged, a picture of stern resolve thinly masking a simmering rage held just beneath the surface.

"The man you took in, did he give you his name?" he asked.

The girl's lips pressed together in a tight expression as if she did not want to divulge any more information than she already had. Her eyes narrowed. Lieutenant Pike was struck by her beauty even through the tense expression. He made a point to soften his face by arching his eyebrows and leaning his weight back onto his feet and off of his wrists.

"I cannot help you if you will not speak to me," he said. "From what it sounds like to me, you were seeking justice for your father and found yourself in the company of these pirates. That is not a crime. If you did not participate in the taking or sinking of a ship, I believe I can gain you some leniency, but, you have to help me."

The cold stare on the girl's face broke for a moment. Her lips parted slightly as if she were about to speak. But, after only a moment, she returned to the same steely expression she had held before. Lieutenant Pike took a deep breath and let it go in a long sigh. He chewed at his lower lip before pacing around the end of the desk and lifting one leg to sit on its edge in front of the young woman. With folded arms he furrowed his brow and decided to try one more time.

"There is a prisoner in Kingston who was taken from the wreckage of a slaver vessel off the coast of Haiti. From the sound of his story, it could be the very same man you are looking for. Give me the name of the man who killed your father."

The girl's eyes widened. Her posture went rigid with expectation and Lieutenant Pike took note that her hands curled into fists and pulled the chains binding her iron shackles taut. "His name was Tim Sladen."

4

'U.S.S United States'
12 May 1809
36 degrees 4' N, 74 Degrees 5' W

A piercing shriek filled the air. It was followed by another and then another. The horrid noise of crunching and cracking timbers followed. Captain Woodhaven tried to lift himself from the deck of his ship only to find his weight thrown back down with a savage shudder that jarred his limbs. Screams sifted through clouds of acrid cannon smoke while his officers called out to their sections to ascertain damage. His broadside had landed, but so had theirs.

"Mr. Porter! Marines to the main deck, prepare to repel borders!"

The call reverberated through the air and nestled its way into Captain Woodhaven's mind. It sent icy fingers up his back and wrapped his spine with ribbons of fear and doubt. Repel borders. They were about to be boarded by a hostile force, or so the voice that had called the command thought. Repel borders. Swords, pistols, bayonets, rail pins, fists, teeth, these were the weapons it would come down to. Swivel gun and musket fire billowed through the rigging. The captain tried again, bunching his arms beneath his body and forcing his weight up off of the deck timbers and onto his hands and knees. More screams ripped through the smoke-filled air. A warm sensation tickled at his cheek. He lifted one hand and ran his fingers along his face. It was liquid. He withdrew his hand and held it in front of his eyes. Blood. Was it his? He felt no searing pain. No hot pang of sword or pistol wound. With a shove from his arms, he managed to hoist himself up onto his feet. United States was damaged, her railing had been battered by the incoming volley. Bodies lay in various contortions of pain and agony across his main deck. Severed lines crossed the seams of shattered timbers where blood collected in tiny rivulets along coarse wood grains. The captain stumbled forward and braced himself against the main mast as his crew swarmed around the deck removing the bodies of the dead and wounded. Marines armed with muskets and cutlasses began to form a line along the shattered railing and the call went out to fix bayonets.

A gust of breeze swept over the chaos of U.S.S United States' deck taking the thick cloud of gun smoke out to sea with it. For a moment he could see them. They were lined up on the deck of their own ship a mere thirty yards apart from his. Their officers were scrambling on deck, sailors hurried away their wounded while royal marines prepared to engage in a close quarter fight. Their ship had not gone untouched. Captain Woodhaven could see a section of the railing blown away, shredded deck timbers and torn lines. He scoured the enemy vessel for a moment as the cannon smoke continued to clear. They had sustained one wound he had not. Courage and hope built in his chest. Suddenly, the screams of his wounded sailors seemed to fade away as if they had not cried out at all. With a shove, he lifted his weight away from his main mast and paced toward the shattered railing of his ship. Across the sea gap, amid smoke and chaos and pain, he could see the enemy's mast and the twisted shreds of shattered wood at its base. It wasn't severed. The mast was still holding, but it would only take a small strain before the wounded timber would succumb and fall to the surface of the sea.

For a moment, it seemed as if time slowed to a crawl. The finest details became glaring. Blood puddled on the deck beneath his feet. The shouts of his crew. The report of muskets from marine marksmen high aloft. His heartbeat throbbing through his chest and into his neck. The feel of the breeze brushing against his skin. Sweat trickling down his face. Captain Woodhaven reached to his side and felt the familiar curved handle of his officer's sword. He drew the blade in a single sweeping motion and forced his feet to propel him to the battered rail of his ship where sailors and marines locked shoulder to shoulder.

"Come on over then, you tea swilling cowards!" The voice that escaped from his throat didn't feel like his own. It was as if he had been possessed by a revenge bent demon. He waved his cutlass and swept his eyes over the men to either side of him. "Kill every last Brit that dares to set foot on this ship! If it takes your last ounce of strength, make them pay dearly for every inch!" A roar of shouted agreement rose up from the deck of United States. "If they kill us all, let the last man blow the powder magazine! They will not have our ship!" Another roar of shouts and yells drowned out the captain's last words while ropes with grapple hooks attached to them sailed through the air toward his ship. The first few hooks landed inertly into the sea separating the two vessels. More taunts flew through the air while marines loosed accurate musket fire onto the attacking crew. The first hook that landed bit into timber amidships before its rope was swiftly cut away by a quick sailor with an ax close at hand. Swivel guns erupted throwing scatters of lead shrapnel whizzing in both directions. Captain Woodhaven heard the commands of gun captains on the deck beneath him. Another grapple hook thudded down onto the deck before its rope was pulled taut.

"Cut away that line!" he shouted.

A flurry of sailors hurried to execute the order when the roar of a swivel gun erupted from across the small gap between ships. The impact of lead balls and scrap iron sliced into wood and flesh and ripped more of United States' rigging. A second grapple landed and was quickly being pulled tight by the enemy crew.

"The lines! Cut away the lines," Captain Woodhaven shouted, "and for God's sake, somebody find out why the gun deck hasn't fired another volley yet!"

The deck of United States erupted in zips and pops of incoming musket fire. Splintered shards of wood ripped into the air and more sailors fell from accurate shots. Captain Woodhaven could see the situation deteriorating around him. Accurate fire prevented his sailors from cutting away the grapple lines, his ship was wounded, his men were being cut down in volleys of musket and swivel gun fire. Something had to be done. He couldn't just stand by and watch his vessel be boarded. Across the narrowing gap of sea separating United States from her enemy he could hear the British sailors preparing for a boarding. They heaved at the grapple lines and shouted taunts and insults. Pistols fired. Swords were brandished into the dying light of the evening. Desperation clutched at the captain's throat. His deck was littered in dead and wounded. The sailors and marines still fit to fight were clinging to their courage by thread. He feared that one more blow would make them break. Thoughts of one of America's prized heavy frigates falling into the hands of the enemy arose in his mind. He felt his hands go ice cold. More grapple lines were thrown across, too many to cut away. Panic threatened to seize him. He felt it creep into his chest, threatening to squeeze the air from his lungs.

"Captain! Larboard battery ready to fire!" a voice filtered up from below.

As if a wave of rage had crashed over him, Captain Woodhaven drove away his fear and drew a deep breath before screaming at the top of his lungs, "Fire!"

The roar of the gun battery bellowed in the narrow space between ships. Smoke curled from the snouts of cannons protruding from United States' hull. The entire ship seemed to tremble from the reverberating thunder of the volley. It rang in the captain's ears and shook through his chest so hard he could feel it in his bones. A breath of silence followed and for a moment nothing existed between the two ships but a thick cloud of gun smoke. One heartbeat elapsed, then another. Screams filled the air. High pitched wails of pain and anguish that made Captain Woodhaven's blood run cold as the hair on his neck and arms stood on end. The screams were interrupted by a creaking noise. Wooden fibers that had been conditioned to holding against strain were cracking and splitting. As the breeze cleared away cannon smoke, Captain Woodhaven braced himself against a stay line and focused on the deck of H.M.S Cutlass. The volley had caused a slaughter. The enemy deck was strewn with broken lines and shattered timbers, bodies and body parts were scattered in a gruesome scene of gore and destruction. It was a horrid sight, worse than United States' losses just at first glance. But, the threat was not over.

"Look out! Her mast is going to give!" a sailor shouted from aloft in the rigging.

Captain Woodhaven glanced up toward the British warship's main mast. It had been damaged in their first exchange, but now it had taken a second hit just above the first one. The massive timber trunk cracked and groaned under the strain of its own weight. Captain

Woodhaven could see the higher portions of the mast were wavering back and forth in a deadly wobble. The splitting sound of wood cracked through the air as the mast leaned over and finally succumbed to wind and gravity. The panic and fear that had seeped into every fiber of Captain Woodhaven's body relented and was replaced by a rising rush of sheer determination.

"Now boys! While we have them on their heels! Cut away those lines," he shouted, "get those guns reloaded and fire when ready! We might just carry the day!"

On the deck of H.M.S Cutlass, her crew was beginning to recover from the barrage United States had just loosed on them. Sailors were dragging the dead and wounded away while more men appeared from below deck with weapons in hand. It was a race to open a gap before the Brits could board their ship. Axes cut at grapple lines amid exchanges of pistol and musket fire. A group of royal marines raced to extend a gangplank between the two ships while Woodhaven's crew struggled to cut away the lines holding their ship in the enemy's grasp. Musket fire sizzled and whizzed through the air cutting into wood and flesh. Men dropped to the decks of both ships, screaming and writhing in agony. The first of the enemy to cross decks did so over the battered wooden rails of both vessels. They were met with cutlasses, hand axes and bayonets. The clatter of a gangplank being placed sent a rolling wave of action flooding across United States' deck. Marines rushed forward to meet the first attackers attempting to board. They fired their muskets and jabbed with their bayonets while Captain Woodhaven barked commands to his sailors to free their ship from the enemy's clutches.

"Cut away those lines!" He bellowed forward to the bow where three grapples remained in place. "Helm! Steer us hard a-starboard and give us some standoff for another volley!"

His shouts seemed lost amongst the din of battle. Swords clashed and pistols barked. Men shouted commands and encouragements to their shipmates while others hurled taunts and insults at their enemies. The first wave had come aboard, and the fighting was intense. Captain Woodhaven wheeled his cutlass and stabbed at an approaching British sailor as the man attempted to swing an ax at him. He stepped between a pair of fallen sailors and raised his pistol to line up a shot at the enemy's helmsman. With a careful pause, he lined up his sight as best he could and squeezed the trigger until a satisfying thump reverberated up his arm while a belch of bluish smoke coughed from the barrel of his weapon. He watched as the helmsman across decks fell while clutching his chest. H.M.S Cutlass' wheel spun freely for a moment and her hull slowly began to drift in the direction of her fallen mast as the current of the ocean dragged her away.

More pistol shots sounded. The clash of steel clattered between the reports of muskets and cries of sudden pain. With the ships finally separated, the crew of the United States fought to retake their own deck from the handful of enemies that had crossed over. The gangplank had fallen away into the sea and with nowhere to retreat, the last of the enemy sailors surrendered as Captain Woodhaven and his men advanced on them with swords, bayonets, pistols and muskets. It had been a pitched fight. The United States barely managed to get away in time. Had their ship been locked together with the enemy any longer than it had, Captain Woodhaven knew, the outcome would have been very different. A cheer rose up into the wind as the last light of day faded from the world. While he couldn't quite call it a victory, they had survived their scrape with a British heavy frigate.

Fort Charles
13 May 1809
Kingston, Jamaica

He was a pitiful sight, really. His beard had grown wild and unkempt during his weeks of incarceration. The treatment he had received at the hands of the guards however, was unacceptable. Admiral Torren made a note to take the issue up with the captain commanding his marine detachment. The cold, damp conditions within the stones that formed the foundations of Fort Charles gave the admiral a slight chill even as he sat on a cushioned chair and sipped at a cup of hot coffee delivered by his men. It seeped into his joints and brought a slow, churning throb to his knees and ankles. The admiral shrugged off the pain. He would walk it away on his journey back through Kingston to the governor's mansion. For now, though, he sat through his discomfort and stared at the

American prisoner as he wolfed down the coffee he had offered.

"I suppose a proper meal is in order for you, should you be of further use to us," the admiral said before taking a healthy sip of the rich, dark coffee. The warmth felt good in his throat and fought away the chill that was creeping into his joints.

Tim nodded after draining his cup. "I can tell you quite a bit about the organization, but, I am afraid I don't know the details of their current plans. Things being as they are."

Admiral Torren cradled his coffee cup in between his hands and let the heat radiate into his fingers. "Where does it start? The Order. Every snake has a head. This one is no different."

Tim shook his head and extended his empty cup toward the admiral. "That, I couldn't tell you. I do know the British lords who hold stake of ownership in the East India Trading Company play their part, but, so does Napoleon. There is also involvement from the Vatican, little pieces and snippets I picked up in conversation with my former employer. He had spies from many different nations in his employ, Brits, French, Spanish and Dutch. He even received reports from some of the Jesuit missionaries along the coast of South America from time to time. It is like I said, admiral, you have no idea what you are facing. The slave trade is only one arm of this. The Order has dealings in the far east, you may have heard, the emperor of China has forbidden the import of opium."

Admiral Torren arched his brows and filled Tim's

coffee. "I have, actually. I have also heard it has given rise to a fleet of smugglers that could rival the strength of my own navy."

Tim snorted and leaned back into the plank bunk suspended from his cell wall. "The problem is, admiral, the bulk of the smuggled opium is being moved by company ships. The left hand doesn't know what the right is doing."

"Are you suggesting, Mr. Sladen," Admiral Torren replaced the pot of coffee onto a small table by his chair and folded one leg over the other, "that the King of the British Empire is somehow involved in all of this?"

Tim shook his head and sipped at his coffee. "You still don't get it, admiral. You are thinking on too small of a scale. This goes beyond your monarch, which I assure you, is completely oblivious to the threat."

Suddenly, the coffee seemed utterly inadequate to fight the chill threatening to overcome him. "What do you mean?"

Tim smiled and set his coffee on the plank bunk where he sat. "The Vatican, admiral, think about this for a moment. Since the rise of Protestantism in England and its subsequent spread overseas to the Americas, the British Empire has made itself the greatest threat to the spread of the Catholic Church and thus, the power of the pope. When explorers found the new world, the pope declared South America the dominion of Spain and North America the dominion of France. What gives him this authority? The church. The power of the faith of millions upon millions of people. If he were to excommunicate a sitting monarch, he could have their head on a spike and a new, more cooperative man installed within a fortnight. But, after the reformation, he no longer wields that type of control over the English. England becomes Britain, expands, and reaches its fingers into the new world. Do you see now? Do you understand? This goes beyond the power of kings."

Admiral Torren sat in silence as the warmth faded from the cup of coffee nestled between his hands. "What could the Vatican possibly hope to accomplish by smuggling opium into China?"

"How many Chinese do you think are converting to Catholicism?" Tim asked with widened eyes.

"Very few, if any," Admiral Torren replied.

"But, if the East India Company were to be discovered as part of the opium trade, how do you think the Chinese would react? Would they allow them their influence in Hong Kong?"

"Certainly not," the admiral said as he saw a greater picture being formed.

"It is not about slaves, or opium, or spices or any other specific medium. It is about eroding the power of the British Empire until it collapses in on itself. Do you think the gunpowder plots were organized without outside encouragement? Or the first shot at Lexington? You'll never be able to prove it with any certainty, but I promise you, The Order has their fingers in all of it."

Admiral Torren leaned back in his chair and drew a breath of the damp air within the cell. It felt as though a ship's worth of ballast stones had been dumped onto his shoulders. These accusations were preposterous, so outlandish and far-fetched that if he were to take them before the sitting authority in Britain he would be laughed off as a crackpot. But, logically, if he dismissed the grandeur, it made sense. The protestant reformation and its subsequent offshoots presented a growing portion of the world's nations which the catholic church could not exert its influence.

"The struggle in Ireland, with the papists?"

Tim nodded his head. "Now, you are beginning to see. This is bigger. Every move they make, they create another struggle for Britain and reap profits at the same time. It is a steady, constant stream of gold flowing toward the Vatican, which then goes back out and is used to fuel yet another conflict."

"And you know all of this, how? You are a foot soldier in this war, are you not?"

Tim plucked his cup off of the bunk and drained it in one long draft. "I am. But, I listen, I pay attention. My employer used to an officer in the British army. He was instrumental in getting The Order involved in the slave trade. He is a vicious, unforgiving man, and he would cut my throat from ear to ear if he knew that I shared any of the information I have discussed here with you today. Some of which, he isn't aware that I know. But, like I said, I pay attention."

"So. The Order is an arm of the catholic church?" Admiral Torren folded his arms across his chest to fight the chill from gripping his torso. His desire to leave the dungeon cell grew by the heartbeat as Tim began to solidify the fear that had been nagging at the back of his mind for months. Something sinister was afoot, and it had a far-reaching breadth, greater than even he had first imagined. It had been difficult enough to picture a smuggling conspiracy involving officers of the East India Company subverting parliament, and the involvement of a governor, but this was too much. It was too big. There were too many unproven details, too many facets that would never be able to be nailed down. How could he ever hope to combat this? The cell he sat in with the American prisoner seemed to shrink around him. His joints were stiffened by the cold and damp while his mind buzzed with the information, he had just taken in.

"The catholic church as a whole, I am sure, knows little to nothing of these dealings. Information like this, a conspiracy like this would rip at the pious fabric they wrap themselves in. No. This has to be controlled by a select group, a few very powerful men."

"Who?" Admiral Torren pressed with narrowed eyes.

"That, admiral, is a very good question," Tim replied before leaning back against the stone wall of his cell. "It is a question I have had myself. Is the pope himself involved? Some bishops or some such? There is no telling, really. Whoever knows that sort of intelligence is likely well in their grasp. The only reason I know as much as I do is that I delivered messages for my employer, Mr. Clyde Ritten. He organized the backing of The Order for the continuation of the slave trade, he hailed their intervention when the tides of fervor in the new world favored war for independence. He knows far more than I do."

The admiral scoured Tim's face with his stare, searching for any sign of deception. This was the man who had twisted the minds of his own ship's marines to stage a mutiny against him, at the cost of many lives and very nearly his own. What could he have to gain by lying?

"Can you prove any of these things?" the admiral asked with a cocked eyebrow.

Tim shrugged and shook his head. "No. That is the point, admiral. No one man could ever hope to prove anything beyond corrupted government officials. That is why your friend Admiral Sharpe is dead. He started poking around, asking too many questions."

"And the captains of the Indiamen. They don't have questions of their own?" the admiral prodded with a doubtful frown.

"Gold satisfies most curious minds, admiral. But, your friend, Admiral Sharpe, he was not the type to be bought off. Same as you." Tim replied with a defeated slump of his shoulders.

Admiral Torren could feel warmth returning to his chest at the fond memory of his old friend. "No, Mr. Sladen. You are right about that. He was not, and, neither am I."

Tim rattled the shackles binding his hands together. "But, you are a man of your word, admiral. Are you not? You promised that you would stay my execution and deliver me into the hands of my countrymen."

Admiral Torren nodded and panned his eyes around the damp, dark cell. "I did, Mr. Sladen. And I will have you know that I am a man of my word. I will stay your execution, which is far better than you deserve. As far as delivering you to the American authorities, well, perhaps the next time my flagship makes port in an American harbor. Though, I doubt that will be anytime soon given the tense state of affairs between our two nations. In fact, before we had the wretched misfortune of bringing you aboard as a prisoner, my fleet was engaged by an American frigate. No, Mr. Sladen, I doubt we will be seeing any hospitality from the former colonies for quite some time."

Tim narrowed his eyes. "You son of a bitch. You never intended to release me in the first place."

Admiral Torren did his best to feign a smile as his knees and ankles ached with pain from the cold dampness of the fort's stony bowels. "Nonsense, Mr. Sladen. I was quite upfront and honest with you, we just never discussed a time line for these events to take place. All in good time."

Admiral Torren grit his teeth and forced himself up from his seat. He nodded to the American sitting on the plank bunk and turned to make his exit. "I will return for another of these productive conversations. More cooperation on your part just may purchase you a change in your situation. In any case, I must leave you now. I have letters to write."

As the admiral made his way out of the stone walled cell and into the corridor he could hear Tim's voice issue one final rebuttal to their exchange.

"Be careful those letters don't become a dagger in your back, admiral."

'Drowned Maiden'
22 May 1809
12 degrees 26' N, 72 Degrees 08' W

"Land in sight!" The call echoed down to Lilith's hearing as fingers of dawn stretched toward the heavens. The brilliance of night was fading as hues of pink and orange invaded the inky black of night and drowned away the glitter of the stars. Along the southern horizon, at the very far edge of sight, a sliver of darkness extended from east to west. Lilith shielded her eyes from the early dawn glare and studied the coastline that lay far ahead. In the growing light she could make out shores of jagged rock and thick vegetation where tall trees overhung the surf zone. Through the distance it appeared as one long stretch of solid landmass though Lilith knew better after the hours she had spent pouring over charts in her cabin with Chibs. The South American coast was littered with coves and inlets, jutting fingers of land and river deltas that would offer the Maiden a plethora of opportunities to seek cover. In addition to its varied coastline, the north coast offered a list of towns and villages longer than Lilith's cutlass. The waters off of the north coast played host to shipping lanes that saw some of the most frequent traffic of anywhere in the world. All of the commerce, over time, attracted some of the most famous pirates to ever don a black flag to the Caribbean winds, and where there are pirates, the world's navies will surely follow. All of this weighed heavy on Lilith's mind as more of the horizon was dominated by the looming trees and rising mountains of the South American coast.

"Looks like our friends are tacking off toward the west," Chibs noted through a breath of pipe smoke, "want we should shadow them Cap'n?"

Lilith studied the sleek hull of Batard De Mur in the growing morning light. Her sails had shifted and her bow slid through the water at a slight angle before heeling over toward the opposite direction and bearing slightly southwest. "Aye, follow them. They are probably wanting to find somewhere to hole up for a spell. I can't imagine their captain is mad enough to sail these waters under red canvas." She paused for a long spell before nodding toward Chibs. "Let's follow them, but keep a wary distance, fast friends have a way of turning into foes."

Chibs replied with throaty growl that seemed to begin in his barrel chest and sweep into the wind along with the bluish cloud of smoke it was mixed with. "Aye, Cap'n. Seems like you stole the thought right out of my head. Fast friends indeed, but a band of pirates shouldn't be so easily trusted."

"Have the guns readied Chibs. If they are leading us to an ambush, I wont go without a fight."

Chibs pulled the stem of his pipe from his teeth and nodded. "Aye, I'll have the guns ready, perhaps we would do well to have the crew armed up."

Lilith shifted her gaze back out across the sea and watched as Batard De Mur slid through the slight waves that rolled away from the coastline as the tide slipped away beneath them. She was a sleek vessel, smaller than the Maiden, but that made her nimble. Her deck was loaded with cannons and swivel guns. If her armament was handled half as well as her sails, she would be formidable in any fight. But, her captain had ordered her about in the face of the big British line ship. He wasn't out to chase glory or valor. Lilith wondered if he would prove to be a stalwart friend should the Maiden ever need one. Somehow, even though the captain had shown himself to be a loyal friend to Dr.LeMeux, she doubted that would carry over to the rest of the crew.

"Sail on the horizon! Due west of us, and coming on fast!"

The cry from high in the rigging took Lilith by surprise and lit her blood with a jolt of lightning. In a swift fluid motion, she dashed to the starboard rail of the Maiden and clasped onto a stay line with one hand while searching the horizon for any sign of the sighted ship. Pale blue skies with wispy white clouds met the briny gray sea surface but belied no form of the white canvas she searched for. With a look aloft she searched for the lookout who had sighted the ship and called out, "Where away?"

"Off west, captain. Near dead even with our main, square rigged and sailing this way!" The voice was that of Jilhal, one of Lilith's most experienced sailors and the mother of her one legged helmsman.

"Any sign of colors?" Lilith called back.

Jilhal shook her head before answering, "She's too far out to tell captain, but I'll keep watching for them."

Lilith's mind raced with possibilities. The unknown ship could be anyone, another pirate, perhaps someone in league with her newfound cohort. It could be Spanish, French, British, even Dutch. All of those possibilities spelled bad outcomes for the Maiden. She was already damaged from her encounter with the big British line ship. Another engagement could spell disaster. She tried to recall exact details from the charts she had studied. The north coast held a trove of places to seek refuge. But, could they beat the new found ship to the coastline?

"Chibs, rig all sails, come about with the wind at our beam, I don't want that ship getting within range," Lilith said as she studied the fill of the Maiden's sails.

"Aye, Cap'n, but, what of Batard De Mur? Should we warn them?" Chibs replied through a puff of his pipe.

Lilith shot a glance forward to the red sailed pirate ship sliding its way through the low Caribbean waves. "I'm sure they are keeping watch on the horizons, same as us. If they haven't seen it by now, they will soon."

As if cued by Lilith's words, Batard De Mur shifted from its southward heading. Shouted orders floated over the gap of seawater as her red sails adjusted to a new sailing condition. Her crew had noted the newcomer, and like the Maiden, they wanted nothing to do with a fresh engagement. Lilith watched as the nimble ship piled on more red sail. Their bow slid through the low waves with ease at first, but started to take them with more impact as the ship gained speed.

"They're making quite a run for it," Chibs noted over Lilith's shoulder as the pair of them watched the red sailed vessel fly even more canvas. "Suppose they know something we don't?"

Lilith narrowed her one good eye as Batard De Mur's hull cut through a wave and bobbled under the force of her sails for a split second. "Whatever that ship is, it appears our new friends want nothing to do with her. Seasoned pirates on a maneuverable vessel armed to the gills with every manner of cannon and swivel they can carry. I'd say we ought to pile on some more sail, Chibs, if we can."

The salty quartermaster drew a long puff from his pipe and cast a look up into the rigging. "We can still fly top gallants and sky sails. The mast is in good shape, we may even be able to get away with running out stunsails. We won't make as much speed as they are, but, hopefully we will make enough to stay out of that other ship's range for a time."

Lilith followed Chibs' gaze back to where a white sail was barely beginning to protrude from the horizon. The morning chill traced along her skin while the wind stung her remaining eye. Batard De Mur was sailing with all speed to escape contact with the distant but approaching ship. A knot formed in her stomach as Chibs shouted orders to the crew. A tone of urgency laced the edges of his voice. Lilith had heard that tone before, but never when the Maiden was sailing in favorable winds. It reminded her of the icy tone Chibs' orders had carried when the Maiden was being stalked by a pair of British warships, both of which had the gunnery power to lay her on the bottom of the sea. She had managed to come out on top during those engagements by the razor's edge of her wits and those of her crew. Seamanship, smart maneuvering and clever tactics had forestalled the Maiden's doom several times in the past. She hoped that if the pursuing ship managed to come within range, the combined strength and smarts of her and her crew would somehow be able to pull off another victory.

Expectant stares and grudging glances over the Maiden's stern dominated most of the morning. As the sun rose from its low break over the eastern horizon toward its zenith overhead the sails that stalked Lilith and her crew grew ever larger to the west. Her colors were still obscured, but the bluff lines and rigging of her sails made Chibs announce his opinion that she was Spanish made. Spanish made did not necessarily mean Spanish navy, however, the salty quartermaster was quick to point out, she could be a privateer, a trade galley, or even another pirate. Lilith didn't like any of those options, save for the off chance she was a trade galley. A merchant vessel would have steered well off from two unfamiliar ships and made her inert intentions well known. This ship hadn't.

"Do you suppose she is a pirate hunter? Or maybe even another pirate?" Lilith asked.

Chibs squinted hard as he stared at the approaching canvas. "Hard to say, Cap'n. Whatever she is, she's definitely taken an interest in us, or in our cohort with red sails. They are gaining ground on us, or so to speak, Cap'n."

Lilith matched Chibs' gaze. The white canvas stalking its way toward them had become larger even as they spoke. "How soon do you think until we are within range of their chase guns?"

"Three hours, four at the most," Chibs answered with a resigned breath of smoke.

"And how far are we from making the coast?"

Chibs turned and looked over the bow while rubbing his chin and drawing a lungful from the pipe clenched in his bite. "Two hours if the winds hold. But, it's a dicey proposition, Cap'n. Its one thing to lose a chasing ship at the edge of daylight, or in fouled weather, its entirely different with clear skies at midday. We could make for a cove, or tuck into some inlet, but they'll see us and follow."

Lilith scrunched her nose while keeping her eye locked onto the pursuing vessel. She made a silent calculation in her mind before closing her eye and drawing in a deep breath. Her whole crew was counting on her. She had failed them once already, she wouldn't do that again. With a determined sigh, Lilith opened her eye and focused back onto the Spanish built ship stalking behind the Maiden.

"Pull the charts Chibs, and find me a cove to duck into." She turned toward Renly and extended a finger toward the long rowboat battened down just forward of the main mast. "Prepare a shore party, Renly. I want strong backs and able hands. Rig up one of the long nines and a gun carriage, shot and powder to go with it."

"Cap'n," Chibs interrupted, "do you want to signal

Batard De Mur?"

Lilith shook her head before turning to scour the coastline. "No. If they are with us in our cause, they will find us again, or they will turn and fight with us. We are going to spring a trap, if they care to join, the more the merrier."

PART TWO
"A King's Ship"

5

'U.S.S United States'
13 May 1809
36 degrees 4' N, 74 Degrees 5' W

The utter blackness of night had taken U.S.S United States and swallowed her whole. Without a trace of moonlight, waves gently licked at her hull and slipped away into the darkness. On deck, the crew was working frantically to recover from their ordeal with the British ship. The most serious of the wounded had been taken down to a lower mess for the ship's doctor do what little he could. Footfalls on wooden deck timbers clunked and padded while the rope lines of the rigging creaked and groaned. Whispers were exchanged, sailors comforted the wounded and dying while others continued the work of sailing their vessel as best they could. Captain Woodhaven made his rounds of the main deck. He checked on the more serious wounds and spoke words of comfort and praise to those he knew would not live out the night. United States had survived, her crew was battered and disheartened, but they would live to see action another day. The ship itself had not escaped unscathed either. While the captain anxiously awaited his damage report, he noted the sections of railing that had been blown away, the decking that had been shredded by cannon fire and the sections of the upper hull that had sustained hits. Not all of the enemy's fire had penetrated, however. Captain Woodhaven was pleased to find that there were several indentations that appeared to be from direct hits. The thick white oak timbers gave ground only slightly. He imagined what the Brits must have thought when they saw their shot score a direct hit onto his hull only to watch the heavy shot careen off to land in the sea. This brought a fast grin to his lips that lasted only a moment until his first lieutenant arrived with the damage report.

"Captain," Lieutenant Smith reported with a dutiful salute, "the hull has suffered three serious hits, all larboard side. Two of those breached the hull level with the gun deck, the other, well, the other tore through your cabin, sir."

"Any further damages?" Captain Woodhaven asked.

Lieutenant Smith shook his head. "Your personal effects all seemed to be in order, sir. Your sea chest survived unharmed, but there were a few books on your desk that took splinters right through their covers."

The captain exhaled a deep breath before grasping the lieutenant's shoulder in a firm grip. "Damn my personal effects, son. I want to know about the ship. Is there damage to the yards? The masts? Can we make sail for somewhere to refit the damage?"

Lieutenant Smith dipped his brow as he replied with a wince of sheepishness. "She is still seaworthy, sir. The masts appear to have remained untouched, I will assess them better in daylight, but for now, they will hold. The main top was shredded to ribbons by a shot of grape from a swivel, I have the top men working on replacing it. As far as the butcher's bill… forty three hands, thirteen dead, the ship's doctor believes that number will double before the night is out. The remaining wounded are either being treated now by the doctor's mates, or they are being taken care of by capable hands here on deck."

Captain Woodhaven shook his head as a tremble of apprehension embraced his guts. He fought away the urge to be sick over the ship's rail. It wouldn't do for the remaining sailors to watch their captain's bearing waver in the face of hardship. Forty three casualties. Thirteen of those already perished and just as many well on their way. They had been short handed when United States left Boston, another forty three short would put them near skeleton crew levels. Granted, some of those men would heal in due time and return to their full service, but for the days ahead, his ship was dangerously undermanned.

"Very well, then, lieutenant," Captain Woodhaven replied with a sigh, "see to it the remaining wounded are cared for in the most humane way possible. Instruct the doctor to use my quarters if the need arises. I want every last one of them to have every chance we can give them. I will see to things here on deck, you are dismissed to go below and see to it."

Lieutenant Smith saluted smartly before departing while sailors scurried around him while attending to their tasks. Captain Woodhaven acknowledged the salute with a brisk nod before turning to a pair of sailors carrying one of their shipmates up from below deck. Both men knuckled their foreheads after they lowered the lifeless body down to the deck in as dignified a manner as they could muster.

"One of our lost shipmates, I presume?" Captain Woodhaven asked the sailors.

"Aye, sir. Able Seaman Pembly, from Boston, I believe. His leg was shattered by shot, the doctor tried to amputate it but the poor sod lost too much blood in the process." One of the sailors reported before leaning on one arm against the aft castle bulkhead. "He won't be the last, by the looks of things down there. Its almost like we have taken on more blood than water. I can only imagine what the hold looks like. Probably something close to the Nile in the days of the plagues."

Captain Woodhaven offered both men a solemn nod. "Tend to our wounded before the fallen. If we can spare any of them, we owe them that chance. The ship will keep for now," he paused as he noticed one of the sailors wipe away a spot of blood that appeared from his hairline. "See the doctor and get that addressed at once. It does us no good to lose able bodies to infection in the days ahead."

The sailor offered a touch of his brow with bloodied

fingers. "Aye, sir. Much appreciated, but I should be fine, it is just a bit of a scratch, shouldn't even leave a scar."

"All the same," Captain Woodhaven insisted, "get it looked after."

Both sailors acknowledged and disappeared below deck while Captain Woodhaven looked over the lifeless body they had placed on deck. A heavy feeling rested on his shoulders as he took in the gaunt features of the perished sailor's face. He was a younger man, maybe twenty, twenty two at the oldest. Feelings of guilt pulled at his insides as he tried to recall anything about the young sailor who had died under his command. Pembly, from Boston, it struck no memory for the captain.

"Your sacrifice out here won't be forgotten sailor," Captain Woodhaven muttered in a low voice, "and the next time we come across those damned Brits, we won't make the same mistakes again. That, I promise you, son."

The cool of night settled over U.S.S United States while small rises in the sea washed against her hull. Her progress was slow and during the course of the night it was discovered that her foremast had been damaged by cannon fire during the exchange with H.M.S Cutlass. It was a deep gouge above the topsail extension that one of the top men said was as broad as his arm. Captain Woodhaven ordered the gallants to be reefed until the section of mast could be repaired or replaced. Slowly but surely, the order of life aboard ship returned to its typical routine. Sail adjustments were made with the crew available. Watch rosters were altered to reflect the new level of manpower, and on the quarterdeck the careful registry of events and readings resumed. Time on deck, ship speed and heading, and each adjustment and order were dutifully recorded into the ship's log. As the ship proceeded on her course through darkness, the number of dead sailors placed on the main deck slowly grew. It seemed to Captain Woodhaven that his crew was shrinking with every passing hour and he silently cursed the sighting of the distressed ship which had led him into the engagement with the British. By all counts, he and his crew had done their duty. But, it had cost them grievously.

The first hints of dawn were playing on the eastern horizon when at last the ship's doctor came up from below deck to deliver his report to the captain. The front of his shirt was stained by the blood of the sailors he had fought all through the night to save. In his hands, he carried a rag which he was using to clean bits of dried blood from his hands and arms.

"The final tally, doctor?"

The ship's doctor shook his head. "I did what I could for them. Much of it was beyond what any doctor could, especially at sea. I believe the original count was thirteen dead?"

Captain Woodhaven confirmed the number with a grave nod. "Yes."

The doctor wiped at his forehead with the back of one hand, inadvertently smearing some blood on his face. "We can add fourteen to that number. I will say, there was less than a chance for most of them. Shattered bones and loss of blood, mostly. Most of those wounded that are still breathing should manage to recover, as long as we don't let infection set in."

"How are you on supplies in that regard?" Captain Woodhaven asked.

The doctor shook his head again before leaning against one of the few spots of ship's railing that was still intact. "Nearly out, captain. We need bandages, proper bandage material, not sailcloth. Iodine, laudanum, silk thread, just to name a few. We have sailors with wounds that will need to be cleaned and treated daily to avoid infection, some of them will be unfit to sail. There is one man, O'Donnell, I believe his name is, who may yet not make it. He has an abdominal wound. I was able to retrieve the pistol shot that wounded him, but deep wounds in the chest and belly can be confounding things. It only takes the smallest fragment of foreign material within the body to remain and it will fester. I do believe I got it all out, but he lost a barrel's worth of blood in the process. I am amazed he is still breathing."

Captain Woodhaven clenched his jaw. His ship was in no fit state to fight, his crew was in a more dire state. Returning to port seemed to be the only feasible option remaining. He had no idea what had become of the British warship. They could be floating on the sea, unable to make headway with a damaged mast and their hull taking on water. Or, they may have made hasty repairs and were now prowling to claim their next victim. Whatever the case, U.S.S United States had to return to port.

"Lieutenant Smith," Captain Woodhaven called toward the quarterdeck.

"Aye, sir," the first lieutenant replied.

"Come about with the wind at our quarter, once the sun is up, get a fix on our position and make your course for Charleston. We will refit there as needed, get our dead and wounded ashore, and take on whatever crew we can. See to it that the purser is provided a list of supplies and provisions we need so he may handle his business in port with all haste. I want the carpenter and his mates working on repairs immediately, every watch will assist them until we have made her fit to fight again. Work on what we can until we get her into port, that will ease the burden once we begin the major repairs. Have the gunner inspect every piece, deck guns, cannons, cannonade, swivel guns and small arms. I want to know exactly what is in good order and what will need to be replaced, and I want you to do a full inventory of the magazine. Shot, powder, wadding, bags, all of it."

"Aye, sir." Lieutenant Smith replied with a touch of his hat brim, "Would you like for me to work up a rotation for shore leave, sir?"

Captain Woodhaven shook his head and locked eyes with his first lieutenant. "No, lieutenant. Once we have made the ship ready, we will put back out to sea in search of H.M.S Cutlass. We had to break our engagement, that couldn't be avoided, but, I mean to finish the job."

Governor's Mansion
18 May 1809
Kingston, Jamaica

A lifetime spent at sea had given Admiral Torren a special appreciation for certain things. After decades spent on a variety of ships of the fleet he had grown so accustomed to life at sea that when he was on land it felt more like a peculiarity than normalcy. Floors that did not move beneath his feet. When he had first moved from a fleet admiral to a headquartered billet, he thought that having solid ground beneath his feet was a nice change of pace. It did not take long for him to miss the constant sense of motion. In fact, there were times he would awaken in the dead of night and wonder if the wind had been lost only to remember that he was indeed not aboard a naval vessel. Personal space was another creature comfort which he had mostly gone without for many years. Granted, an officer certainly enjoyed more personal space than anyone else aboard a man of war, but by landsmen standards, all sailors were creatures of shared common space. A sea chest, perhaps a ward room, or, when one ascended the ranks high enough, a personal cabin. To the common man who lived his life on land, the lack of personal space seemed an insufferable torture. But, to Admiral Torren and many men of his majesty's naval service, the lack of personal space was a shared bond. Forced proximity and shared hardship creates a stronger camaraderie than just about anything else. Shipmates begin to understand one another on a level few who have never served under such conditions could comprehend. The food at sea often left quite a bit to be desired, especially on an extended voyage. But, sailors often got to sample foods from far flung places that the ordinary civilian in dear old England could only dream about. One thing that Admiral Torren had least suspected he would miss was the noise. A ship at sea was a creature of constant sound. The creak of timber under constantly changing pressure, footfalls and chattering voices, the sound of the ship's bell tolling out the hours or the constant wash of the sea against the hull. There were times when Admiral Torren found the sheer absence of noise to be maddening, none more so than when he was trying to fall asleep.

Sleep on land was an elusive beast to Admiral Torren. He stalked it, yearning to achieve a restful night by ensuring he had sufficiently exerted himself throughout the day. He tried different manners of sleeping aids, warm milk, late night reading, teas with herbal blends that were fabled to help him achieve the sleep he so desired. But, each night he wound up staring at the ceiling of his chambers while the grandfather clock in his office ticked away each passing second. The nights in Kingston had been insufferable. He longed to return to sea and let the details of reconciling the colony of Jamaica become someone else's problem. Since he had moved his personal effects into the governor's mansion in Kingston, Admiral Torren had been plagued by nights of restless and elusive sleep. No matter how much he walked during the day, or what foods or drink he consumed or avoided, it seemed the evening hours had become a never ending personal hell where he repeated the same habits of tossing and turning before pulling himself out of bed to pace his room and brood over one of a hundred issues that kept his thoughts.

Each day in Kingston, the admiral had made progressive steps toward restoring the colony to a place of productivity, safety and security. Signs of life were already beginning to show throughout the town and commerce was beginning to move as well. But, as the curtain of night fell over the island each night, the long list of tasks that still needed attending would loom over Admiral Torren like a headsman's axe over the neck of a doomed man. After the conversation in the bowels of Fort Charles, Admiral Torren's mind was consumed by a different set of problems entirely.

"Be careful those letters don't become a dagger in your back, admiral."

The warning could not have been more clear, and it came from someone who had nothing to gain by sending a threatening message to him. The American mercenary, as big a pain as he had made himself, was trying to warn him. Of this there was no doubt in his mind. It was quite possible that he could be trying to string him along, giving him bits and pieces of information in order to forestall his execution. Admiral Torren considered this as he lay in bed, staring at the stark ceiling of his chambers. But, what if he wasn't? What if the treacherous bastard had finally had enough and was ready to cooperate? He thought of the typical offices which he would send his reports to. How could the letters he would send out become daggers in his back? The thoughts and questions continued to torment him until Admiral Torren rose from his bed and, as he did on most nights, began to pace in his chambers.

Thoughts broiled through his mind as moonlight traced a long, pale silhouette from the window along the floor. Memories of his protege, Admiral Sharpe, flooded into his consciousness and grappled with his concentration of the problems at hand. As he paced the floor of his extensive bedroom chamber he began to mutter aloud for the shadows to hear.

"If this conspiracy has reached its grasp all the way to London, who can I trust?" his words echoed within his bedroom as they did in his mind. "Lord Becker is well placed enough, if he were somehow involved with this, that would explain how this business has been allowed to continue. But, what does he have to gain by betraying his country? What do any of them have to gain, really? Did they think that their plots and schemes would not be revealed?"

Another leg of pacing across the room brought his conversation with Mr. Sladen back to the forefront of his mind. The American had eluded that The Order was responsible for many of the crown's woes over the last century. The struggle with Ireland, the gunpowder plots, the war of succession in the Americas, and now, a scheme which from an outside perspective would seem to be a subversion of parliament by the sitting monarch.

"This isn't about slaves, or gold. This is an attempt to bring calamity against the king, to use his own subjects against him. If this smuggling operation was discovered, it would land squarely on the king's shoulders. It would appear from the common perspective that he has ignored the will of parliament, and therefore, his subjects, in order to line his pockets." The words spilled out in a mutter that died away in the dark recesses of his room. Admiral Torren ceased his pacing at the far wall and turned abruptly to face the room at large. He paused for a long moment and noted where the silvery light of the moon fell onto the floor. It had traced its path from one end of his bedchamber to the other. The admiral sighed and tried to shake away the notions he had been contemplating. It was folly. Paranoid ideations brought about by a conversation with his American prisoner. A man that only a lunatic would fully trust.

Admiral Torren did not trust the things Tim Sladen had told him in the bowels of Fort Charles' dungeon, not fully. But, the accusations did hold some truths. Logic bore out that if the same people were responsible for all of the other plots and schemes against the crown, they could very well be pulling the marionette strings to create this massive scandal in hopes of bringing about a fresh domestic problem for the king. It was maddening. The pieces were there, laid out in his mind beneath a thin veil of shadow. He could fit a few together. Governor Alton, possibly Lord Becker, some of the commanding captains of the East India Company, but there was still something that eluded him, pieces of the puzzle that couldn't quite fit together. What was the end goal? How would the Vatican benefit from the overthrow of the British monarch? How were the individuals involved brought into this scheme?

An ache had formed in the admiral's knees and ankles. He cursed the chill of the night and his foolishness for pacing around his room in bare feet. With narrowed eyes he cast a glare at his bed along the far wall. It seemed a foreboding structure rather than a place of respite. An instrument of torture where he would spend countless hours whiling away time while tossing and turning, switching between staring at a painting of a sailing ship of the line on one wall and the stark moonlit window on the opposite wall. He squeezed his hand that would have normally been clutching the ornate curved handle of his cane and realized he had forsaken the instrument when he had set to pacing his room.

"Damn fool, no wonder these knees ache so fiercely," he muttered to himself as he crossed his bedchamber and eased himself back into the large feather bed.

As the aches and pains of age and a hard life wracked his nerves, the admiral scoured his mind for another course forward. Upon his return to the governor's mansion earlier in the day, he had penned three reports. One, to the assembly of admirals in London, another to Lord Becker. The third report remained unsealed. He had not yet addressed the envelope, nor was he finished writing the report. It was lengthier, by pages, and far more detailed than the other two reports he had penned. Admiral Torren wrestled in his mind with not only who to send the report to, but also if he should send it at all. In the third report, he had included every detail of his interview with the American mercenary, Tim Sladen, as well as a lengthy assessment of the working relationship Tim had with the deceased Governor Alton. The implications of this report, if landed in the correct hands, would shake the foundations of the British Empire. If it should fall into the wrong hands, it would simply be laughed off as the ravings of a mad old sailor well past his prime, or worse, they would result in the dagger Tim Sladen had mentioned in his cell.

'H.M.S North Wind'
16 May 1809
17 degrees 6' N, 76 Degrees 13' W

Tensions thrummed through rigging and brace lines as H.M.S North Wind slid through low rolling waves on a north easterly course toward Kingston. The sun was out in its full glory, baking the deck planks and shining off of the freshly mended canvas that was taut from the power of the wind. Lieutenant William Pike kept a watchful eye aloft from his place on the quarterdeck just aft of the helm while the crew kept about the business of sailing their ship. Sail adjustments were called out on the fly and the top men responded quickly and efficiently while a steady pattern of readings were relayed from the leadsman.

"Nine knots and holding steady," the leadsman reported with an edge of pride in his voice.

It was decent speed, for a ship of the line. Lieutenant Pike watched as the midshipmen, second and third lieutenants and the sailing master all made their navigational notations. Not long ago, Lieutenant Pike observed to himself, it was him who was knuckling his hat brim and reporting knot readings every ten minutes. He drew his lips into a tight grimace. Those days were simpler, it was not that long ago, but somehow, it also seemed like a distant memory from another lifetime. These men all looked to him, to his guidance and leadership. He was the master and commander of this ship. It was unheard of, even preposterous, that a lieutenant would be entrusted with such a valuable asset of the King's Navy. But, desperate times had called for desperate measures. The sacking of Kingston had left few officers on hand with enough sea experience to handle such an assignment while the hardships that Admiral Torren's fleet had endure left them similarly shorthanded. The admiral was in desperate need of capable commanders, and Lieutenant Pike was determined to prove himself as just that. His temporary command of H.M.S North Wind would be short lived, he knew. The minute a ranking captain was available, Lieutenant Pike would find himself relegated back to a first lieutenant posting. He knew he should be thankful just to be alive, and even more so to retain his commission in the navy, given the circumstances he had been entwined with in Nassau.

"Thirty two fathoms, bottom of sand and broken coral."

Lieutenant Pike watched while midshipmen hurried to notate the findings in their individual logs. Noon was approaching and the time would soon be ripe for a latitude reading to be taken by way of sextant. He had always enjoyed the finer points of sea navigation. While many struggled with the complex equations of spherical trigonometry, Lieutenant Pike excelled in it. The reckoning of a ship's position at sea was a matter of grave consequence should a lackluster captain allow for improper calculations to hold. There were documented cases of crews being decimated by dehydration and starvation after their officers had blundered the most critical piece of navigation. Figuring where a ship currently sat in relation to a specific point allowed for all of the following calculations. A mistake made in the early parts of reckoning became catastrophic if it was not recognized and corrected immediately. Lieutenant Pike recalled reading a report of an East Indiaman whose officers had incorrectly calculated their navigations on their return voyage to England. One missed land sighting had alerted the officers to their problem. In order to get a fix on their position, the captain had ordered a course change until land was sighted. Unfortunately, for both the officers and the crew, there was no sighting of land for the next several days. The crew had watched while their stock of supplies dwindled and rations were tightened day by day until a tipping point was finally reached. The crew mutinied in order to save themselves from their incompetent leadership. In the end, most of the officers died gruesome deaths at the hand s of their own men, and once the ship finally encountered another British vessel, the crew responsible for the mutiny were immediately slapped into irons and brought to England to stand trial for their crimes. It was a cautionary tale, but not an uncommon one. It was also not the worst outcome Lieutenant Pike had ever heard either. There were cases, of East India ships and Navy ships alike, where the crew did not mutiny, but suffered through a slow torturous voyage of death a deprivation until their commanders were finally able to either correct their navigation, or receive aid on the high seas. A shudder threatened to creep up his spine, but the lieutenant shook it off. His sailing master was as skilled as any and he made it a point to double check all navigation calculations.

When the reckoning was completed, North Wind's first lieutenant approached and informed Lieutenant Pike that Jamaica should be sighted off the larboard bow shortly after noon. After doing a mental run through for himself, Lieutenant Pike squinted his eyes at the horizon. He thought it would be closer to the afternoon watch change, but he kept his figuring to himself. It hadn't taken him long since becoming an officer to learn that it was better to keep doubtful remarks to himself, lest he be proved wrong and then forced to reconcile with a young lieutenant or midshipman who had made a more apt calculation than he had.

The scars North Wind carried from her encounter with the pirates were plentiful, though none of them impeded her handling the lieutenant thought it would be a good stroke of work to have the cosmetic damage repaired as quickly as possible.

"No doubt, after all this time on shore, the admiral will be wanting his flagship back," he said aloud with a slight grin.

"Pardon me, sir?" one of the midshipmen standing near the helm inquired.

"Nothing, lad. Just talking to myself," Lieutenant Pike replied with a slight shake of his head.

The midshipman returned to carefully watching as the helmsman held steady course, but not before exchanging a charged look with one of his fellow junior officers. The look communicated a silent exchange between both of the young men, a knowing look and a look that Lieutenant Pike knew well.

"Land sighted! Two point off the larboard bow." The call came down from a lookout stationed high aloft in North Wind's rigging.

Lieutenant Pike scoured the horizon with his eyes. From his position on deck, the land still remained hidden from view by an endless horizon of bluish gray sea against the wispy pale blue of the sky. A sighting was a sighting, he had been wrong about his estimation of their progress and he thanked himself for maintaining his reserve and not challenging the collective reckoning of his midshipmen.

Kingston. The thought brought up a feeling of excitement he could hardly contain. He would get to deliver the report he had painstakingly prepared to the admiral. It had taken him hours under lamplight in cabin. He had written and rewritten it until he felt like his pen would have to be removed from his cramping fingers by the ship's surgeon. It detailed North Wind's movements and sightings around the island of Jamaica and the subsequent engagement with the squadron of pirate ships. Also included in his report, was his accounting of the ship that Admiral Torren himself had sent to the depth within that cove on the coast of Haiti and its present state. Try as he might, Lieutenant Pike could not venture a guess as to how the admiral would react to the news. He may scoff and try to pass it off as a case of mistaken identity, but there were scores of witnesses aboard North Wind who had seen the Drowned Maiden sink beneath the waves. If that didn't sway the admiral's mind, the prisoner North Wind held deep inside of her hull surely would.

"Sail ho!" A call rang down from high in the tops.

"Where away?" Came the response from a grizzled looking petty officer.

Lieutenant Pike began to scan the horizon aft and to the starboard beam. His mind raced with the possibility that the two remaining ships from the pirate squadron could be setting an ambush as North Wind beat her way toward Kingston. It would be the logical direction to lay a trap, after their engagement, it was almost a given that they would return to port to offload their prisoners.

"All hands, beat to quarters," Lieutenant Pike called over the quarter deck, "Run up the colors!"

6

'H.M.S North Wind'
16 May 1809
17 degrees 6' N, 76 Degrees 13' W

Creaking wheels and straining ropes sounded from the gun decks of H.M.S North Wind. The clatter of wooden gun ports being lifted open sounded one after another while grunts and groans of sailors heaving at heavy lines filled the narrow spaces between each gun. Each gun crew scrambled to removed the barrel plug covering the bore of their individual piece before ramming home a small canvas bag of powder. A leather wad was shoved into each gun and driven down the barrel, followed by a ball of iron shot. Once these steps were completed, a sharpened iron spike was pushed through the breech of each cannon to pierce the bag of shot. A small amount of powder was poured into a flash pan to prime the gun to fire. When each gun was ready, the whole crew would run the gun out by   One by one the ugly snouts of oiled black iron protruded from their open ports.

"Larboard batteries loaded and ready!"

"Starboard batteries loaded and ready!"

The calls echoed throughout the cavernous gun decks almost simultaneously while gun captains inspected their gun elevations and ensured their cannons were ready to fire.

On the deck below, the ship's surgeon set out bandages in his quarters. He prepared various instruments including clamps and tourniquets, scalpels and a thick, rigid, bone saw. Sand was spread onto the floor to prevent him from slipping on deck timbers that could soon be covered in the blood of wounded crew members. On deck, H.M.S North Wind's shrouds and ratlines were filled with top men and marines hurrying small arms up into the rigging. These 'fighting tops' would target crewmen and officers from their elevated positions on North Wind's masts and yards. Preparatory commands were called out and smartly answered in kind. Each order was promptly repeated back to the issuer so that every hand within hearing had a clear understanding of exactly what was being done.

From the moment her commander had issued the order, to the moment every hand was ready for action, H.M.S North Wind was a hive of frenzied activity. It was a well rehearsed dance, with every hand moving to their station without delay. The guns were loaded and run out, the sails were adjusted and top men remained at the ready for rapid adjustments, and the surgeon prepared for his task of treating wounded sailors and marines. Every officer aboard promptly reported to their place of duty whether it be on the quarter deck or down by a gun battery. When the ship was cleared and ready for action, each station officer reported to the first lieutenant who then reported the entire ship ready to the commander. When the ship was cleared and ready, Lieutenant Pike nodded toward the drummer who ceased the rattling roll of snare strikes on his instrument.

"H.M.S North Wind is cleared and ready for action, sir." Lieutenant Thatcher reported.

"Very well," Lieutenant Pike nodded and pointed toward the horizon, "Make your course for the sighted ship. I want chase guns loaded and ready to fire."

"Helm, make two points to larboard! Trim the foresails and stand ready to loose royals." Lieutenant Thatcher called out in response to Pike's order.

"Two points larboard, aye aye," the helmsman replied.

"Trim foresails and ready on the main royals, aye aye," replied the sailing master.

Lieutenant Pike watched while the crew diligently carried out his commands. H.M.S North Wind shifted onto her new course with ease while the gunner's mate raced two gun crews through the process of preparing the nine pounder chase guns.

"Extra lookouts fore and aft, Mr. Thatcher, I won't have us caught with our pants down if this happens to be a trap devised by those pirates we encountered."

"Aye, sir. Lookouts fore and aft."

North Wind surged forward under the Caribbean

sun while sort choppy waves broke along her wooden hull. The sun was beating down and the skies were clear. The rattle and chaos of a ship beating to quarters settled into a long stretch of quiet tension as crewmen awaited their fate. On the gun decks, men crowded each open gun port in hopes of catching sight of the ship they were sailing toward. The heat below deck was insufferable and soon each sailor that manned the guns was covered in a layer of thick droplets of perspiration. The only relief was the occasional breaths of wind that snaked their way into the open ports. Minutes stretched on while the quarterdeck kept the ship steady on course. With every passing waves that broke along the ship's hull and every pitch and roll of her deck the crew grew more tense with anticipation. Only the intermittent commands of the quartermaster broke the monotony of creaking timbers and straining lines as North Wind forged her way ahead in search of the sighted vessel.

After only two hours on their new course, Lieutenant Pike spotted the stack of billowing white sails with his own eyes. Through his telescope, he tried to glean as much detail about the strange vessel as he could. His attempts ended in frustration as the ship was too distant to decipher much beyond her presence. She was flying white sails, so unless the vessel he had encountered accompanying the Maiden had switched out all her canvas, doubtful, it was not her. There was a possibility that it was the Maiden herself, but Pike thought that her trusty quartermaster, Mr. Chibs, would surely have advised against a straight on approach to Kingston. Lieutenant Pike shook his head and squinted at the dark form of ship beneath those white squares.

Distance and heat shimmered off of the sea surface. One square of white became two. Lieutenant Pike extended his telescope and re-examined the distant vessel to see if they had maneuvered to evade North Wind. The glimmer of sunshine on waves made it difficult to distinguish detail. He relaxed his brass telescope away from his eye and stared at the horizon. One square had become three as he was staring at it, as he looked again three had become five. The form of five white sails became clear to him even through the glare of sun and the shimmers of heat and evaporating seawater. He raised his telescope back to his eye and studied the white shapes on the horizon. They were square, facing full on toward North Wind. The form of five distinct hulls separated in his sight. Five ships. His stomach tightened into a knot. A chill ran up his spine and saturated his blood.

He had watched Captain Grimes engage three ships while he served aboard H.M.S Valor, at the time, Lieutenant Pike had thought that the captain was brash beyond reason. Five ships against one was not an engagement, it would be suicide, regardless of how large North Wind was or how fast her gun crews could reload and run out. They would be maneuvered on and gunned to shreds. Even as he studied their forms through his telescope the ships seemed to be changing course and fanning into a wider formation.

"They are moving to intercept while sending ships

wide to flank me," he said under his breath, "I still have the wind, though. Five against one, damn the luck."

Whispers and mutters rippled through the crew like a shock wave from a disturbance on the sea. Lieutenant Pike could hear their grumblings, even if they didn't reach his ears. It was written on their faces and the looks they passed from one sailor to another.

"Is he mad?"

"Five ships? We're doomed!"

"Why isn't he turning to and running like hell?"

The lieutenant crossed North Wind's quarterdeck with a burst of quick strides. He snapped his telescope shut and pulled the brim of his hat low over his eyes.

"Gentlemen, we don't know who those ships are out there." He paused and took a look around the faces on deck. Their courage was hanging on a precipice, ready to slide into a state of panic at any moment. Lieutenant Pike drew a deep breath and mustered as much of his own courage as he could. "Did Nelson hesitate when his moment came at Trafalgar? Did he turn and run when he faced a French fleet far larger than his own? No! He charged right into their teeth and carried the day for king and country! We face five ships on the horizon, we know not who they are, nor what their intentions may be. Courage, men, courage. I won't have it said that North Wind didn't have the courage to face her nations enemies head on! Onward to victory, or onward to defeat, but onward we press! It may be a squadron of French men of war, it may be a whole fleet of pirates, but they will write about what we do on this day for years to come! If we fire every last piece of shot we have and fight down to the last man, that is what your nation expects of you! Great Britain rules the waves, from the stretches of the far east, all the way to the channel that separates us from Napoleon! Will you stand with me?"

Wind whipped over North Wind's deck and strained her stay lines. The sound of creaking and groaning as the ship held steady under the stress of force was deafening as it met Lieutenant Pike's ears. He could feel his face grow hot under the shade of his hat as a solid moment of silence from the crew elapsed. Had his rallying cry fallen on deaf ears? Just as he was about to begin cursing himself for such a brash speech a roar of approval erupted on deck. It drowned away the noise of the ship, echoing between the fore and aft castles. Shouts of solidarity rang down from the rigging and bellowed out from the gun decks below his feet. North Wind seemed to be shaking with the war cries of his crew. The chill that had threatened to engulf his blood retreated as a ball of fiery vigor rose into his chest. He wrapped his fingers around the hilt of his officer's sword and drew the blade in a single motion. Sunlight glinted off of the polished steel as he raised the weapon high overhead amid the shouts and cheers of North Wind, the roar intensified. "For Admiral Nelson," he shouted. The roar grew louder. "For Admiral Sharpe and the fallen sailors of Kingston harbor!" The deck board beneath his feet seemed to be alive with the rumble of shouts and screams from below deck. He thrust his sword forward into the air in front of him in a stabbing motion. "For England!"

'Drowned Maiden'
22 May 1809
12 degrees 14' N, 71 Degrees 55' W

Lush stands of dense foliage rose up all around the Drowned Maiden. Chibs had selected this cove not for its size, but for its proximity. The mouth of the cove was narrow, so narrow that it looked to only be traversable to one ship at a time, two at the most. Just inside of that, however, the cove opened into a broad body of seawater that seemed large enough to make maneuvers. On the chart, there were only a scant few depth readings. Once inside the cove, every turn would be a gamble. It was a risk, but Chibs felt that Captain Lilith had the right of it. She was taking a page out of the late Captain James' book by displacing a gun onto the shoreline near the mouth of the cove. If the Drowned Maiden could lure the pursuing vessel in, they would effectively trap her. The mouth of the cove was narrow enough that once the guns all opened fire, there would be no escape. It was a plan with a double edge though, their pursuer wouldn't be able to slip away, but neither would they.

"Hard over larboard, Chibs, and drop anchor. Let's make sure the guns are loaded and run out." Captain Lilith said as she crossed the quarterdeck to study the mouth of the cove through her narrowed eye.

"Aye, Cap'n," Chibs replied even as the deck of Drowned Maiden began to shift beneath his feet.

Omibwe, ever dutiful and obedient to his captain's orders, didn't wait for Chibs to repeat the command. He muscles the wheel over and oriented the Drowned Maiden exactly as Captain Lilith had commanded. It brought a smile to Chibs face. The lad was born for a life at sea, even though the path that had brought him to it had been fraught with pain and injustice.

"Loose sheets and spill the wind, lads. Let the canvas hang in case we need to move quickly," Chibs shouted aloft with his hand cupped around the side of his mouth. "Deckhands, drop anchor and run below to man the guns. Load them all and run them out."

Footfalls thudded across the Drowned Maiden's deck as her crew sprung into action. Within moments the ship had eased to a halt on the calm water of the cove with her larboard broadside facing the narrow mouth that led out to the open sea. Gun ports popped open one by one and the sound of wooden wheels rolling across the lower deck reverberated through the ship's timber structures.

"How long do you think until they are ready ashore?" Lilith asked Chibs without moving her gaze from the mouth of the cove.

Chibs shrugged and stuck the stem of his pipe into his mouth. He searched for a flame for a moment before finding that all the lanterns had been extinguished when the day had dawned. "Renly is a top hand, Cap'n. I imagine he will have that gun ready to fire any time now."

"And how long until our Spanish made friends come around the mouth of the cove there?" Lilith asked, her gaze still unmoved.

"Less than an hour, I'd say, they were gaining on us pretty steadily. The question in my mind is, will they sail into the cove?" Chibs paused and chewed at his pipe stem for a moment before continuing, "Any captain with a sound mind and sharp wits will see this for what it is and stand off in the distance. They'll bottle us in here and wait for us to make a move. Our broadside is facing the entrance. Only a fool would run at us with his bow exposed to our broadside."

"Let's hope their captain is a bold one then," Lilith muttered.

Chibs smiled. "Let's hope."

As the words left Chibs mouth and trailed away into the light breeze that traced its way through the cove the form of a ship began to show itself at the mouth of the cove. White sails billowed above a wooden hull built with bluff lines and a high bow and stern. She was of Spanish build, there could be no doubt, and her captain seemed to pay no heed to the fact that the Drowned Maiden was anchored with her broadside oriented directly in his direction.

Chibs had to fight to keep his jaw from dropping as he witnessed the very act he had just described as foolish and brash unfolding before his eyes. "I'll be damned. He's either ignorant, or mad."

A cloud of gun smoke protruded from the bow of the newly arrived ship just before the report of the shot echoed through the cove. A whistle shrieked through the air and passed close to the Maiden's stern as the first shot missed.

"Ranging fire, Cap'n. They'll have their mark on the next one!" Chibs shouted over Lilith's shoulder as she continued to stare at the vessel that had sailed into their trap.

A long pause passed. Chibs could feel his chest tighten as precious seconds slipped by. Lilith remained at the larboard rail of the quarterdeck, seemingly locked in a trance as she stared at the incoming Spanish vessel with her narrowed eye.

"Cap'n..." Chibs said as the seconds slipped away.

Lilith lifted one hand and raised a finger as the Spanish vessel pushed further into the cove. A second shot erupted from their bow and hissed through the air. Chibs could feel the shriek of the shot down into his bones. The whistle grew louder, and louder still until it screamed through the rigging just above the Drowned Maiden's deck. It missed, but just barely.

"Cap'n!" Chibs shouted as the scream of the shot died away.

"Now!" Lilith cried out, "Fire the larboard batteries!"

A heartbeat passed before the Drowned Maiden's guns roared to life. In ones and twos the cannons fired their projectiles in thunderous roars that sent billowing clouds of bluish gray smoke racing out into the air above the cove. With a flutter in his chest, Chibs moved to the larboard railing to watch and see how the broadside would land. A plume of seawater rose high into the air in front of the Spanish ship. Chibs could feel his heart drop into his stomach as a second plume rocketed into the air. Another missed shot landed next to Spanish ship's hull. Just as Chibs was about to consign the broadside as a loss, an explosion of shattered wood erupted from the Spanish ship's bow. First one impact, then another sent jagged shards of wood flying over the enemy's decks. In all, Chibs estimated that four of the Maiden's cannons had found their mark.

"Ready on those guns! Reload! They are coming about!" Lilith shouted over her shoulder.

Chibs watched with baited breath as the Spanish ship's bow began to swing over. Her captain was maneuvering to bring her guns to bear. As her bow nosed around, the first of her gun ports began to come into view. Chibs watched as wooden hatches popped open and the cold iron snouts of cannons protruded from their dark openings. Panic crawled up his back and threatened to seize his chest.

"Cap'n!" Chibs shouted.

"Fire when ready!" Lilith screamed as the Spanish vessel came further around.

The last of the Spanish guns ran out, her broadside fully exposed and facing the Drowned Maiden.

"Here it comes Cap'n! All hands, brace yourselves!" Chibs cried out in terror.

Lilith raced inboard from the larboard rail. "Fire! Fire the guns or it'll be the bottom of the cove for us!"

Even as the words left her mouth, Drowned Maiden shuddered with massive tremor as her cannons fired in near unison. Smoke belched from her gun ports as her cannons all recoiled into the recesses of her gun deck. Across the cove, the Spanish ship answered with a near simultaneous volley and the air filled with the shriek of speeding balls of iron that passed each other in mid flight.

A heartbeat elapsed. Chibs felt lightning run through his blood as he heard the shriek of approaching fire. Images of the Maiden being torn to shred flashed through his mind. They had lost so many that day, Trina among a score of others. It had cost him his hand and Captain Lilith her eye. More than that, Chibs knew it had changed her. Lilith emerged from the waters of that cove a different person. Whereas some would be more cautious after facing down death, Chibs felt that the disastrous encounter had made her more brash, even to the point of recklessness. His breath seized in his chest and he struggled to force out a shout for the crew on deck to take cover as he dove onto the wooden planks.

Impacts sounded. It was like being in the midst of a thunderstorm that shook Chibs to his core. He had been under fire before, but this was otherworldly. The closest comparison he could make was the day that the Drowned Maiden was sunk. Splintering and cracking filled his ears. Shattered timber flew through the air in torrents of deadly shrapnel. The Maiden trembled under the force of impact after impact. Chibs felt the force wash over him, it penetrated his body and shook his bones down to the marrow. His mind raced. He felt panic creeping in around the edges of his thoughts. His eyes were shut against the terrors he knew he would find. He waited to hear the screams of pain and agony, a sound he had heard too many times before.

"Reload! Fire the guns again!" Lilith's voice cut

through the chaos.

Chibs rolled to his side. He opened his eyes, unsure of what he might see. Smoke drifted over the deck of the Maiden. Lines hung in disarray. As a cloud of bluish gray smoke filtered away, Chibs found Lilith standing with one foot resting against a shattered deck gun, her cutlass in one hand and a hanging line in the other.

"Fire when ready! Fire the guns, fire! Fire! Fire!" Her shouts carried over the sound of wounded crew.

Chibs shifted his good arm beneath himself and struggled to his knees. He was surrounded by shattered wood and carnage. The Maiden's larboard railing was all but gone. Her aft castle stairs had been obliterated. The deck timbers just forward of the quarterdeck were splintered and buckled by a cannon ball that had blasted it's way through the gun whale and torn across the width of the deck. The creak and rumble of wooden wheels echoed up from below deck. Chibs felt the next shot before he heard it. He forced himself to his feet and looked toward the mouth of the cove. The Spanish made vessel had not escaped the Maiden's fire unscathed. A section of her hull was damaged near the bow quarter and her starboard railing had been shattered. There were holes and tears in her sails and one of her mainsail yards hung suspended by shreds of canvas and fouled lines. They were wounded, but they weren't finished.

"Cap'n, they're reloading same as us." Chibs said as smoke stung his eyes and throat. "I don't know if we can take another broadside from her."

"She'll hold, Chibs," Lilith replied in a cold rush before turning to the weather hatch. "Reload and fire them again! Fire when ready!"

Another cannon roared from the Maiden's gun deck, followed by a second and then a third. Chibs watched as impacts blasted the Spanish built ship and sent wood flying in all directions. His nerves were aflame as the seconds slipped by. Her guns would be ready any minute and her broadside was still oriented directly at the Drowned Maiden.

"Cap'n, we need to set the sheets and pull out of her line of fire. The next volley could be the end of us!" Chibs shouted as Lilith crossed the deck again and pulled a crewman to his feet.

"She will hold, Chibs," Lilith replied with an edge in her voice.

'H.M.S North Wind'
16 May 1809
17 degrees 6' N, 76 Degrees 13' W

A shift in the wind caused North Wind's sails to flutter for a heartbeat before her crew reacted and trimmed them accordingly. The minor offset brought a cringe to Lieutenant Pike's sun burned face. Wind off his larboard beam. He hoped it would shift back to his quarter, though seep in his stomach he knew it wouldn't. The small variance had erased the only edge of advantage he held over the quickly approaching squadron of unknown ships. Their sails loomed tall in front of him and with every passing breath they beat their way closer. The five sets of sails had fanned into a line of battle with three large vessels in the middle and two smaller ships on either end. Pike judged the two smaller ships to be sloops of war. The center most ship sailing his way looked large enough to be a second- or third-class line ship. She would be carrying the heaviest firepower. At least two gun decks with twelve or eighteen pounder guns. Flanking her on either side were ships of only slightly smaller stature, most likely frigates.

Lieutenant Pike agonized over the origin of the squadron. Though he had originally feared that the encounter was an ambush from pirates who were sailing in league with Lilith and the crew of the Drowned Maiden, their ship handling was too good. They were sailing in a formation and the synchronized maneuver of the two far flanking vessels indicated that signals were being passed between ships. Pirates didn't sail or fight in such an orderly manner. In his guts, he feared he was facing a squadron of French ships bent on seizing control of the waters surrounding Jamaica. An edge of hope sliced through his fear when the thought crossed his mind that the fleet could indeed be reinforcements from another British colony. Admiral Torren had sent dispatches to Barbados, St. Kitts, Nassau, Bermuda and London. The arrival of a fleet would be a welcome relief.

"Hold fast, wind steady on out larboard beam. Helm bring us about one point over larboard."

The sailing master's orders broke Lieutenant Pike's course of thought and he focused back onto the approaching ships. If they held course, and if the wind did not shift again, they would be within firing range within an hour. His chase guns were loaded and ready. North Wind had her guns loaded and run out on both sides. He and his crew were as ready as they could be.

"Direct action and aggressiveness will be our cutlass today," he said aloud for the benefit of the officers and crew near him. "We will carry the day with bold action and fast gunnery."

Nods of agreement spread across the quarterdeck. Five against one seemed to be more of a suicide mission than bold action, but Lieutenant Pike had steeled their nerves. Onward to victory or onward to defeat, whatever awaited them, North Wind would sail right into the teeth of their enemy and give them everything they had.

"Lieutenant!" The gunner's mate called back from the bow, "We should be close enough for the long nines. Shall I range them?"

Lieutenant Pike took a deep breath and studied the opposing vessels for a long beat. Once he opened fire, the course he had planned was inescapable. If the ships proved to be hostile, they would know his intentions. "Aye, fire a ranging shot."

The gunner's mate went to work dialing his elevation while carefully estimating the distance. A few words were exchanged amongst the gun crew and another elevation adjustment was made before the crew cleared away from the gun carriage and the gunner's mate pulled on a lanyard to trip the brass mechanism which released a spring powered flint and showered sparks into a pan primed with powder. The report of the gun firing thundered over the sea. A cloud of gun smoke bellowed forward of North Wind and was quickly carried away by the breeze. Lieutenant Pike watched while the gray cloud filtered away to reveal the stark image of five warships on an intercept course with North Wind. A plume of seawater rocketed into the air just short of one of the middle three warships. They were not close enough to hear the reaction of the opposing crews, but Lieutenant Pike imagined the reaction on deck. Gun crews would be scrambling to respond in kind to the ranging shot. North Wind's first shot had not been far from its mark, both sides of the confrontation would be within range of each other by the time a reload was completed.

The lieutenant extended his telescope and studied the approaching vessels for signs of activity. Sail changes were being made on the largest ship in the formation. Her tacks were run up and sheets tightened as she prepared to maneuver. The two vessels to her flanks edged their bows outward in order to open the formation into a broader line. Lieutenant Pike scoured for any weakness he could exploit, a vessel maneuvering slower than the others, a sign of sluggish handling or poor discipline on the helm, anything. His eye found nothing. The squadron of ships were performing their tasks in near synchrony with each other. These were sailors of another caliber entirely. The sail changes came in perfect timing, the ship handling looked superb. These would be stout opponents. His mind wandered as he scoured each ship with his telescope. Perhaps this would be a glorious end for him and the crew of North Wind. His aggressive approach would surely allow him to inflict serious damage on whatever ships he sailed between, but the end result would surely be his demise along with that of the crew and the ship. North Wind would fire both broadsides as she passed dealing whatever damage she could. The reload would be furious and surely interrupted by a return volley from both sides, whatever gun crews were left would continue to fire and reload as North Wind was maneuvered on and eventually boarded. They would be overwhelmed by superior numbers, or blown to bits as each enemy ship loosed their volleys in turn while carefully sailing in circuits around them. A knot formed in the back of his throat. This would be it.

"Lieutenant!" a voice called down from high in the rigging, "Lieutenant, look at her pennant flying from the main mast! She's British!"

The knot in Lieutenant Pike's throat disappeared and was quickly replaced by a chill running up his spine. He adjusted his telescope and studied the top pennant of the biggest warship's main mast. A thin banner with the likeness of Union Jack billowed in the wind coming out of the west.

"Chase guns, hold your fire! Those are friendly vessels," he shouted while collapsing the telescope down to its smallest form. "Helm, bring her larboard four points and put us close haul to the wind, let's make sure they can see our colors." He raced to the weather hatch and shouted down a command for the gun decks. "Gun crews, make safe your guns and haul them in, it is a friendly fleet off our bow!"

North Wind's hull shifted and slid through the sea at an angle as her helmsman reefed at the steering while top men scrambled to make a hasty sail adjustment. Tacking up to close haul from a broad reach required a significant change in the canvas to avoid losing momentum. Below deck the rumble of wooden wheels on deck timbers signaled that the gun crews were running their pieces in, within a few minutes their gun ports began to close with a series of clattering thunks that sounded one after another.

"Drummers to your station," Lieutenant Pike called over the quarterdeck, "Gunner's mate, prepare to render honors from the chase guns as they come alongside." He paused for a moment before cracking a smile, "I don't suppose the shot we have already fired would count. Would it?"

The gunner's mate beamed back with a smile of his own. "Aye, sir. I reckon it could count as rendering honors. But, I will have the chase guns ready nonetheless."

"I will undoubtedly be explaining myself before the day is out," Lieutenant Pike mused as the smile faded from his lips, "carry on then."

"Aye, sir," the gunner's mate replied while knuckling the brim of his hat.

"Lieutenant, the fleet is coming about on a course parallel to ours!" Lieutenant Thatcher reported from across deck, "and they are flying an admiral's pennant."

Lieutenant Pike shook his head and let his gaze settle on the line ship which was now only a half mile away and sailing abreast to North Wind. "I will surely be explaining myself."

A call came down from the aft lookout. "Signal flags!"

Pike tensed as Lieutenant Thatcher opened his private log and flipped to the section dealing with signals. The younger officer frowned and drew his face into a deep squint as he studied the flags with his naked eye before switching his attention down to the logbook in his hands. He repeated this gesture several times before announcing his decipher. "Remain on current heading," he paused and looked back at his log of signals before continuing, "Pardon me, sir. Belay my last. Heave to immediately, commander to come aboard."

The tension Lieutenant Pike had felt dissolve when he had learned that the fleet was British now reared its ugly head again. A knot formed in his throat. He had no idea what Admiral Torren had included in his letters, and the newly arrived admiral was surely going to be curious how a lieutenant was given command of a line ship. His post aboard North Wind had come to an end. At least, in the capacity as her commander. There had to be a senior captain commanding one of the lesser ships accompanying the line ship. North Wind would be promptly handed over and Lieutenant Pike would be fortunate to retain a first lieutenant billet. A far more likely scenario would be this fleet admiral installing one of his senior captains as North

Wind's commander and an ambitious lieutenant of his choosing from among the men he knew and trusted.

North Wind's decks shifted as wind spilled from her sails. Top men high in the rigging reefed the canvas as deck hands worked lines to secure the ship from movement. Lieutenant Thatcher reported no depth reading from the chart so North Wind maintained one set of top sails to keep from drifting. A longboat was prepared and boomed over the side with the aid of strong backs at the forward capstan. Lieutenant Pike retired to the commander's cabin to retrieve the reports he had compiled up to this point on the voyage. The stack of papers felt heavy in his hands as he turned to return to the weather deck. Before he left the dim light of the cabin, he glimpsed himself in a dully polished brass mirror hanging along the bulkhead by the door. His uniform. It looked a mess. It was a poor fit, too short in the arms and too long of torso. One look and the newly arrived admiral wouldn't be outside of his rights to accuse him of being an impostor. The scars on his face had healed, but they remained a garish pink that betrayed their recency. A drum roll from out on deck snapped Lieutenant Pike back to his task at hand. He turned and faced the hatch leading outside. With a deep breath, he took the door handle and plunged himself forward to meet his fate.

7

'U.S.S United States'
26 May 1809
32 degrees 44' N, 79 Degrees 50' W

"Cast lines and pipe our departure," Captain Woodhaven ordered. "First lieutenant has the ship, take us out and plot our course southward."

"Aye, I have the ship," the first lieutenant replied before turning inboard to the quarterdeck. "Lookouts fore and aft, I want a sounding every five minutes until we have forty fathoms under the keel. Helm, come about with the wind and make your heading east by southeast, full mains and top, leave gallants and royals reefed until we are out in the swells."

"Aye aye, sir, east by southeast," the helmsman repeated. "Coming about with the wind."

"You heard the first lieutenant, sheet those mainsails and tops, stay lines for the foremast," the sailing master shouted orders through a speaking trumpet. "Haul the spanker over, we mean to come about with the wind!" He turned to the first lieutenant and growled, "Some of these replacements aren't the sharpest, but our boys will have them in ship shape in no time, sir. Mark my words, we will be ready next time we see that Union Jack flapping in the wind."

The first lieutenant exchanged a look with Captain Woodhaven before turning back to the sailing master. "See to it, once we are clear of the coast the captain means to run through maneuvers."

Captain Woodhaven stood firm on the quarterdeck. His eyes surveyed the deck of U.S.S United States while his mind scoured the events of the previous evening as he had been preparing to set sail. United States' refit had been a rushed affair, due in no small part to his own urging. The damage his ship had taken in her engagement with H.M.S Cutlass had been repaired, inoperable cannons were replaced, deck timbers and mast sections painstakingly torn away and fit with fresh live oak. Replacements for the dead and wounded had been added to the ship's log. A week in port, and by the captain's reckoning, a week he could ill afford. The situation he had been briefed on had only grown worse. U.S.S Constitution was said to be on her return voyage from the Mediterranean, where she had been successful at interdicting pirates off the Barbary coasts. Her return would not be for several weeks, and even then, she would need to refit and resupply before she could lend her strength to any fight. Acts of British impressment were the hot topic of port, both in the naval offices and in the taverns. Merchant ships were being stopped within sight of the

American coastline and sailors were being pressed against their will into the service of the crown.

"It's dark days ahead, I can smell it in the air!" a tavern keeper had regaled Captain Woodhaven with his thoughts on the matter. "There is another war with Britain coming, and this time, we may not fare out so fortunate. The French are too busy trying to conquer all of Europe to care much for our problems."

With the wind in his face, and his ship setting out to sea, the tavern keeper's words rang as clear as the ship's bell in his ears. The old man wasn't wrong. Another war with Britain was looming, and this one would be just as stacked against the fledgling nation as the revolution had been. He muttered to himself, "Oh how the bravado of town halls and taverns has glossed the reality of history. The amalgamation of states had barely managed their victory. They had faced a fraction of the British Empire's total strength, most land battles had resulted in the ranks of the Continental Army breaking in retreat. The situation at sea was no different, aside from a few key victories, the Americans were regularly embarrassed by a well-supplied and well-disciplined Royal Navy. If it were not for the timely intervention of the French, the whole endeavor would have been a loss.

"Helm, two points over starboard," the first lieutenant's command broke Captain Woodhaven's train of thought. "Hands aloft and ready sailing master, stand by to fly gallants and royals."

"All hands at the ready, gallants and royals!" The sailing master called aloft with his speaking trumpet.

U.S.S United States had cleared the harbor and was making her way past the last slip of shallows before turning beam reach with the wind and slugging her way southward. Captain Woodhaven watched closely as top men made their way across the yards high over the deck. The replacements United States had taken on were mostly assigned below deck, working the capstans and manning guns, the natural progression of an enlisted sailor began in the bowels of the ship. There were a few though, a few new men who had come to the ship with enough seafaring experience to convince the sailing master to rate them as ordinary seaman and assign them up in the rigging. The problems of finding able bodied recruits who were willing to hazard their bodies at sea for what amounted to a paltry sum compared to the wages available to merchant sailors seemed to be easing as time went on. Sailors had either been aboard a merchant ship forced to heave to by the Brits or had heard tales of those who had. The merchant fleets were becoming almost as risky as a regular navy ship. If not more so, in certain circumstances.

The American states had enjoyed a run of good fortune with the wars in Europe, as far as trade was concerned. British blockades of French ports drove the prices of foodstuffs higher, the Royal Navy's constant harassment of French trade to and from the French West Indies had driven it even higher. American merchant ships had enjoyed a season of lucrative trade. Smugglers fared even better. The tides were shifting, however, and British attention had settled its eye yet again on the Americans. Vessels were being seized, sailors were being forced to serve against their will, and blockades of French ports were growing ever tighter. Even seasoned smugglers were having trouble getting their goods into the hands of French buyers. To make matters worse, the struggle against the Barbary pirates had both cost the Americans in terms of lost goods and ships as well as brought additional presence from the Royal Navy. The sword that cut both ways.

"Helm, two more points over starboard," the first lieutenant called out over the quarterdeck, "hands, to the braces! Let fly tacks and jib!"

U.S.S United States' bow crept further to the south, her hull listed as the force of wind caught her sails from beam reach and propelled her through the rising swells of the open ocean. The Carolinas fell away behind her stern and clear blue skies stretched out as far as the eye could see. The winds held steady out of the west and the seas rolled to a manageable swell of around eight feet. The waves broke along the wooden hull and rippled outward before disappearing into the mix of the sea. The ship was sailing well, as Captain Woodhaven observed, but they were in calm seas and favorable winds. It was time to push his ship, and his crew. He turned to the first lieutenant.

"Bring her about with the wind on our larboard quarter. Beat to quarters."

Lieutenant Smith faced the quarterdeck and called repeated the captain's orders. "All hands, hard over a-larboard. Standard tacks and sheets and beat to quarters!" He turned back toward Captain Woodhaven and lowered his voice, "quarters, sir? I thought we were going to drill maneuvers."

"Our last encounter demonstrated to me that it is quite necessary for us to practice both forms. Hard training, Lieutenant Smith, rigorous training under less than ideal conditions. We have fair seas, for today that will have to do. But we can test the top men's agility in the rigging and train the gun crews to perform their tasks under the strain of maneuver," Captain Woodhaven replied. "When we meet H.M.S Cutlass again at sea, nothing less will do. The British method of naval warfare involves close battery with heavy cannonades, rapid reloads that pummel the enemy before they have a chance to recover. I believe, if we can engage them from a greater distance with superior accuracy, we will be able to inflict enough damage while closing with them that by the time their tactics finally come into play, we will have sufficiently wounded them to turn the odds in our favor." He paused and watched while United States swept hard to her larboard side, the deck listed hard and rocked as the swells broke against the beam of her hull. Officers, midshipmen, and sailors all steadied themselves as the ship reeled from her maneuver. The sounds of blocks straining under effort crept up from the gun decks as crews readied their cannons to fire on command. Captain Woodhaven had drawn nearly double the powder and shot allocated to a ship of war. He intended to make good use of the surplus. The next time he met Cutlass on the high seas, he would be ready.

Governor's Mansion
19 May 1809
Kingston, Jamaica

"This is both highly irregular and an affront to over three hundred years of tradition and sacrifice!" Admiral Roland's voice filled the chamber of Admiral Torren's office as it bordered between the verge of disgust and outright rage. "A lieutenant, given command of a vessel that would normally serve as a flagship! And, not just any lieutenant, but one that you openly admit has a record of taking up with pirates! Admiral Torren, you will have to forgive me, but are you well? Have you lost your senses?"

Admiral Torren let a long moment of silence elapse. The familiar tick of a grandfather clock served to fill the absence of speech. He shifted his gaze from the offended admiral to the mural painting of the famous last victory of Lord Admiral Horatio Nelson at Trafalgar and tried to imagine what the old man would think of the situation. Not only his unorthodox handling of Lieutenant Pike, but also the borderline insubordinate rebuke he was receiving from a man who was his junior not only in seniority, but also in billeted position. He fought the urge to return Admiral Roland's words with a thorough dressing down.

"Extraordinary circumstances, admiral. I can assure you, I fully understand your concerns. But, I stand by my decisions. Lieutenant Pike made some grave mistakes after the loss of his commanding officer and then subsequently his ship. The young man was fell victim to mutinous sailors, twice by my count. Had he not taken up arms to defend me when a handful of my own marine detachment tried to take North Wind, the outcome would have been drastically different." Admiral Torren paused for a moment to let his words sink in. He placed his fingertips onto the polished dark wood desktop in front of him and rose to his feet. "Kingston was sacked by a mercenary group. The fleet was all but annihilated. When I arrived here, the fort lay in ruins and the town was left in a near state of anarchy. I had precious few officers with command experience at my disposal." He lowered his chin and his voice. "Would you have preferred that I handed over command of North Wind to a midshipman? Or perhaps, left it at anchor in the harbor? Tell me, Admiral Roland, what exactly do you think I should have done differently?"

Another long, uncomfortable silence filled the office. Admiral Torren let it stretch on as his detractor wrestled with how to reply. Kingston had sweltered all through the afternoon and even as evening brought relief from the heat, the admiral's office remained well above a comfortable temperature.

"Sir, my concerns are not without merit. Had the lieutenant decided to defect and take up piracy again, there would be a first rate ship of the line in the hands of brigands," Admiral Roland said. His face was not only a deep shade of red, perspiration had formed a thin sheen on his forehead and neck. Admiral Torren knew he would not change this officer's mind in the course of a single conversation. Especially while both of them were broiling in his office.

"Let us both cool ourselves, and our tongues," Admiral Torren said with a halfhearted smile, "there is a balcony off of the upstairs dining room which will serve nicely. We can discuss a plan to move forward from the mess in the Caribbean, something I am sure we can both come to some sort of agreement on."

Admiral Roland nodded his assent. "A breath of fresh air will serve us both. My apologies, admiral, if I have overstepped with my rhetoric. I was not present for the situation, I could not speak to what I would have done were I in your position."

Admiral Torren allowed a genuine smile to break through his reserve. "As I said before, these are extraordinary times, I will not begrudge you a spirited disposition. After all, admiral, your words come from your zeal for our shared nation of origin and your dedication to her king. Now, let's take in the cool of the evening before we both drown in our own sweat." He gestured towards the door. "Shall we?"

The two officers made their way out into the lamplit corridor. The walls had not yet been redecorated since Admiral Torren had taken over as the interim governor and their footsteps echoed as they walked all the way to the formal dining area. Admiral Torren crossed the dining area and opened the double doors that led out to the balcony. The night air was considerably cooler than his office had been and Admiral Torren instantly felt relief. Sunset was fading into the late evening and a cool breeze swept in from the sea. The westward horizon blazed bright orange which faded into reds and violets skyward. The first twinkling stars were just becoming visible while the lamps of Kingston were being lit.

Admiral Torren inhaled deep through his nose and savored the smell of sea air coming in on the breeze. A hint of woodsmoke and native flowers laced the smell of saltwater and washed-up seaweed. The waters of the harbor were placid calm but for the ripples of ebbing tide. A heavy brigantine was taking advantage of the lowering sea to continue the salvage and recovery efforts of the vessels that had been sunk in the harbor while Admiral Roland's fleet and H.M.S North Wind stood vigil just a few cable lengths seaward.

"Who do you propose to take command of North Wind?" Admiral Torren asked as he stared out over the serenity of Kingston.

Admiral Roland let a long pause pass before he answered, "I think it only fitting that the senior captain from my fleet be given the privilege and opportunity to take her. Captain Thomas Williams. He is a sound sailor and one hell of a tactician, leads with a firm but fair hand and he isn't much of a drinker. I think he is the obvious choice."

"Obvious choices have disappointed me, as of late," Admiral Torren replied with a side eyed look over to his colleague. "We need someone who is bold but calculated. A man who knows when to take risks. These are desperate times for the empire, my friend. Not a good time to put a conservative captain at the helm of a ship I intend to send into the teeth of our enemies. Make no mistake about it, admiral, Your fleet will be hunting down these pirates and patrolling for French vessels, but North Wind will be the tip of the spear. I want an aggressive commander for her."

"Are you proposing to leave this lieutenant of yours as her commander?" Admiral Roland's tone began to take an oppositional note once again.

"No," Admiral Torren answered with a quick shake of his head, "no, it wouldn't be proper while there is a senior captain available. But, Williams needs to understand, I want aggressive leadership on North Wind. It is what is needed. Otherwise, I would be better to relinquish my temporary posting to you and take command of the fleet myself, to ensure she is sailed as intended."

"Captain Williams is such a man, admiral. I can assure you. He studied amidships at the elbow of men like Nelson, I can think of none better than the grand old man himself. You want someone who will sail her straight into the enemy's jaw and hammer out three broadsides to every one of theirs," said Admiral Roland. "Williams is the man for the job, admiral."

Admiral Torren conceded. "Very well then. You have me convinced. Captain Williams for North Wind," he paused for a beat and then continued, "that leaves the matter of what to do with Lieutenant Pike."

"A short drop with a sudden stop, admiral. He committed piracy on the high seas, he contributed to the sinking of a vessel of his majesty's navy, and he was a co-conspirator in the assassination of not just one, but two of the king's governors," Admiral

Roland's response became more heated as he continued. "Were it any other officer, he would already have had his neck stretched and been buried in a pauper's grave, or better yet, dumped into the briny blue and left for the sharks. It is beyond me that you of all the flag officers in the king's navy have turned a blind eye to this man's crimes."

"Admiral Sharpe seemed to have faith in the lad," Admiral Torren replied, "and let's not forget, he stood against a mutiny that would have been my end and seen North Wind in the hands of a band of rebellious brigands under the influence of an American conspirator." The admiral tapped his cane twice on the balcony rail and turned inboard to face Admiral Roland. "He was mutinied on even as he was trying to fill the shoes of his previous commander. His decisions had some unfortunate consequences, yes, but let's not forget that both of those governors were involved in what amounted to treason. The ship he sank was full of mutineers, for God's sake! I have no intention on hanging him. In fact, I have a mind to promote him."

"His posting as first lieutenant aboard H.M.S Valor was generous, but for argument's sake, I will say the lad may have very well earned that. But, his conduct since leaves much to be desired in terms of a captain."

Admiral Torren took his cane up by the shaft and tucked it under one arm. "I disagree. He has exhibited both sailing prowess and a capacity for bold decision making. A rogue streak, yes, but then again, the captain he last served under had a similar reputation."

"Grimes was bold, yes, I will give you that, admiral,"

Admiral Roland said with a defeated tone, "and I cannot say exactly what I would do, were I in the same position that young man found himself in. But, this sets a dangerous precedent. Especially if it is confirmed by the admiralty."

"Confirmed?" Admiral Torren stifled a chuckle. "I am on the promotions board, Admiral Roland. With my signature, his promotion will be done and confirmed in a stroke. Like it or not, he will be a captain. The only matter we have to set to terms will be which command he will receive."

Admiral Roland stood silent with his face slack and his shoulders slumped. "You will not be swayed on this. Will you?"

"No, admiral. I will not," Admiral Torren replied. "He will be promoted, and he will be given command of a man of war. A sloop of war, a frigate, hell, even a prize ship. It makes no difference. He will exceed expectations wherever he is placed, of that I am sure." He paused and took a deep breath of the cool evening air. "And, of his alleged transgressions, we will speak no more of it. He has paid dearly for them; he will not make the same mistake again."

"You did punish him," Admiral Roland muttered.

"Aye, I did," Admiral Torren answered, "his punishment would have killed lesser men. In fact, at the time, I had intended for it to kill him. He survived, and still came to my aid in what I would call the most desperate hour of my entire career at sea."

Admiral Roland looked perplexed. "My apologies, admiral. I should not have assumed. It, just, it seemed almost as if you had wanted to sweep it all under the rug."

"On the contrary, admiral," Admiral Torren replied in a graveled voice. "I had him keelhauled, three times over. As I said, sailing with pirates is not a folly he will make again."

Renly
22 May 1809
12 degrees 14' N, 71 Degrees 55' W

Thunderclaps of cannon fire echoed through the cove as the Drowned Maiden exchanged fire with an unknown, Spanish built warship. Clouds of smoke enveloped the space between the two vessels as hardly a heartbeat elapsed without a roaring report from one ship or the other. The fire slowed for a few moments, and Renly thought that he could hear faint voices across the stretch of water that separated the two vessels from his shore position near the mouth of the cove.

His mission had been frantic from the outset. As Drowned Maiden had made her turn into the narrow inlet of the cove, he and two more crewmen from the Maiden had been lowered over the side in a long rowboat. With them, they took a long nine pounder cannon, the gun carriage to go with it and as much shot and powder as they could load into the small boat in such a hurry. There had only been minutes to prepare. Renly chose the first two men he had seen when he received Captain Lilith's order, a tall African man that Chibs had nicknamed "Hammer Hands" because of the massive sized fists he sported on the ends of his tree trunk forearms and a lighter skinned man named Crowley that had come to the Maiden when she had sunk the Boston Autumn. Both men were capable hands, but Renly soon realized his folly when he began to set up the single gun emplacement on the beach of mixed sand and pebbles. The two men he had chosen had been trained up in the sails, among the rigging, the knowledge they had of cannons was from a rudimentary class they were given by Chibs, a man who valued skill in the rigging to be far more valuable. It had been Lieutenant Pike that had trained most of the Maiden's more capable gunners, and he seemed a distant memory to most of the crew.

When the three men had managed to haul the cannon out of the rowboat and onto the beach, the next challenge became seating it onto the carriage and then lashing it down. Renly decided to begin setting up a charge for a ranging shot while his two companions muscled the long iron into place. To Renly's frustration and dismay, he discovered the cannon had been lashed down with its touch hole facing the sand. At that moment, the Spanish built ship made her turn to angle her way into the cove.

"Unseat her, untie those lashings, you damn fools. Her touch hole has to be facing up!"

Hammer Hands glared at him with a narrowed stare and began to work the rope lashings he had just secured loose. "You might have said that before we tied it down…"

"There's no time for that, hurry!" Renly snapped and dropped the bag of powder in his hands to aid his green gun crew. "The captain will be counting on us to fire accurately on them, and we have but a few minutes."

The first of the Spanish vessel's ranging shots rang out as if to emphasize his point. Renly froze and glared across the glimmering water of the cove. A plume of seawater rose into the air beyond the Drowned Maiden. The Spanish vessel had missed her mark, but Renly knew that the next salvo would be far more accurate.

"Come on captain, you have got to move," he muttered to himself as he turned his attention back to the task at hand. Hammer Hands and Crowley had managed to lash down the iron gun in the proper position. Without a breath of pause, Renly fetched a bag of powder and the ram rod. He shoved the powder home as another roaring report echoed through the cove. A sense of panic began to grip his guts. He rammed a leather wad down the iron gun and grumbled out loud, "Damnit, girl. Return fire!" He turned to his companions and pointed to the load of cannon shot they had packed into the rowboat. "Load the piece with one of those balls while I prime it and get it sighted."

Using a sharpened metal hook, Renly punctured the bag of powder through the cannon's touch hole and pulled a small amount of powder into the brass pan. As Crowley hefted the nine-pound ball into the muzzle, Renly adjusted the threaded elevation screw beneath the cannon. He looked down the side of the long iron weapon to get a rough idea of how the gun was oriented. The long iron barrel stretched forward from the gun carriage. Renly pressed the side of his head next to the cool metal, the Spanish ship was partly occluded from his view by the muzzle of the gun.

"That will have to do for now, we will adjust after our first round," He grumbled before pointing toward the stash of shot and powder in the rowboat. "Hurry and get us shot and powder for the next round, we will need to fire as quick as we can to have any effect on them."

Renly dug a small leather pouch from a pocket in his trousers, he unfolded the thick leather and withdrew a piece of waxed canvas that held within it a smoldering wick. As his fingers gripped the braided cotton string he noted the absence of any heat. His stomach gripped into knots and his heart rose into his throat. The match he had intended to use to fire his cannon had gone out. A roar erupted over the water. Renly looked up just in time to see a furling cloud of bluish white cannon smoke drift into thin wisps in the breeze. The Spanish ship had loosed her broadside.

"Damn the luck! The embers on this wick have gone cold," He looked to his two companions and asked, "Do either of you have a flint and steel?"

The two hastily recruited gunners exchanged a look. Crowley shrugged and returned Renly's stare with a wide-eyed look of dread. "I don't," he paused for a moment before continuing, "can't say I would even know how to use them in the first place."

Renly shook his head and drew in a breath through his nose. "We have to find a way to light the powder or the captain and everyone else aboard the Maiden is doomed!" His mind raced. He had no flint, no burning wick. His eyes scanned the sand and pebble shoreline. By the time he gained an ember to build a fire, the Maiden would be sunk.

"What about your pistol?" Crowley said with an extended finger pointing toward Renly's waistline.

A heartbeat passed, then another. Renly thought about the suggestion for a moment. The flintlock mechanism of his pistol put out a shower of sparks into a small brass pan. It was approximately the same mechanism that regular navies had on their guns. If he held the pistol in a certain position above the breech, it should allow a spark to fall into the pan and ignite the powder, thus firing the gun.

"Crowley! It's genius!" Renly said with an exuberant gesture. He drew the pistol and held it out toward the Spanish built ship. With a quick squeeze of the trigger the pistol discharged and sent its small projectile out over the waters of the cove. In a scramble, Renly positioned himself next to the gun carriage and gave the cannon one last check. The long cylinder of iron was pointed straight at the hull of the Spanish ship. Another roar of cannon fire erupted from the cove. He exchanged a quick look between Crowley and Hammer Hands before cocking the pistol and holding the flash pan directly over the cannon's breech.

"Abandon hope, lads. If this works, they'll likely turn

their next broadside on us."

With a held breath, and his heart clamoring within his chest, Renly pulled the trigger of his pistol. At first, he thought the attempt a failure. A heartbeat, then another. He began to let out his breath when a sizzle erupted from the cannon's breech and a bluish smoke rose from the top of the touch hole. The nine-pounder cannon roared to life and belched a cloud of smoke that obscured their target and the Maiden until the breeze carried it away. The cannon fire exchange was ongoing between the Spanish ship and the Drowned Maiden. Little explosions of wooden shards erupted from both vessels causing havoc and destruction. Renly watched closely for an impact from his shot. No plume of seawater rose into the air, he had either hit her directly and couldn't distinguish his shot from those fired by the Maiden, or he had missed entirely.

"Reload! Reload her as quick as we can!" Renly shouted.

Hammer Hands and Crowley burst into a frenzy of activity. A bag of powder was rammed down the bore of the cannon. Renly went to work priming the pan as soon as a spot of white fabric showed itself through the gun's breech. A wad was pushed in and then followed with a nine-pound ball of shot. In the matter of a few seconds, the small gun crew had made their piece ready to fire. Renly gave another look down the side of the long barrel and took away some elevation with the screw mechanism. Satisfied with the gun's aim he drew his pistol, cocked it, and held it over the breech.

"Stand clear boys!" He shouted before pulling the

trigger of his pistol.

A long moment stretched by. Renly expected the same blossom of bluish smoke to appear from the breech that he had seen last time. It didn't come. He grumbled and re-cocked his pistol, through a grimace he watched as the flint striker sent a shower of sparks into the breech as he pulled the trigger. Almost instantly, a hiss sounded and a small cloud of gunpowder smoke burst from the cannon's breech. The cannon roared and shuddered violently as it sent its projectile hurling over the cove. Renly watched through the clearing cloud of smoke as his shot impacted onto the Spanish ship's quarterdeck railing. It shattered wooden rail, sending deadly debris flying above her deck before blasting into the ship's wheel. Hammer Hands and Crowley let a victorious shout fly and Renly squeezed one fist in a triumphant gesture. More cannon fire sounded between the Spanish ship and the Maiden. Both vessels were locked in their deadly standoff.

"Another round lads, we need to keep it up!" Renly shouted even as Hammer Hands and Crowley were making the gun ready. Powder was rammed home, the gun primed, and a shot was loaded within a few heartbeats. Renly made a slight adjustment to the elevation screw and positioned his pistol. He pulled the trigger and waited for the tell-tale hiss of powder igniting. Nothing. With a groan of irritation, He re-cocked the weapon and pulled the trigger again. It took three attempts, but a spark finally found its way into the breech and ignited the powder. The nine-pounder cannon thundered. Renly looked up in anticipation of a solid impact. His hopes were rewarded with a resounding crash and the sound of shattering timbers. Their shot had hit home on the Spanish vessel's transom just above the waterline and smashed its way through the crucial timbers that kept the seawater at bay. So far he had taken out the helm and opened a hole in her hull.

"Again! Again! Reload!" Renly shouted as Hammer Hands and Crowley scrambled to make their cannon ready. A staggered line of cannons fired within the cove. Renly looked up for a moment to see that the clouds of smoke had spewed forth from the Maiden's cannons. She was still in the fight! A touch of lightning raced through his veins. Captain Lilith and the Maiden could still prove to be victorious. He cocked the hammer of his pistol back to the locked position and examined the flint. It was well worn. Renly tried to remember the last time he had replaced the flint. As worn as the flint was, there was still enough left for a few more rounds.

8

'Drowned Maiden'
22 May 1809
12 degrees 14' N, 71 Degrees 55' W

The sound of splitting timbers and cracking beams sent shivers up Chibs' spine. He'd heard it before, and it hadn't ended well. Another volley of cannon fire thundered, and a fresh wave of smoke clouds filled the air. On the deck of the Maiden, men and women were preparing to repel an incoming attack. Swords were drawn, axes and knives, hammers, rail pins and muskets were being taken up to defend the ship. Though he could not see the damage, Chibs knew it had to be severe. They had taken a partial broadside full on the beam and another up toward the stern. The rigging was in shambles, but that was to be expected from an exchange of gunnery within such close quarters. Lilith had set her trap, and the Spanish ship had quickly turned the odds back into their favor. Another cannon shot fired. Chibs listened for the impact. A shrill whistle pierced the air and Chibs winced in anticipation of the damage it was about to inflict. The slam of the cannon ball sounded, an initial boom of the impact followed by cracking timbers. It sounded different than the others, somehow more distant.

From his position near the stern, Chibs looked out over the cove toward the Spanish vessel. Her guns hadn't run out after her last partial volley, there was no fresh cloud of smoke drifting away in the breeze. The shot hadn't come from her.

"Renly, you bastard. You got her now!" Chibs shouted out to nobody in particular. He looked back over the crew on the Maiden and raised the pistol gripped in his good hand. "Our shore gun has her in range lads! Keep up the fire, we may just make it out of this!"

Another shot fired and Chibs winced until he realized it was Renly's gun again. Their rate of fire was impressive, and so far they had managed two hits.

"Grapples! Grapples to the larboard rail!" Lilith's voice cut through the chaos on deck.

Chibs' felt a pang of fear and confusion hit his guts. He looked up and down the length of the Maiden for any sign of grapple lines coming from the opposing ship. They were still too far away. He looked across the deck and found Captain Lilith holding a rope with an iron grapple attached to it on one end. She was ordering grapples, not warning of them! For the span of a heartbeat, Chibs didn't know what to say, or to think. He stood frozen, watching as his captain crossed the deck and wound the iron grapple through the air in a tight circle.

"Captain! What in God's name?" Chibs cry was lost to another round of cannon fire from the Maiden's guns. Lilith released her grip of the iron hook and the curved iron flew through the air in a high arc before thudding onto the Spanish ship's deck. Lilith seized the rope in both hands and pulled with every ounce of her weight. A half dozen more lines with grapple hooks sailed through the air even as Chibs issued another protest.

"Cap'n we don't have the numbers for this fight," Chibs called only to have his cries fall on deaf ears.

The ship was battered. There were wounded men and women on deck. Their best chance was to heave to and run. He looked out to the enemy ship. The crew was in disarray. Sailors were running back and forth between opposing rails, orders were being issued from the quarterdeck. What little Spanish Chibs knew, he could make out that things were not going well for them. Another cannon shot reported from the far shore of the cove, Renly and his mates were putting in work to keep the Spanish ship from gaining an edge. Lilith knew exactly what she was doing. A swell of pride rose in his chest, she had seen the pandemonium aboard the enemy vessel and she wanted to take full advantage of it. Captain James would have been proud. Chibs leveled his pistol at the enemy vessel as the Maiden's crew hauled her closer with grapple lines. With a quick eye he found a sailor moving to cut away one of the grapple lines and pulled the trigger. The sailor toppled over backward from the force of the ball.

"No quarter!" Lilith cried as the crew hauled on grapple lines to bring the Spanish ship in close. A roar of approval rose from the deck of the Maiden.

Chibs looked on toward the enemy crew. Their disarray had gone from bad, to worse. Sailors had glimpsed the motley band of escaped slaves and ex-royal navy men, some braced for the fight about to come, some fled over the opposite rail. A smile spread across Chibs' lips. With a simple act of aggression, Lilith had turned the tide.

"Gangplank! Drop the plank and board her!" Lilith shouted as the ships came close enough for the crew to cross decks.

A few more sailors turned to flee. One of them fell to a musket shot from the Maiden. Two of them made it to the opposite side of the ship. An officer on the Spanish ship shot one of the fleeing sailors with a pistol before shouting something in Spanish. Chibs searched his immediate surroundings and found a pirate that had been with the Maiden since before Captain Lilith holding a musket in his grip. With a quick snap of his wrist, Chibs grabbed the musket away from his shipmate and braced it against the crook of the elbow above his half amputated arm. He cocked the hammer and sighted in on the Spaniard who had just fired at his own crew. A cloud of smoke blew into the air when Chibs pulled the trigger and as it cleared in the breeze he watched the Spanish officer topple down the aft castle stairs and sprawl onto the weather deck.

A reverberating wooden thunk announced that the Maiden had dropped her gangplank in place, as soon as the sound uttered forth it was drowned away by an uproar of shouts and curses from the crew of pirates. Bloodcurdling screams and pistol shots erupted from the deck and rose high into the rigging. Panic had set in aboard the Spanish ship, her crew had gone from chaos to cowardice as only a handful of sailors stood ready to repel borders. Lilith was first across, with a cutlass in one hand and a pistol in the other she raced over the double wide plank and dropped to the deck of the enemy ship. Before her boots touched the timbers she had discharged her pistol into a defender and deftly spun the weapon in her grip to use as a bludgeon. Her cutlass was next in use, and she used it with a level of skill that seemed to take her opponents off guard. First, she parried away an attack from a sailor swinging a crude looking machete, she stepped around her opponent and slammed the butt of her pistol against the side of his head in a savage upward blow that caught him just below his chin. A raking slash sent her opponent to the deck, blood dripped from between his clenched fingers as he tried desperately to stop the onrush from the wound she had opened. Chibs hefted his sword as the press of pirates made their way across the Maiden's gangplank. Lilith was in the thick of fighting, she parried away another attack before stepping into a lunge and plunging her blade into a defender's chest. Pistol shots roared. Swords clashed amid the screams of dying sailors and pirates. The intensity pitched as a handful of men emerged from below deck to rally for the defense of their ship. Their efforts died almost instantly as a broad-shouldered African man let fly with a swivel gun and cut through half of the advancing sailors.

Almost as quickly as it had begun, the fight waned to a handful of scraps and a pair of sword fights. Amidships, two of Lilith's crew were exchanging sword strokes with a tall, lean sailor who wore an officer's coat. Near the bow, a group of three sailors were failing to hold off advances from two of the pirates who had them cornered against the bowsprit.

"Captain! Ship in sight, our friends with the blood-red sails!" A voice from high in the Maiden's rigging called down.

Every eye aboard the Spanish ship shifted to the north and landed on Batard De Mur with her sails of crimson red billowing in the wind. She dominated the entrance of the cove. There would be no escape, even if the Spanish crew managed to repel the pirate attack on their weather deck, they were bottled in. Swords fell to the deck of the ship. The first to surrender were the sailors trapped against the bowsprit. Next, struggle amidships came to a halt as the Spanish sailors recognized their defeat.

"We've taken the ship!" Chibs cried out from his perch on the gangplank. He had yet to strike out with his blade. Lilith had led this charge, and he couldn't be prouder. "She's ours!"

A roar of approval and celebration rose from the decks of both ships as pirates pushed their newly taken prisoners into more compromising positions. The sailors retreated at the point of swords or the cold muzzles of pistols.

"Bring me the senior survivor," Lilith ordered as she paced toward the aft castle of the Spanish ship, "take anything of value to us and rig her to burn. We will get what we can from her crew and leave her for the sea."

A pair of stout hands grappled one of the last surviving sailors toward the aft castle. Both were broad shouldered men that Chibs knew well. Handsome Jon had been aboard the Maiden since the days of Captain James, he was a seasoned hand in the rigging and even better in a fight. The other was a brick house that Chibs had taken to calling Jack, he had come aboard the Maiden from the Carolina Shepherd and he was one of the few survivors of all of the Maiden's successive encounters with the Royal Navy. The two men half dragged and half marched the sailor up the aft castle stairs, one at each of his shoulders, holding his arms immobile.

Lilith rested her cutlass along the iron grate of a lit brazier. She motioned to her two crewmen with a nod of her head. "Open his shirt and hold him at the fantail railing." Both men complied without a response. They knew what was coming, even if the sailor had no idea what he was about to endure. Chibs followed the party up to the high stern. He knew the terror that was about to unfold, and he knew he couldn't stop it even if he wanted to.

"Who is this ship that would try to send the Maiden to her grave?" Lilith asked as she stared into the flames of the brazier with her remaining eye.

The sailor struggled against his captors for a moment before surrendering to his fate. "This is the Cazadora De Olas, a ship of his majesty's navy."

"Wave Hunter? Is that right?" Lilith asked, her eyes unmoved from the flames.

"Si," the sailor answered.

Lilith turned the blade of her cutlass and Chibs could see that the color was distorting as the metal grew hotter. "You chased us into a cove and opened fire on us without warning, or provocation. Why?"

The sailor nodded over the ship's rail at Batard De Mur's crimson sails. "Because you sail with them."

"Pirate hunters," Lilith smiled as the words left her mouth. "It seems you have failed your mandate. How disappointed your commanders will be, what a shame." She hefted the cutlass from the flames and held it vertically in front of her face. Chibs could feel the heat radiating from the blade as Lilith crossed to the stern where the prisoner was being held. "How many more are there?"

"How many what?" The sailor looked confused and afraid.

Lilith nodded to her men holding the sailor by his arms before moving in to administer the Drowned Maiden's brand of coercion. His screams rose until Chibs was sure he would never forget the sound.

Fort Charles
20 May 1809
Kingston, Jamaica

The snaring rattle of drums echoed within Fort Charles' stone walls. Admiral Torren stood painfully still facing a formation of sailors at rigid attention. The sun had crested over the fort's eastern wall and the temperature was rapidly rising beyond the threshold of comfort. On the far flank of the formation, Lieutenant Pike stood ready to move into position in front of the admiral. The rattle of drums continued, and the admiral narrowed his eyes as he panned his gaze over the formation one last time, his stare landed on the drummers and he offered them the slightest nod. In unison, the drums silenced, their final notes reverberated through the fort before finally dying away. Lieutenant Pike snapped into motion and marched directly in front of the admiral before performing a snapping right face movement. The admiral drew in a deep breath before taking a long pause to examine the lieutenant. His uniform coat was crisp, his scarred face shaved clean and his posture as rigid and proper as the day that the young officer had stood within the board chambers in London. A spark of pride nestled in the admiral's chest. He pulled out a pair of wire framed glasses and pulled them onto his face, unraveled a rolled parchment and held it up to read aloud.

"Hear ye, hear ye. To all gathered parties and those of concern, hear that on this twentieth day of May, in the year of our lord 1809, given by my hand as the acting governor in his majesty's colony of Jamaica and by direction of the Admiralty in London, in the service of his majesty's navy, I do hereby appoint William Pike from this day forward as a captain in the Royal Navy. As a captain of the fleet, I do hereby charge him with the command and care of those subordinates assigned to any vessels under his charge as well as require such subordinates to follow his direction and orders as given according to the Articles of War. Captain Pike will take forth a ship or ships given his command and orders from higher authority and seek the enemies of our king and country, he will protect the national interest on the high seas and abroad, and he will leave no effort unspent, either be it his life or the lives of his subordinates, should service demand it from him."

As the admiral finished reading the promotion warrant, he could feel the intensity of the Caribbean sun growing on his face and warming the thick wool of his uniform coat. He appreciated warmth. It eased the ache of his arthritis riddled feet and legs, but this was another level of heat entirely. Within the courtyard of Fort Charles, the breeze was shielded away by thick stone walls that also radiated heat inward. It was almost insufferable. A sheen of perspiration was forming on his head and neck as the admiral opened the lapels of his newly promoted captain's jacket and applied new epaulets, signifying the freshly attained rank. With a slight grin and a crisp salute, Captain Pike performed a rigid left face movement and marched to the flank of the formation where an edge of shade offered some respite from the beating sun.

Admiral Torren gave a slight nod to the next ranking officer before turning the formation over to him. He returned the captain's salute and walked with a brisk but dignified pace to the far flank where Captain Pike stood at attention, awaiting the dismissal of the hands. As cool shade overtook the sun beneath the high reach of Fort Charles' walls. He retrieved a sealed envelope from an inside pocket in his uniform coat and extended the packet to the new captain.

"Orders for you and your new command, Captain Pike," Admiral Torren said. "I know you will make us all proud. It isn't a line ship, but it is a fine vessel for a first command."

Captain Pike offered a nod and a grin as he opened the envelope and scanned through the first few lines of the document. "H.M.S Redemption, sir?"

Admiral Torren nodded before removing his hat and swiping at his brow with a linen kerchief. "Yes. She was a frog vessel, a prize captured by Admiral Roland's fleet during their voyage along the coast of Brazil. I thought a renaming would be appropriate, the damned French and their flowery prose doesn't belong on the fantail of a ship in service to our king."

"Redemption," Captain Pike repeated, "I hope I can live up to it, sir."

"You will, captain. Of that, I am most sure," Admiral Torren replied as he replaced his hat on his head. "She is a heavy frigate. American made, according to what Admiral Roland has told me. Her hull timbers and frame are constructed of live oak. I have heard it said that it is harder than white oak. The Americans, they know a thing or two about building ships, as disturbing as that may seem."

"Thirty-six guns, sir?" Captain Pike asked. His tone implied that the answer would be a given.

Admiral Torren broke his legendary reserve and allowed a smile to cross his face. "Oh, no, captain. She is a forty-four gun frigate. Every bit the ship H.M.S Valor was, but with more firepower. Swift with the wind all the way to beam reach, as maneuverable as a sloop and shallower on draft than a line ship." He paused and tipped his brow forward toward the new captain. "If you want to serve the king's navy, there is hardly a better ship to do it with."

Captain Pike stood quiet for a long pause. He appeared to be processing his new position and everything that went with it. Surprise and awe quickly faded and the weight of responsibility seemed to settle over his disposition right before the admiral's eyes. "The crew, sir?"

"Right," Admiral Torren nodded, his eyes flitted to Admiral Roland as the formation of soldiers, sailors and marines were released to return to their duties. "Some sailors, as well as one officer, who were assigned as her prize crew will remain aboard. Admiral Roland will reassign men from each of the ships under his command," he paused for a beat before continuing, "and we are pressing some local sailors into service. Not ideal, I know, but it is the right of the king and his navy."

Captain Pike's eyes lowered. He drifted away,

appearing deep in thought. After a beat, his head snapped up, eyes filled with resolve. The admiral saw something in him that validated his decision, there was a spark there, a glimmer of the officer that had stood before him within the walls of the Admiralty.

"Our orders, sir?"

Admiral Torren pursed his lips and drew a breath in through his nose. "You are to screen for Admiral Roland's fleet as he searches for the pirate vessels that you encountered on your cruise with North Wind. You will signal any sighting and engage the enemy until the fleet can reinforce you."

Captain Pike's face remained stony. He looked down toward his feet and shifted his weight between his feet. "There is something I haven't told you, sir. The pirates we engaged; they were in the company of the Maiden."

Admiral Torren pursed his lips. He drew in a sharp breath through his nose. "Are you certain?"

"As sure as I am standing here speaking to you, sir. It was the Drowned Maiden. I would recognize that ship anywhere. She looks, different, of course. But her crew brought her up from the depths and make repairs." Captain Pike's stare met Admiral Torren's and the admiral could see it was no jest.

"We fired no less than a half dozen broadsides at that ship. There is no way anyone aboard could have survived, Captain Pike. Perhaps you are mistaken. Perhaps you saw what your mind wanted you to see. It is impossible, son, she sank. I watched her succumb to the water myself." Admiral Torren lowered his voice and stepped close to the new captain. "But, if it is her, you will do your duty, sailor. You will engage her without mercy or reservation, you will fire every one of your cannons until she is only a field of flotsam bobbing on the sea's surface. Do you understand? I am giving you command of a heavy frigate, Redemption, son, not disappointment. You have been given a second chance. There will not be a third." He gestured toward the ramparts. "Come, walk with me. We should be able to see your new ship."

The admiral led with a brisk pace. His knees and ankles protested, but after the first score of steps the pain subsided to a dull ache. On the ramparts, the view of Kingston and the harbor opened up below the fort. Broad leafed green trees bordered the town and hugged the shoreline. The morning sun had worked its way high into the first quarter of sky, it cast a glimmer over the blue green water of the harbor that radiated like jewels. North Wind loomed over the rest of ships at anchor, her tall masts towered compared to the others and her massive hull seemed to dwarf the smaller vessels making their way in and out of Kingston. Several other warships were anchored in the harbor, vessels that had sailed in with Admiral Roland's fleet. Two brigantines, H.M.S Elizabeth and H.M.S Sea Otter, were anchored together and had dropped gang planks across their railing. H.M.S Elizabeth appeared to be stepping a new foremast. Further out, top men on the frigate H.M.S Tiger were running new lines and replacing blocks. Admiral Roland's flagship, H.M.S Reliant, was anchored near North Wind. She wasn't as large as North Wind, though in her own right she seemed to dwarf the brigantines and even the frigates.

The admiral motioned toward a long wooden pier that stretched out from the shoreline on the far end of the harbor.

"She is being made ready as we speak. I have ordered enough shot and powder loaded onto her for you to do live gun drills. Your crew will need to be first rate in order to stand up against a French man of war, or a seasoned band of pirates. Drill them until you can complete three broadsides in a minute, once they can do that reliably, execute gun drills while you do maneuvers. If you want a top-notch crew, that is how it is done." Admiral Torren faced outward and took in a deep breath of the sea air. "Her new name is being painted on the fantail in the morning, she should be loaded and ready by then. Check with Admiral Roland and see when he plans to hoist anchor. He is an aggressive man, I would assume that he will want to make way as soon as possible."

"I hope he has a heading in mind. We met the pirates out on the open sea, far from any shore. I haven't the foggiest clue where to begin our search," Captain Pike said with a shrug. "After the initial exchange, the Maiden and the other ship accompanying her turned southward. They may be cruising Spanish routes looking for prey, but I wouldn't even know where to begin."

"In that, I know for a fact Admiral Roland does not have a specific heading in mind," Admiral Torren replied. He faced Captain Pike and narrowed his eyes, hoping to see the reaction he wanted. "But, I would imagine, if you questioned that girl you brought in as a prisoner, you may find her useful."

The breeze brushed at Captain Pike's uniform, and the admiral could see conflict welling inside of him. The seeds of doubt were there. Was he committed?

"I will question her. I'm not sure how useful she will prove, she seems to be every bit as fiery as the pirate captain she was following."

There it was. Admiral Torren chanced a grin. "If she is willing to divulge anything, I am sure you will make the best use of the information. Whether or not we agree with her mission, captain, piracy on the high seas cannot stand. The Maiden, and any ship in her company is a direct threat to the peaceful passage of commerce. They may see themselves as avenging saints. It makes no matter. They must be blown from the water. I expect nothing less."

Fort Charles
20 May 1809
Kingston, Jamaica

There hadn't been a noise for hours in the bowels of Fort Charles. Emilia was starting to wonder if she had been completely forgotten by her captors. The stone walls and floor were cold, the air was damp and smelled like a mixture of unwashed bodies and raw sewage. Cold dominated her every waking moment, and even in her sleep she curled on the hard slab of wood suspended by two iron chains from one wall of her cell and shivered. Occasionally, a gust of breeze would enter the small, barred window and bring with it welcomed fresh air and a taste of the tropical warmth she yearned for. These were conditions she had never feared to endure in all her years. The bread she had been given was stale at best and riddled with weevils or rot at worst. The nights were intolerably cold and the days seemed to drag by with no end in sight. The guards didn't deign to speak to her, let alone check on her wellbeing. It seemed that she had been taken prisoner to be left to rot. At first she had cursed at them and rejected the meals she was brought. As time wore on, and her hunger took hold, she kept her insults to herself and picked at the bread to remove any unwanted portions before eating what she was given. She had determined that they were trying to break her spirit, and she would not be broken.

Iron clanking broke the silence that had been Emilia's only companion. At first it was only a slight noise, a distant rattling that could almost be mistaken for a trick of the mind. Her ears perked up when the noise grew. Footsteps accompanied the rattling noise as it grew louder. Fears that she had finally been forgotten and left to die eased from her mind only to be replaced with the dread of what the visit was for. It was not evening, not time for her paltry ration of stale bread and fouled water. The sunlight still beamed bright through the iron bars of her cell's window to the outside world. The footsteps changed cadence, grew louder. Something was off about them, different from the other times she had listened as the guards approached with rations. A cough echoed up the stony corridor that led to her cell. Emilia eased herself up from the slab bench that served as her bed and listened intently for any detail she could glean from the echoes. The cough repeated, more footsteps. The sound of leather soles crunching on hard granite. A slight metallic rattle. Keys. It had to be a guard carrying keys. But, it was different than the other times she had heard the guards making their way to her cell. Usually they were conversing amongst each other and paying no mind to any of the prisoners. The footsteps grew louder, whoever it was, was almost to her cell. It clicked in her mind. The guards came in pairs. She was hearing the footsteps of a solitary individual as he approached her cell. Emilia ran her fingers through her hair, it had become a mussed mess in the last few days, a matted tangle. She eyed the last edible crust of bread from her ration the night before and tucked it away in her waistband before looking toward the cell door as the footsteps finally came to a halt. A rattle of iron keys and the solid clunk of her cell lock sounded before the hinges screamed in protest. Her cell door opened and she saw the naval officer who had been her captor.

"Good afternoon, miss," Captain Pike said with a forced smile. "I apologize for the intrusion, but I have some questions I would like to ask you."

Emilia pursed her lips. She would have preferred a visit from the guards with more stale bread and vile water. "Whatever questions you could have for me, I have no answers for you."

He nodded. "I thought you might say that, but, I

determined to come and try to speak with you anyway," he paused and looked at her. She noticed the scarring on the side of his face and on the edge of one of his hands.

"It makes no difference. Ask all the questions you want. I don't know anything."

"Somehow," the captain replied, "I doubt that." He nodded toward the empty plate sitting next to her on the wooden bench. "Are you being fed regularly?"

She nodded. "If you can call it that."

He shook his head and looked down at the floor where he shuffled his feet. "It is unfortunate, the conditions in which prisoners are kept. I will inquire into your situation and see if I can find you better circumstances. I understand all too well the torment of being a prisoner of the crown."

Emilia felt a rush of disdain, she fought the urge to attack the officer standing in her cell and managed to pare her rage down to a sneered lip. "How would you know? You are the one who took me captive. Remember?"

Captain Pike grimaced, his eyes narrowed for a moment before his face softened. "Actually. At one point, not long ago, I sailed with the very pirate crew you were in the company of."

"Lies," Emilia sneered and averted her stare to the stone wall opposite the captain.

"It is truth, I assure you. I came to the Caribbean as the first lieutenant of the H.M.S Valor. A series of events passed that had me mutinied against, twice actually. Captain Lilith and her crew took me and several of my officers, sailors and marines aboard the Drowned Maiden. I sailed with them for the better part of a year."

"Likely story," Emilia could barely contain her contempt, "You happen to know the ship's name and her captain. There's probably a thousand sailors who know of her. That doesn't mean they have sailed with her."

Captain Pike nodded his understanding. "Well, I doubt thousands of sailors know Trina, or the African boy Omibwe who mans the helm with one leg beneath him, or his mother Jilhal." He paused and squinted at her as her gaze landed on him. "Fewer still would know that her quartermaster, Chibs, is absolutely smitten with Jilhal. Or that Omibwe lost his leg when the slaver crew who raided his village shot him. Fewer still would know that it was Captain Lilith's own doctor, Doctor LeMeux who did the amputation."

Emilia's blood tinged with lightning. Only someone who had been aboard the Maiden could know these things. Her eyes narrowed and her eyebrows crowded into a frown. "How is it you went from a pirate back to being a navy man?"

The captain's face went slack, his eyes drifted back to the floor and his voice lowered as he spoke. "Lilith had found evidence that the governor of Nassau was involved in the slave smuggling operation. She sent me ashore with Governor Alton and a member of her crew to ascertain just what was being done on the island. When we met with the governor, her crewman, a man she had rescued from a plantation in Haiti, killed both governors right in front of me. It was never meant to be a reconnaissance effort. Lilith had planned for it to be an assassination and left me there on the island."

"And yet, you have somehow regained trust with the navy," Emilia said, still unsure if she could believe what she was hearing.

"The admiral who held me as his prisoner," He pointed to the scars on the side of his face, "the man responsible for these scars, and many more across my back. I saved him from a mutiny." He paused for a long moment. Emilia could see a flicker in his eyes, as if he had recalled something important. "The man who started that mutiny is the same man responsible for the murder of your father."

"Tim Sladen," Emilia spat. Her blood went hot with a wave of fresh hatred.

"Indeed," he turned toward a corner of the cell and looked at her from beneath his lowered brow. "In fact. Mr. Sladen is currently being held as a prisoner here in Fort Charles."

Her face shriveled. She wasn't sure how to feel about what she was being told. Was he going to torment her further by parading her in front of him? Or perhaps he would have her cell changed so that she was imprisoned within earshot of him. She remembered the sight of the ungrateful American running for his life as she chased after him with her father's sword and pistol. "Why are you telling me this?"

"Because I sympathize with you, believe it or not. I understand your plight better than anyone in this fort, likely anyone in Kingston, or Jamaica for that matter.

You took up with these pirates out of necessity, as did I. My necessity was survival, yours was a desire for justice."

"Not justice. Vengeance." Emilia interrupted between her clenched teeth.

"Be that as it may," Captain Pike continued, "you now find yourself a prisoner of the crown for the high crime of piracy. There are only two options before you. Full cooperation, or death by hanging. Since I sympathize with you and your situation, I feel compelled to offer you every opportunity to find your way out of this mess and back into the good graces of my king and his representatives abroad." He paused for a moment before continuing with a grave note in his voice. "Tell me everything you know of the Maiden and her plans, tell me what you know about her companion ship with the red sails, and give me a heading I can sail on. Do this, and I am assured by the governor that he will stay your execution. Forgo this opportunity, and he will have you hanged before the fleet sets sail."

"I don't know where Captain Lilith plans to sail the Maiden. She is in the company of a pirate I knew only from the tales my father had told me," Emilia replied in earnest. She opened her hands and extended them forward. "I was a deckhand, they never told me their plans."

Captain Pike leaned one shoulder on the stone wall of the cell. He peered out of the heavy cell door and into the corridor. "You overheard nothing? Not even in exchange between her and her newfound friends?"

Emilia shook her head, she could feel her chance at freedom slipping away, like the cell she was in was tightening its grip even as she spoke. "Your battleship chanced upon us almost immediately after we encountered the ship with red sails. We all thought it would be a battle between us and her, until you showed up."

The captain looked back at her over his shoulder, his weight still leaning against the cell wall. "You have to give me something, anything. What about the red sailed ship? You said your father had talked about it before his death."

Emilia felt a pang of pain lance through her chest as she remembered the conversation. It had actually been between her father and Tim Sladen. "My father heard about her down at the dockyards. He worked for the shipwright and often spoke with sailors from all manner of different ships. He said their captain is a Frenchman, and he never sets foot aboard a vessel without taking a life. He flies red sails and a red banner. It isn't known where he calls home, but father said that he was known for sinking ships without taking a scrap of goods. Almost like he was doing it for sport, or to send some kind of message."

"The ship with red sails is a lead that I will work on," the captain replied. He continued looking out the cell door into the corridor. "In the meantime, I would encourage you to scour your memory. A repeated sailor's tale handed down from your father will not suffice to stay your execution."

'U.S.S United States'
10 June 1809
26 degrees 35' N, 76 Degrees 54' W

Gentle rocking and pitching had lulled Captain Woodhaven into a state somewhere barely on the edge of alertness. He was not asleep, yet his mind drifted aimlessly. The slung canvas hammock he occupied in his cabin cradled his weary body and the pitch and yaw of the ship eventually eased his mind into a relaxed state that left him teetering on the edge of sleep. The last two weeks had proved grueling, he had drilled the crew mercilessly through maneuvers and gun drills, until the top men could nearly anticipate his next order and the gun crews were some of the fastest and most efficient he had ever seen. He ran them to quarters at night and during meals, he had interrupted sailing maneuvers with orders for a different heading, at one point during gun drills he had walked the gun deck and began tapping individual sailors on the shoulder to tell them they were now casualties and their respective gun crews must carry on without them. He was sure the men were beginning to hate him. Grumbling on deck hadn't contained itself to the landsmen or even the enlisted sailors. Captain Woodhaven had heard the mutterings coming from several of the ship's midshipmen and even the second lieutenant. But, he pressed on, driving the men as hard as he could. They had sailed south, beating a course for the edge of the Caribbean. He had suspected H.M.S Cutlass would need to refit from their engagement, just as United States had. Nassau was the closest British port with a deep water harbor. He laid his bets they would be there, refitting, restocking and rearming. As hard as he had pushed his crew, a strange thing had occurred only an hour before he finally retired to his cabin for some rest for the evening. He had called the off watch up on deck and summoned the hands in for what he thought would be a short, informal briefing.

"Men," he had started, with the wind whipping at his back. "By morning we will be within a stone's throw of the Caribbean, and with any luck, the Cutlass." A cheer arose from the crew and Captain Woodhaven had to mask his surprise. He hadn't judged them eager for action, he was wrong. "She is a stout enemy. Her guns fire true and they fire quickly, her captain is a sound tactician, and her hull is every bit as thick and hard as ours." He scanned the faces in front of him and found a stony resolve that made his heart beat a little quicker in his chest. "The Brits fancy themselves the finest sailors in the world. That is fine, they have been for centuries. They pride themselves on total domination of the world's oceans, in truth, they have more control over the seas than any nation on earth ever has in history. But, the world is changing. Thirty-four years ago, our first continental congress put paper to pen and cast off the yoke of the crown. No other nation in the world has defied the British empire the way we have, and we continue that defiant tradition to this day. The ship you are standing on represents the future of naval warfare. The forty-four gun frigate is the pride of the republic and the bane of

Brits. They may have regarded themselves as the worlds finest sailors, but we will teach them a lesson next time they see our banner, that I promise you!" Another cheer rose from the deck and lifted through the tops. Sailors stomped their feet and clobbered one another on the shoulder. Captain Woodhaven held up his hands and waited until the frenzy died away. "I have pushed you hard these last two weeks. As hard as any commander has a right to. But, the service demands your absolute best, and by God, I will get the best you have, out of each of you. Our broadsides are down to two in a minute, which is better than any crew I have heard of in our navy. The fact that we are hitting flotsam targets at six cable length is even better!" Another cheer ushered forth, and the captain had to hold his hands up to quell the voices. "We will find the enemy, and this time, we will show them what it is to truly taste defeat at the hands of the United States. I want your absolute best, at all times. Watchmen remain alert, top men keep your lines clean and tight, and gun crews, keep your guns and your men ready. Officers, take care of your charges and see to it that everyone remains ready. We will carry the day. That is all, men, as you were."

The crew had come together. Captain Woodhaven felt a pride that carried him through his evening meal and lasted well after he slung his hammock in his cabin for the night. U.S.S United States was among the finest ships sailing the oceans of the world, and he had forged himself a fine crew to man her. He relished the southward voyage, every passing hour brought him closer to the quarry he sought. He would find H.M.S Cutlass and exact justice upon her. No formal declaration of war had been issued, he could not take her as a prize, but that was not what he truly desired. He wanted to watch her submit to flames and sink beneath the waves. He wanted vindication for his lost and wounded sailors and marines. He wanted vengeance.

A knock sounded on his cabin door.

"Enter," he said in a gruff, sleep riddled voice.

"Beg your pardon for the intrusion captain," the voice was that of Midshipman Stewart, a lanky young man from Boston with fiery red hair and an eagerness to serve that had endeared him to the captain immediately. "Land sighting, three points over starboard bow on the horizon."

Captain Woodhaven wiped a hand over his face and fought the webs of encroaching sleep from his mind. "Have you reckoned our position? Is it man-o-war cay?"

"I believe we are slightly farther south, sir. Elbow cay, by my reckoning," Midshipman Stewart replied with an unsteady voice.

Noting his tone, Captain Woodhaven lifted one brow as he sat upright in his hammock. "Elbow cay, huh? Did any of the lieutenant concur with your reckoning?"

"Well, not exactly, sir," Midshipman Stewart answered. "But, I am confident, sir. Elbow cay."

"You are confident, but the lieutenants would not concur with you. Why?" Captain Woodhaven asked as he rose from his hammock and stepped into his trousers and boots.

"Sir, they believe we are just east of man-o-war cay, as you said." Midshipman Stewart replied in his unsteady voice.

"And, yet, you still believe that your calculation is correct and all of theirs are wrong?" The captain pulled on his uniform coat and began fastening buttons. "Have you ever heard the phrase pride comes before the fall?"

"Yes, yes sir. I have," Midshipman Stewart's voice grew more unsteady as he spoke. "But, I believe my calculations to be correct, sir. We are too far to the east for the land sighting to be man-o-war, and we are farther south. The next possible spit of land would be Elbow Cay."

"Your logic sounds reasonable," Captain Woodhaven said, "but, if your calculations aren't correct, you will spend the next week standing every other watch and making every calculation side by side with the sailing master. Never announce your findings as an identified landfall unless you have the concurrence of the first lieutenant and the sailing master. Do you understand?"

Midshipman Stewart went to rigid attention. "Yes, sir."

"Do you understand how catastrophic it can be if the commander of a vessel is given an incorrect appraisal of his ship's whereabouts?"

"Yes, sir. I do," Midshipman Stewart answered with his eyes locked straight forward onto the cabin's bulkhead.

"Not all commanders are as thorough as I am. Many would take an announced landfall as just that and proceed with their navigation as such. Incorrect navigation can lead a ship to drift aimlessly. Countless British crews have made just that folly, running out of food and fresh water, mutinies, sailors dying of thirst and starvation, scurvy. We don't want to get into the habit of making that mistake in our own navy."

Satisfied that he had sufficiently corrected the young officer's exuberant error, Captain Woodhaven left his company and made his way up to the weather deck. The night was cool, with a steady wind from the northwest that filled United States' sails and had her clipping along through gently rolling swells. A waxing moon flew high in the night sky and drowned away the light of stars in its immediate vicinity. The captain studied her position for a moment and panned the sky to see what constellations he could identify. Taurus the bull was rising from the southeast. He turned over the fantail and looked to the northern horizon, the big dipper was still prominent in the northwest, with the little dipper higher still and almost due north. He took a minute to examine the watch log and noted the last calculation of latitude, the headings and speed United States had been making over the past several hours and the leadsman's depth readings.

"Nineteen fathoms," Captain Woodhaven said aloud for no one in particular to hear.

"Pardon, sir?" Lieutenant Smith said from his place near the helm.

"Nineteen fathoms," Captain Woodhaven repeated, "that is the average of the last twelve depth readings."

Lieutenant Smith looked at the watch log under the light of a lantern and nodded. "Yes, sir. That appears to be so."

"Tell me, Lieutenant Smith. Do you recall the depth readings off of man-o-war cay?" The captain inquired with a stony reserve.

Lieutenant Smith shifted on his feet and rolled his eyes skyward as he tried to recall. "I believe I would have to have another look at the chart, sir. I do not recall."

Captain Woodhaven drew his lips into a tight grimace. He inhaled through his nose and folded his arms in front of his chest. "I can tell you what the charts say. The average depths east of man-o-war cay are over thirty fathoms, the average depths east of Elbow Cay are between eighteen and twenty. Tell me, lieutenant. Did you factor this into your reckoning of our position before you refused to concur with the midshipman?"

Lieutenant Smith shook his head and lowered his gaze. "No, sir. I did not."

"I just delivered a first rate dressing down to that young man, and it turns out he was likely correct," the captain said with a terse tone. "See to it that I am not put into this position again, young man, or you will be standing every other watch and doing your navigation parallel to the sailing master, just as I have prescribed for him!"

Lieutenant Smith snapped to a rigid position of

attention. "Aye, aye sir."

"The sailors are performing at an exemplary level, lieutenant. I expect the officers of this ship to set an even higher bar for performance and conduct. This," he pointed to the log entry detailing their land sighting incorrectly, "falls well short of that standard."

"It won't happen again, sir." Lieutenant Smith snapped a crisp salute and returned to his duties.

The captain paced to the stern railing and looked down toward the inky dark waters. Ripples of wake washed out from United States' hull as she plowed her way southward. Silvery moonlight served to illuminate the frothy white caps that edged their way outward from the ship before dying away and blending into the rolling seas. It was a beautiful night and despite his weariness from the day he decided to spend some time on deck in the cool night air. The stars were out, despite the flood of light from the moon they sparkled in the sky like ten thousand diamonds scattered across a carpet of black. Sailors in the tops were enjoying the chance remaining on a steady course afforded them and skylarking at the moon and stars just as he was. Captain Woodhaven recalled his early days at sea and the rudimentary telescope he had purchased with his first wages, he'd spent far more time gazing the moon through it than looking for sightings of land or sails. A glance over United States' deck revealed Midshipman Stewart holding just such a telescope. The captain smiled and pulled his own from inside of his uniform coat as he walked toward the young officer who he had just recently given an undeserved scolding.

"The depth readings, midshipman," Captain Woodhaven said, "you should have mentioned the depth readings. We are indeed looking at Elbow Cay."

"I, I didn't... It isn't my place to argue with a captain, sir," Midshipman Stewart stammered in reply.

"On the contrary, young man. For the exact reasons I described earlier. When you know you are right, stand your damn ground. A commander needs that, just as much as he needs correct information." He smiled and extended his telescope toward the midshipman. "Care to have a peek at it through this? The magnification is excellent and there is almost no distortion in the glass."

The midshipman smiled and took the instrument. "Thank you, sir."

"I noticed all the other sailors had their glass fixed on the moon. But, not you." The captain asked, "What are you spying out there? Do you have another surprise for me?"

"I sure hope not, sir. But, I thought I saw a shape in the moonlight. My own telescope is quite insufficient, even in daylight." He raised the telescope to his eye and resumed peering toward the spit of land that loomed west of them.

"What do you mean a shape?" Captain Woodhaven asked.

"Well, I wasn't quite sure," Midshipman Stewart paused for a heartbeat, "this telescope really is a fine piece, sir."

"Why, thank you. Find what you were looking at and point me to it." He studied the young officer's face and looked toward the cay with his naked eye. He could see nothing but dark seas with a silvery glimmer from the moon and the darker form of land in the distance.

"There, it is something," the midshipman exclaimed, "I can't quite make it out, but it isn't part of the shoreline." He handed the telescope back to Captain Woodhaven. "A point forward of our beam, sir. There is a dark shape along the shoreline. I can't tell if it is a grounded vessel or a fallen tree. Follow the sand on shore until you find the dark spot."

Captain Woodhaven followed the young officer's instruction and scanned the shoreline with his telescope. He found the white sandy beach glowing under the moonlight and traced southward approximately one point forward of the United States' starboard beam. Just as the midshipman said, he found a dark spot that interrupted the silvered glow of moonlight on sand. He focused on the dark spot for several heartbeats, studying the outline and asking himself if he was seeing what he thought he saw. More shapes came into view. White squares unfurled and billowed in the breeze above the dark form. It was a ship, a ship that had been sitting in hiding.

"All hands," Captain Woodhaven bellowed, "beat to quarters!"

PART THREE
"The Bitter End"

9

'Drowned Maiden'
22 May 1809
12 degrees 14' N, 71 Degrees 55' W

"All hands," Lilith cried out, "hoist anchor and make ready to sail!" Panic was forming at the edges of her mind even as she wiped away the blood and burned flesh from her cutlass blade.

"What did he say Cap'n?" Chibs asked through a cloud of blue pipe smoke. "I couldn't hear after his last screams."

Lilith shook her head and looked at her faithful quartermaster. "Nothing good, Chibs. We need to make sail, now."

She stormed off of the quarterdeck with her sword in hand, cutting away grapple lines that had been drawn tight between the Maiden and her most recent prey. "Cut her away, boys! Loose the sails and bring her about. Get us out of here!"

"Cap'n, we'll need to fetch Renly and his gunners off of the beach. And, the Batard De Mur, we should signal them that we are leaving. It looks like she is about to drop anchor." Chibs called after the Lilith.

"No time, Chibs. Signal Renly to load his gun and men and make for the mouth of the cove, we will collect them as we pass, if we can." Lilith called back over her shoulder as she hacked through another grapple line. "We need to leave this cove and this whole damned coast behind us."

"Cap'n! We can't just leave Renly behind," Chibs shouted after her, she could feel anger welling in his voice. "What did that Spaniard say?"

Lilith turned to face him, her sword held low with the point nearly touching the wooden planks of the Maiden's deck. "He said that they were pirate hunters, Chibs. One ship of a fleet that numbers more than two score, and they are searching the coasts for any and all manner of pirate vessels. Forty ships, Chibs. There is no surviving that, and there is no running from them once we are spotted. We have to sail, now. Run for our lives."

Chibs' jaw went slack as he heard what his captain had to say. The pipe he had clamped in between his teeth fell to the deck and spread a pinch of burned tobacco and ash as it rolled to a stop. "Forty ships..." he breathed out a puff of smoke before darting down to retrieve his lost pipe. "Aye, sail with haste. Damn hoisting the bloody anchor, Cap'n, cut the bitch away and be done with it!" He raised his voice and shouted high up into the rigging for the hands scrambling to loose sails. "Hurry your damned selves! Loose those sails and tighten the sheets, run the mains and tops up, cut away anchor and bring her about with the wind! Put your backs into it, we haven't a moment to lose!"

Lilith turned and resumed cutting away the grapple lines that held her tight to the Spanish ship she had just defeated. Every second, every heartbeat that passed brought a feeling of impending doom. The ship that had followed them into the cove could have been with a squadron, it could have been screening for a fleet or sailing on the far flank of one. Every second presented a new and wholly awful scenario in Lilith's mind. When she cut away the last grapple line, she closed her eyes and saw sails on the horizon, closing in around her and the Maiden. Dozens and dozens of sails. The oceans of the world suddenly didn't seem big enough. The Spanish ship that they had just fought had chased them down with ease. The Maiden was a fast ship, in waters dominated by the Brits or the Americans. Lilith hadn't chanced upon a ship that could run her down when she donned full sail and hit a strong point with the wind. But, the Spanish vessel had gained on them as if they had been at anchor. She had felt petrified on the waves, like when she tried to run from danger in a dream and all her limbs seemed to be trapped by some invisible force dragging them down. And that was only one ship.

Lilith turned inboard and surveyed her ship. Her sails had holes and tears from the Spanish pirate hunter's cannon fire, the railing, gunwales and deck were in tatters. The aft castle ladder had been smashed midway through by a cannon ball. There were severed rigging lines hanging from the yards and one of the spars swung loose where it had been blasted free from the rest of it's form holding taut canvas. She was in foul shape, but she could still make sail. Lilith clenched her jaw and pressed onward. "Hold her hard over larboard, Omi. Steer us out of this death trap and get us back into open water!"

Run. It dominated every thought in Lilith's mind. They had to run. Maracaibo was east of them, and countless Spanish ports lay to the west. They had to beat a course northward, and fast. The Maiden lumbered away from what remained of the Spanish pirate hunter and entered a dogged turn in front of the defeated ship's prow. Lilith had made her way to the bow and stepped up by the bowsprit as the first quarter of her ship cleared away from the pirate hunter. Batard De Mur was sailing straight towards them, her crimson sheets carried her slowly inward and opened the mouth of the cove.

"No, damnit, we need to be sailing the other way!" Lilith muttered under her breath. She sprinted along the shattered remains of the Maiden's larboard side and waved her arms. "No! Turn back, we have to leave!"

Aboard Batard De Mur, Lilith cries were met with looks of dumbfounded confusion. Her captain paced the starboard side of his ship, hat slung low over his dark eye patch and a tattered linen shirt showing the effects of the heat blazing down on the cove. He cupped his hands around the edges of his mouth and shouted back to Lilith. "What for? You won, girl! Let's plunder her holds and each take a share!"

A pang of anger struck Lilith's blood, as white hot as the blade of her cutlass had been when she had sharply questioned the pirate hunter only minutes ago. Batard De Mur did not share in the fighting. Why would she share in the plunder? It mattered not. They had to leave.

"She was a pirate hunter, I questioned one of the crew and she is supposed to be sailing with a fleet of many ships. Two score if his words are to be believed!" Lilith shouted back. An edge of hostility was creeping into her voice, despite her best efforts to quell it. She couldn't decide if it was a reaction to the pirate captain's brash presumption that he would share in plundering the defeated vessel, or if it was her reaction to the pressing fear working it's way through her muscles and seeping into her mind. "We sail for open seas. Join us, if you care to live, or stay and plunder this hulk, it matters not to me."

As Lilith's final warning floated across the narrow gap of sea separating the two vessels she reached the stern railing and watched as Batard De Mur's captain met his own stern. He cupped his hands back around his mouth to answer. "The day I turn and run based on the words of a pirate hunter will be the day I order my crew to gut me alive and boil the cowardice right out of my blood. Run, girl. There are more prizes to be had in these waters!"

Lilith stopped as she met the shattered end of her larboard railing. She plucked absentminded at a jagged shard of timber where railing had once stood while staring at Batard De Mur's red sails. Her deckhands were taking in sail and getting ready to board the remains of the pirate hunter's ship. "Damn fools," she said to herself as the Maiden slipped through the cove and approached the narrow opening leading to the sea.

Chibs approached on the remaining intact ladder to the aft castle. "It looks like Renly has his boys loaded and they are rowing out to meet us. I've got a crew on the capstan and we are rigging to recover their gun."

"Very good, Chibs," Lilith replied as she continued to stare at the falling crimson sails. "Once we gather them up, I want to plot our course north. We sail with all haste until we are well clear of these waters."

"Where to Cap'n?" Chibs asked.

Lilith shook her head and turned inboard to find him leaning on one knee with his other foot still on the steps leading up to the aft castle. "I don't rightly know Chibs. We can't return to our cove. The navy will surely search there, now that we have shown ourselves since they sank us."

Chibs steeped up onto the deck and fished in his waistband pouch. He pulled out his pipe and stuck the stem into a firm bite. "Well, Cap'n, she's not in the best shape, but we can make sail, for now. The Maiden sails to free slaves, it is the same crusade Captain James lived and died for. He always talked of sailing up into the gulf, toward New Orleans. That is deep in the wicked heart of slave country. I imagine we could replenish our ranks and set those southern gentlemen all to arms in a matter of a few weeks. But we would needs refit somewhere close before making that long journey." He chewed at the wooden pipe and shifted it from one side of his mouth to the other. "It's one place we could go to disappear from these waters for a time."

"Perhaps we could even take a few of those southern statesmen's ships for ourselves. Maybe blockade their harbor," Lilith said with a devilish smile crossing her lips.

Chibs shook his head. "You really have a death wish, don't you Cap'n?"

"Blackbeard blockaded Charleston," Lilith replied.

"And met his death shortly after," Chibs cut back as he packed a pinch of tobacco into the bowl of his pipe. "There's no happy end in a pirate's life, Cap'n. Not for those chasing fame and glory."

Lilith's gaze drifted away from Chibs as Renly and his gun crew rowed to the Maiden's side. Lines were tossed out to the men who had just been through an enormous effort to drag their gun from the beach and row back out into the mouth of the cove. She could see exhaustion plastered on their faces. "I am not interested in happy endings, Chibs. I gave up on that the day I left my mother."

'H.M.S Redemption'
20 May 1809
Kingston, Jamaica

Captain Pike walked his way up the boarding plank as a fife and drum played to announce his arrival. It was a surreal experience. He had commanded ships before, but never his own. She was grander than he had imagined. Her masts seemed to stretch higher even than the Valor's had. Fresh paint was still drying along the sides of her hull and sailors that had been hard at work preparing her to get underway halted to come to rigid attention. A formation of lieutenants and midshipmen stood at the larboard rail, ready to greet their new captain. Captain Pike took longer than normal strides, eager to meet his new crew and get his ship out to sea. His officer corps saluted in unison as he crossed the threshold and stepped down onto the weather deck from the boarding plank. The captain returned their collective salute and was greeted by a familiar looking lieutenant who stepped forward. Captain Pike would recognize his fresh face anywhere, he did not look like he belonged among the crew about to depart to sea on a pirate hunt.

"H.M.S Redemption welcomes her new captain, sir. Preparations to sail are nearly complete, the last food stores have been loaded, we are waiting on a dozen more casks of fresh water, and you, sir."

Captain Pike did his best not to betray any emotion with his expression. "Lieutenant Thatcher, the admiral didn't inform me that you would be a part of this new command."

Lieutenant Thatcher was unable to mask the emotion from his face. He looked almost wounded. "Yes, sir. I apologize if that is a disappointment, but I have been assigned to the Redemption as a second lieutenant."

"No disappointment here, lieutenant," Captain Pike

replied. "I am sure you will do your duty in a sufficient manner, and see to it that the crew does as well. I am glad to have you. Now, see to it that the last of the water is loaded promptly. The fleet awaits us, and I will not have it said that we delayed the admiral from his task."

Lieutenant Thatcher saluted. "Aye, aye captain!" He departed with a brisk pace to finish the loading.

Captain Pike surveyed the remaining officers, his gaze landed on the lieutenant nearest the ship's railing. "My first lieutenant, I presume?"

A dark haired man around the captain's own age nodded as he replied. "My apologies, sir. I know it is proper decorum for my billet to welcome you to the ship, but the young man has been raving about your assignment with us for days. We thought it permissible to allow him the pleasure." He stepped forward and offered his hand. "Lieutenant Dodran, sir. First lieutenant aboard his majesty's ship Redemption."

Captain Pike offered his first lieutenant a knowing nod and took his hand. "I will be leaning on you for much, lieutenant. Would you care to introduce me to the other officers and show me the ship?"

"Indeed, sir," Lieutenant Dodran replied and turned to the rest of the assembled officers. "Here, we have the ship's gunner. Mr. Jensen." Lieutenant Dodran gestured to the man who was standing directly behind him in formation. Captain Pike noticed that the Mr. Jensen had a face marred by powder burns and he was missing a different finger from each hand, an index finger on his right, and a ring finger on his left. He nodded to the weathered gunner and kept his focus on Lieutenant Dodran's introductions. "Next to him, we have the ship's purser, Mr. Finnegan, and then our master at arms Mr. O'Malley." Captain Pike acknowledged a wiry man with dark hair as Mr. Finnegan, the purser, and then a burly built redhead with scars lacing his knuckles and chin as the master at arms. "And here, sir, we have our sailing master, sir, it is my pleasure to introduce Mr. Bush, formerly of the H.M.S Victory."

Captain Pike paused for a moment. He looked at Lieutenant Dodran and waited for the first lieutenant to correct himself. No correction came. With a frown, the captain pressed his question. "I'm sorry, lieutenant. There must be some mistake. I thought I heard you say that this man sailed aboard the Victory. That cannot be correct."

Mr. Bush cleared his throat and stepped forward. "I'm afraid it is correct, sir. Pardon me for speaking out of turn during a formal introduction, but, I will say, sir. I was not just a sailor aboard the Victory. I was her sailing master."

Captain Pike could not believe what he was hearing. "You were-"

"With the grand old man himself, Lord Admiral Horatio Nelson," Mr. Bush replied when the captain's voice faded away. "I was assigned to Admiral Roland's flagship after being on shore for far too long. I enjoyed serving the admiral, but flagships are a dull affair. When he asked for volunteers to serve aboard a forty four gun frigate, I jumped at the chance."

Captain Pike searched for words for a long moment, unable to find them. Finally, he gathered his wits. "It is my honor to have you aboard, Mr. Bush. I am sure the ship will be the better off for your company."

"Don't go thanking me just yet, sir," Mr. Bush replied with a wink, "wait until we disagree over points of sailing and I get a proper mad on. You'll curse the day I ever set foot on your ship."

"I welcome the added perspective," the captain replied, unable to contain a slight smile at the sailing master's rogue streak.

Behind the lieutenants and warrant officers, a half dozen fresh faced midshipmen stood in aligned formation. Their top hats set them out over the warrant officer's shoulders even though none of them were tall enough to be seen over their shoulders. Captain Pike took in the group as a whole before addressing them. "Gentlemen, this is a new command to the navy, and a new posting for me. It is my first sail as a ranked captain. I will tell you all this once and once only, I expect every man aboard to do his duty. I will accept no less. Treat our sailors with a fair hand, firm, but never abusive. The first instance I hear of heavy handedness over a trivial matter will see the offender scrubbing deck planks next to the landsmen. Is that understood?"

A general consensus was displayed by the faces of the officers. Captain Pike appreciated what he saw. There wasn't a single look of derision, none of them scoffed at him as if he were a weak captain with no clue of what he was undertaking. It seemed, they appreciated the prospect of a level headed commander.

"All right, gentlemen. To your stations," He said, dismissing the gathered officers. "Lieutenant Dodran, you have the ship, take her out and plot us a course south by southeast. I intend to sail a search pattern through the area I last encountered the pirates."

"Aye, aye sir. Out of the harbor and then south by southeast." Lieutenant Dodran replied with a crisp dip of his hat brim before turning toward the assembled crew. "Cast off lines and run up tops and gallants, helm put the wind at our starboard quarter until we have passed out of the harbor."

Captain Pike stood fast on the quarterdeck of his new command and watched while his first lieutenant and the crew eased her away from the pier and through the harbor. A cross wind between stiff westerlies from the Caribbean and the land breeze gave Lieutenant Dodran a challenge to overcome, but the captain felt a sense of reassurance as he watched his second in command recognize the wind and adjust accordingly almost as quick as he recognized it himself. Aloft, top men scurried from ratlines to yards and transitioned from climbing to setting sail and tying off lines in a seamless flow. Commands floated through the air and were repeated. The deck of the ship shifted and swayed as the helm nosed the bow around to exit the harbor under the watchful ramparts of Fort Charles.

"Fife and drum to the quarterdeck," Lieutenant Dodran commanded in a forceful tone that bellowed over Redemption's decks. "Gunner, prepare to render honors as we pass Reliant."

"Honors from the larboard battery as we pass, aye aye." Mr. Jensen replied before hurrying down the ladder well to the gun deck.

A snaring rattle from the drum struck out a rhythm and the fife player began whistling the notes to a march as H.M.S Redemption came abreast of Reliant as she lay at anchor. Captain Pike paced to the starboard railing and presented his passing salute to the admiral. Redemption's larboard battery fired a broadside of un-shotted cannons as she passed. The report thundered through the harbor and echoed back from the rocky faces that led up to Fort Charles. Admiral Roland stood on Reliant's quarterdeck and returned the salute. It gave Captain Pike chills. Here he was, observing proper naval customs and rendering honors to a flagship as he departed Kingston on a ship under his command. Less than a year ago he had been a prisoner in the belly of Admiral Torren's flagship.

"Signal from the flagship, sir," Lieutenant Thatcher called out from the watch officer's stand by Redemption's helm. He paused and looked through his log for the appropriate signal flags to decipher the commands. "Redemption, take up screen position, sail south by east and report all sightings. Fleet to follow."

Captain Pike offered the second lieutenant a brisk nod. "Very well. Signal back our acknowledgment and have the fife and drummer turn to." He turned to Lieutenant Dodran. "I will be in my cabin if you need anything."

"Aye, sir."

As the captain made his way across the quarterdeck and down the ladder, Redemption's deck began the familiar pitch and sway of a vessel moving with the open sea. Sailors stood aside as he crossed the deck and parted like the Red Seas for Moses when he took his first step down the ladder way to go below. He made his way down a short corridor toward the stern and found his cabin door. It looked solid, dark stained planks fastened together by decorative brass fittings. He gave the door handle a twist and entered. Inside, he found the cabin was larger than he had expected. It was not as grand in scale as North Wind's had been, but it was larger than Captain Grimes' cabin had been aboard the Valor. The main cabin, which looked to double as a day room, was well lit by an array of fantail windows. A small wooden desk rested against the bulkhead of the larboard wall, and a wood stove was situated near the front of the cabin in the starboard corner. He stepped in and closed the door behind him. The sounds of the gun deck hushed away behind the heavy wooden door. It felt unreal to him, as if he were standing in someone else's cabin. A pine sea chest rested along the base of the wall next to the desk. He crossed the cabin and took a seat in the small chair tucked into the desk before gently opening the lid of the chest. A neatly folded uniform coat, complete with captain's epaulets, rested within the chest. Captain Pike lifted the uniform coat and found a folded piece of paper lying beneath it. He opened the paper and found an inscription. "I took the liberty of sending some of your personal effects ahead of you. You seemed to be lacking some essentials, so I had your new steward do you the service of acquiring them. Take care of your crew, they will take care of you. All the best -Adm. Torren"

"My steward?" Captain Pike said aloud as he looked over the note. He refolded the paper and examined the bottom of the chest. A pair of pistols, a leather arms belt and an officer's sword in its scabbard all lay on the floor of the chest. He put the admiral's note on his desk and hefted one of the pistols. It was a fine piece with a brand new firing mechanism set into a stock of what looked like polished walnut. A knock at the door sounded the arrival of someone.

"Enter," Captain Pike said as he turned to face the door.

The door creaked open and a red faced man with a severely receding hairline entered holding a platter with a kettle and a covered plate. "I thought you may want coffee and something to eat as we get underway, sir."

Captain Pike nodded and offered a smile. "Indeed. My thanks. I take it you are my steward?"

The balding man returned his smile and nodded an affirmative. "Douglas Reginald Underwood at your service, sir. I have been assigned to the Redemption at the personal request of Admiral Torren." He placed the tray on the cabin desk and folded his hands behind his back. "I see that you have found your effects. Familiarizing yourself?"

Captain Pike nodded his head and looked down at the fine pistol he held. "Preparing for a fight."

'U.S.S United States'
10 June 1809
26 degrees 35' N, 76 Degrees 54' W

The serenity of night was shattered by drums. A rolling snare beat echoed over the darkness of U.S.S United States as it rattled its tattoo and signaled the ship to clear for action. Before his eyes, Captain Woodhaven watched the deck of his ship burst into a frenzy of activity as sailors made ready. He scanned out over the dark seas separating him from the ship that had been lurking along the coast. There was maybe three miles between the ships, no more. With the current wind condition, the unknown vessel could be upon them inside of half an hour, and with the wind closer to their back than to his. If he hove to and beat a course upwind immediately, Captain Woodhaven knew he would be able to salvage some measure of the weather gauge for himself. But, the cost of doing so would take hands away from battle preparation and diminish his ability to fire on the ship as it approached, something that was an essential element of his plans to level the field against a British adversary.

He lifted his telescope back to his eye and focused on the dark spot where he had just watched sails unfurl. Three squares of vertically stacked white canvas appeared in the moonlight. He watched as the sails made way and began to angle out into the open sea. A second mast of sails became visible, and soon after that a third. She was a heavy sloop of war at least, but more likely a frigate. United States had to be plainly visible to them in the moonlight, and with her sails all flying there would be no mistaking her for the heavy class of frigate she was. Whoever was donning their sails to close with them had to be sailing a ship they knew could contend with her. He lowered his telescope and bit his lower lip with his front teeth. "Cutlass... Caught me with my trousers down again, damn them."

"Do we turn and fight?" Lieutenant Smith asked the captain over his shoulder.

Captain Woodhaven kept his eyes locked on the set of canvas sails maneuvering their way away from Elbow Cay. "Nay, they will have the weather gauge on us from the drop, and I don't think we can effectively put gunnery on them as they approach."

"Do you think it is the Cutlass, sir?" the lieutenant asked in a lower voice.

"I do, in fact," Captain Woodhaven replied. "Have the helm come about with the wind, fly the top gallants and the royals, run out stunsails if we must. We have to stay ahead of that damned ship."

"Aye, aye sir," Lieutenant Smith replied before hurrying across the quarterdeck to relay the captain's orders. He called out in a loud voice, "Hands aloft, fly top gallants and royals! Gunner, have the guns made ready but do not run them out, the captain plans a run to give us distance!"

Officer's and warrant officers shouted back their replies as their respective crews hurried to set the captain's conditions. U.S.S United States listed with her turn and heaved as more canvas took on wind to propel her away from the attacking ship. Captain Woodhaven watched the hands aloft as they worked their way up and down ratlines, setting the spars and adjusting sheets until the sails were taut and filled with wind.

"Now," the watch officer called. A pair of midshipmen cast out a line with a weight on it while the watch officer diligently watched sand pour through a small glass mounted near the mainmast.

Captain Woodhaven looked over the stern and found the approaching vessel. Her sails had grown in size, she was less than two miles away.

"Time!" the watch officer called out, prompting the midshipmen to halt their line as it ran out with the movement of their ship. One of the midshipmen hauled in the weighted line hand over hand while counting the knots tied into it.

"Nine knots, sir," the midshipman reported.

"Nine knots," the watch officer replied before opening his log and scrawling the information down on paper. He turned toward Lieutenant Smith on the quarterdeck and reported their finding. "Holding at nine knots, sir."

Lieutenant Smith in turn looked toward Captain Woodhaven, who had been studying the advance of the approaching ship. "Nine knots, sir. What do you gauge their speed to be?"

"Nine knots won't do. Run out the damned stunsails. They have gained on us already, we need twelve knots or they will have us in range by dawn and we will defending borders before I have had a chance to drink my morning coffee. We will fight them, but not like this," the captain said before turning back outboard. "When we face them, I want to set the terms." He looked back over the sea and focused on the sails pursuing him and his ship. They seemed to be growing larger by the minute as a growing sense of dread filled his veins and gripped his stomach. He had trained up this crew to the pinnacle of readiness, the ship was in as good of shape as she could be, and still they had ended up with a disadvantage right from the drop. He grumbled to himself, "We should have stood off from shore until well after daylight. Woodhaven you damned fool! All this preparation, wasted by your damned short sightedness."

"All is not lost, captain," Midshipman Stewart said over his shoulder. "If you don't mind me saying so, we are actually in quite a good position to run them out to sea and maneuver on them. We could open a gap and then turn and fire on them as they pursue. That will allow you to employ the guns in the manner you had hoped for, and if we manage to outrun them for a time, that will cause them to sail with even more reckless abandon."

The captain opened his mouth, about to rebuke the young officer for stepping out of line and speaking out of turn. He was a presumptive young man, and seemed wholly unaware of the decorum with which he should be adhering to. But the words failed to come to him as he considered exactly what he had just heard. The enemy vessel was gaining on them, and quickly. He knew that once the stunsails were run out and he found their optimum point of sailing that they would make the speed he desired, probably even more. They would open the gap with their pursuers, and that would cause them to pursue all the harder. The young man's logic was sound, even if his sense of when to share it was not. He paused for a beat, mouth agape but failing to form words. He blinked and looked Midshipman Stewart up and down. "How much of a sea gap would you create for such a stand, midshipman? Were it your ship to command, that is."

Several of the other midshipmen and lieutenants looked up at the captain with flabbergasted expressions. Their gaze collectively shifted to Midshipman Stewart who looked equally shocked by the captain's response. He shifted his weight nervously between his feet. "If we were to hold true to course, sir, and outrun her for a half a day, we could manage to open enough of a gap to just barely remain within sight. Eight to nine miles, I believe. Then if we shifted to put the wind on our larboard quarter, we would still be sailing within the United States' strong points, allowing us to maintain some speed while opening the possibility of turning to and bringing our guns to bear as they approach."

"That would give us wind at our larboard beam when we come about to fire, captain," Lieutenant Smith added as Midshipman Stewart paused to see the reaction to his statement. "If we shift our sails when we come about to fire, it may give our guns added natural elevation."

Captain Woodhaven nodded as he took in the

excellent advice of his junior officers. The midshipman's thinking was sound, and leagues beyond his limited sea experience. It astounded him how such a junior officer could have such a strong grasp of sailing and seafaring tactics. He glared at the midshipman as the rest of the ship's officer corps looked on. "Where on earth did you learn such tactics, young man? You speak like a man who has been at sea for decades."

Midshipman Stewart blushed and looked down at the deck while continuing to shift nervously on his feet. "Begging your pardon, captain. But, I listen, and I read. I've been reading volumes of biographies since I was a young boy."

Captain Woodhaven turned to the rest of his officers and smiled. "It seems there is something we can all learn from the young man." He shot a glance toward Lieutenant Smith. "In terms of navigation and tactics as well." A renewed wind blew, and United States surged under the added power of her stunsails as the deck hands tied off the last brace lines holding them steady. Captain Woodhaven surveyed their canvas and looked back toward the approaching ship, it seemed their rapid advance had stymied as United States picked up more speed. "It is a fine plan. We will see it through." He turned back to Lieutenant Smith. "See to it that one of the long nines gets moved here to the fantail. If they manage to pile on more sails and gain some speed we can use it to help keep them at bay."

"Aye, aye sir." The lieutenant replied before turning to see it done.

Dawn teased at the eastern horizon. Shades of yellowish hue mixed with oranges and violets. To the captain's eye, dawn was always a sight prettier than sunset. It brought with it the promise of a new day and all the possibilities that offered. The stars faded in their ritual morning retreat as sunlight pierced the darkness and chased away night. He looked back over the United States' stern and saw that their pursuers were falling behind. The gap had opened back up to more than three miles, by his judgment. He played out Midshipman Stewart's plan over and over in his head. As long as they were able to open the sea gap, it would work. They could turn to and loose cannon fire at their approaching enemy with the bonus of added elevation from the natural list of the ship under wind. It was an exceptional tactic, even affording them the opportunity to resume sail and open up another gap should their first salvo of fire prove not to be as effective as they should like. The captain smiled to himself, it was perfect, his enemy thought they were pressing a clear advantage when in fact they would be sailing right into the teeth of his guns. Captain Woodhaven nodded and offered thanks as his cabin steward delivered a piping hot cup of black coffee and a split biscuit with a pork sausage patty folded into it. The captain savored his breakfast and prepared himself for the coming engagement. He sipped at his coffee as Lieutenant Smith made his way up the aft castle ladder.

"The ship and the crew are ready, sir. When you give the command, the larboard battery will range her and we will follow with an accurate volume of fire, sir," the lieutenant reported.

Captain Woodhaven swallowed his coffee. "Well done, lieutenant."

"It seems to me the only thing that could foul our plan would be the sight of another sail," the lieutenant observed with a cautious tone.

Captain Woodhaven considered the thought. It would force him to make a precarious decision, and depending on the nation of origin, it could be catastrophic. He and most of the crew had focused their full attention aft. The captain lowered his coffee cup to the stern railing and turned to face the rest of the quarterdeck. "Lieutenant Smith, I want extra lookouts in the fore rigging-"

His orders were interrupted by a shout from a lookout, panic seeped in around the edges of his voice. "Ship on the horizon! This one is to the east. And she's headed this way!"

10

'H.M.S Redemption'
22 May 1809
12 Degrees 45' N, 72 Degrees 32' W

A pitch in the deck rocked Captain Pike forward in his seat along the fantail window array of his cabin. For the past few hours he had engrossed himself within the pages of a biographic book detailing the life of Lord Admiral Horatio Nelson. The seas had built in size during the course of their sail from Kingston in the last few days, and while a lifetime at sea had made him accustomed to the incessant pitching and swaying, some of the newer sailors were struggling to adapt. Redemption's rails became the sight of frequent visitors as they evacuated the contents of their stomachs overboard. The captain grinned, it reminded him of his first voyage at sea, he thought that he would never leave the ship's rail. But, eventually, he gained his sea legs, and his stomach grew accustomed to the barrage of constant motion and barely edible food. The same would be true for these new sailors, and while some of the pressed men would go on to other endeavors and other professions after their term of service was satisfied, he knew some of them would stay in the navy.

A knock on the cabin door interrupted the captain's thoughts. "Enter," he said without looking up from the pages of his book.

The red cheeked face of one of Redemption's midshipmen protruded through a slightly opened door. "Pardon the interruption, sir. But, Lieutenant Dodran wishes for me to pass on his respects and ask if you could join him on deck, sir. There has been a signal from the fleet."

Captain Pike narrowed his eyes and pressed his lips together in a tight grimace. "What was the signal, midshipman?"

"I believe, sir," the midshipman paused in his reply, "the fleet is altering course due to a sighting on their flank. The admiral has ordered us to remain on our present heading."

Captain Pike fought the ire that the midshipman's shaky statement drew within him. "You believe, midshipman? Is that what the signal flags indicated or not? I have no time for interpretive orders or misread signals."

"That is what it said, sir," the midshipman replied, "exactly. Word for word."

"Then relay the message in conclusive language, young man," Captain Pike said with a tight scowl.

"Aye, aye sir. It won't happen again," the

midshipman stammered.

Captain Pike looked down at the pages of his book and wondered if the old man ever sent his screening vessels ahead of the fleet without an accompanying ship. He let an exasperated sigh escape from his throat and placed the ribbon marker of the book in between the pages he had last read before folding the volume shut and placing it on his desk.

"Have my steward bring up some coffee and inform the lieutenant I will be up on deck presently," he said as he rose from the chair and reached for his uniform coat. "That will be all, midshipman."

"Aye, aye sir," the midshipman replied as his cheeks grew redder with each passing second. He fumbled with the door handle for a heartbeat before finally slipping out of the cabin and disappearing.

The captain stared at his cabin door after it had closed. He drew a breath and wondered if he had been such a blundering oaf when he had first been frocked as a midshipman. Memories came to him, bits and pieces of his formative first years at sea. He grimaced at the realization that he had been just as inept at certain points in his career, and some even more so. Captain Pike pulled his uniform coat on and retrieved his hat from the wooden peg it hung on near the door before exiting his cabin.

Winds from the northwest whipped up a spray of seawater as the captain stepped off of the ladder way and crossed to the quarterdeck. It was a welcome relief from the incessant Caribbean heat. The skies were clear and the sun bore down on them like a furnace to a forge. Captain Pike looked over the sails as he made his way to the quarterdeck. They were trimmed and full, without even a hint of give or slack in the canvas. There were lookouts stationed high up on the fore and main mast and more watching the horizons from the fighting tops.

"Good day, sir," Lieutenant Dodran greeted with a brisk touch of his hat brim. "Signal from the fleet I thought you should be informed of immediately, sir. The admiral is chasing down a sighting reported by a vessel on their left flank, far to the east of us. He has instructed us to remain on our current heading."

Captain Pike scanned the northern and eastern horizons, only to find a never ending line of sea meeting skyline. Not a sail or ship in sight. "He didn't send another vessel to accompany us?"

"No, sir," Lieutenant Dodran replied with a lower tone.

The captain nodded his head and lowered his gaze to the sea immediately surrounding the Redemption. "Some would question the wisdom of that."

"I don't, sir, I know exactly what the admiral intends," Lieutenant Dodran grumbled in an even lower voice. "If we are not within sight of the action, should he take a prize, H.M.S Redemption is not eligible for a share of the prize money. With us being the new command to the fleet, and you a new captain, it makes some sense. But, it is a lowly move in my mind, captain."

"We didn't set sail to take prizes, lieutenant, though I do understand your frustration. Believe me, I share it.

Not for the same reasons, mind you." He paused and gave his second in command a reassuring nod. "I am more concerned with our tactical situation, should we encounter an enemy vessel without the ability to alert the fleet. Admiral Roland may well be chasing down a prize, but he has left us out on a limb, so to speak. Pray that it holds."

"Aye, sir," the lieutenant growled, "and the crew? They're likely to grow restless imagining what famous treasure the admiral will be splitting with the rest of the fleet."

Captain Pike pursed his lips before drawing them tight into a grimace he hid behind a dipped hat brim. He thought of the escalating circumstances aboard the Valor and the Endurance. The last thing he needed was a disgruntled crew as he faced down whatever the horizon may bring. He drew a breath in through his nose and savored the briny sea air. "Alone and unafraid," he mumbled to himself.

"Pardon, sir?" Lieutenant Dodran asked.

"It's nothing lieutenant, a personal mantra, of sorts. We will sail our present course, as commanded. If we sight the enemy we will engage them with everything we have," the captain said. "Our mandate is to locate the pirates I engaged during my last voyage aboard North Wind and sink them. If the admiral has deviated from that course of action, I am sure he has good reason to. We, however, will press on." He paused for a beat before continuing. "As for the crew, there is nothing to distract them from missing out on a prize like an occupied mind. Let's conduct some maneuvers and drill the guns. Shall we?"

"Aye, sir, busy hands and occupied minds," the lieutenant answered with a sharp grin.

"Very well, beat to quarters, let me know when we have cleared for action. I want a full pattern from the top men, put the wind at either beam hard over, and then come about close haul on our larboard side. Then tack us over the wind twice before bringing us about with the wind again. Have the batteries run out when we come about close haul and fire two full volleys each."

"Aye, sir. That should do to keep them well occupied," Lieutenant Dodran replied with a brisk nod and a touch of his hat brim.

Captain Pike observed with a keen eye as his second in command began the maneuvers by calling the Redemption to clear for action. Within seconds a drummer reported amidships and began a rattling roll on his instrument while the crew raced to prepare Redemption for action. Sailors and marines scurried up the ratlines and crowded into the fighting tops. On the gun deck, tompions were removed from cannons and the guns prepped to roll out into their firing positions. From the minute Lieutenant Dodran gave the order to beat to quarters to the point where all stations had reported clear for action took no more than four minutes. Captain Pike checked his pocket watch and offered only a satisfied nod in approval, though inside he was ecstatic. Four minutes to clear the ship for action was an outstanding feat. The crew Captain Grimes had commanded aboard H.M.S Valor hadn't achieved four minutes even after several months of running drills at sea.

"H.M.S Redemption is cleared for action, all men at their stations and ready for battle, sir!" Lieutenant Dodran reported.

Captain Pike nodded and tucked his pocket watch back into his uniform coat. "Very well, lieutenant. Commence with maneuvers."

Lieutenant Dodran touched the brim of his hat and turned toward the rest of the quarterdeck. "Mr. Bush, hard over larboard, bring us to beam reach with the wind."

Mr. Bush raised a speaking trumpet up to his mouth and shouted aloft. "Reef top gallants and royals, slack on the larboard stays for beam reach!"

Redemption nosed over with the wind at her stern, her deck shifted sharply with the hard turn. Captain Pike looked aloft and saw the top hands manage to reef the top gallants and royals just in time. The ship responded with a remarkable agility, the angle of her deck seemed at one point so steep that the captain questioned if they would start taking water over the starboard scuppers. As the frigate reeled through her turn and the wind shifted from blowing straight over their stern to a perpendicular angle over their larboard rail, the deck settled back into its normal pitch and sway. Captain Pike offered the lieutenant a tight grin and a half nod. He was pleased with the efficiency of their handling, but he didn't want to betray his reserve.

"Well done, lieutenant. Now, bring her about," the captain ordered.

"Aye, aye sir," Lieutenant Dodran replied before turning to Mr. Bush. "Mr. Bush, bring her about with the wind, beam reach on the starboard side, smartly."

"Aye, beam reach over the starboard, smartly," Mr. Bush repeated. He raised his speaking trumpet and bellowed out a series of orders corresponding to the captain's ordered maneuver. H.M.S Redemption shifted again, her decks pitched in a tight turn that caused the masts to sway outward from her momentum and the push of the wind until she settled on her new course.

Captain Pike gave Lieutenant Dodran another nod of approval to continue the maneuvers. The crew was performing exceptionally and he was anxious to see how the gun deck would manage their drills under maneuver. Tacking over the wind was not an elementary maneuver, it would put the top men and deck hands through a rigorous pace while keeping the ship in an almost constant state of shift. If the gun batteries could maintain their excellent performance, it would be a marker of success for everyone aboard. Silently, the captain decided that if the combines drills were a success, he would turn the hands to supper early and reward the men with a double ration of their grog.

"Sail ho! Ship on the horizon!" a voice called down from the crow's nest.

Captain Pike felt a touch of lighting in his veins. It started at his feet and worked up his legs and through his back.

"Where away?" Shouted Lieutenant Dodran.

The lookout's voice rang back down through Redemption's rigging. "South by southwest, triple hung sails. She looks to be in our class, but, in rough shape!"

The captain stepped to the railing of the quarterdeck and withdrew his telescope from the inside pocket of his uniform coat. To the naked eye, all he could make out was a small patch of white against the light blue of the low horizon. He extended the brass instrument and held it up to his left eye. It took a moment, but his sight adjusted and the ship in question came into as good of focus as the telescope would allow. The ship was too far off to be accurately identified, but the lookout was correct in his assessment, she was in rough shape. Her sails were in tatters in places and the lines of the ship appeared odd, like she had been refitted in some kind of improvised patchwork of timber. The captain clenched his jaw and drew hip lips tight together. Through the distance he noted the banner flying at her stern. It was black.

"Lieutenant Dodran, I have the ship." He said, in a cold, calm tone.

"Aye, captain has the ship," the lieutenant repeated for all on deck to hear.

"Mr. Bush, bring her about with the wind and put it at our larboard quarter," he paused to collapse his telescope before turning to Mr. Bush and finishing his commands. "All hands remain at action stations, beat us a course directly for that ship!"

'Drowned Maiden'
22 May 1809
12 Degrees 45' N, 72 Degrees 32' W

"Come about, hard over starboard! Bring her around with the wind at our quarter and fly every scrap of sail we have!" Chibs barked over the quarterdeck of the Maiden. A single set of white sails had been spotted on the horizon northwest of the ship. "We need hands to stand on the larboard railing, shift any ballast we can, we need to gain every bit of speed she can muster!"

The sight of the sails had lit a panic inside of his gut worse than he had felt in the inlet on the coast of South America. It was more potent even than the rush of fear he had felt when the Maiden had first taken a broadside from a big navy battleship on the coast of Haiti. The sails on the horizon could not have come at a worse time. Chibs had just walked through the lower decks of the Maiden and found that she had taken on over three feet of water. Her pumps could hold off the onslaught of the sea, but just barely. They wouldn't be sailing anywhere fast, and if they were happened upon by a man of war, they may not be sailing anywhere ever again. His fears came to fruition only a day out of the cove after their confrontation with the Spanish pirate hunters. Chibs cursed the sighting from the instant it was announced by the forward lookout. He wasted no time in ordering a course change and running out every bit of sail the Maiden could fly.

The Maiden made her turn with the wind in a sluggish, lumbering arc that took twice as long as it should have. As every heartbeat passed, hope slipped away from Chibs like sand through an hourglass. They couldn't outrun the ship on the horizon, and as battered as the Maiden already was, a fight would be suicide. Lilith appeared on the quarterdeck. Her face seemed hard as stone as she stared out over the Maiden's shattered stern railing.

"We can't outrun her, Cap'n," Chibs said with a growl of reluctance, "and we are in no shape to turn and fight."

Lilith narrowed her eye and remained quiet for what seemed like an eternity. "What then? Could we at least hold them off for a while? Maybe, mount stern chasers to keep them at bay?"

Chibs chewed at his lower lip and fumbled with his pipe before placing the stem into his bite. "Aye, we could hold them off with stern guns. For a while at least. But, that only forestalls the inevitable. They will overtake us, Cap'n, and when they do..." His voice trailed off. She already knew what he was about to say. No sense in stating the obvious.

"Mount the guns," Lilith said without so much as a look over her shoulder. "If all we can do for now is keep them at bay, then that is exactly what we will do. Keep us out of her reach as best we can and beat a course for the nearest shoreline." She paused for a breath before turning to Chibs. "Do you have any idea who it could be? More Spanish pirate hunters? British Navy?"

Chibs lifted an eyebrow and cast his gaze out over the sea at the sails on the horizon. "Too far out to know for sure, Cap'n. But it could be either. In these waters, they could be from any number of nations. French, Spanish, hell, she could be a Dutchman. But whoever she is, as soon as we sighted her, they came about towards us and started piling on canvas. I don't think we've run across a merchantman looking to make new friends." She looked over the deck of the Maiden and took a deep breath before releasing it in a long sigh. "I don't suppose there are any reefs or shoals nearby that you know of?"

Chibs offered a solemn shake of his head. "No, dear. No reefs. No shoals."

"Who is to say their commander would fall for it anyway. As low as the Maiden is sailing right now, I doubt there is anything she could clear that another ship couldn't." Lilith let her hands both come to rest on the pommel of the cutlass hanging at her hip. "We will sail her in as close to shore as we can and make our stand. Anyone who wants to flee can swim for shore while we hold off these pursuers. I won't surrender, but, I won't lead these people back into bondage."

"A last stand?" Chibs plucked his pipe from between his teeth and frowned as an uncomfortable knot began to form in his stomach.

Lilith gestured out over the stern at the sails on the horizon. "Whoever they are, they won't be letting anyone free. Death or chains will be the only way out of this, unless I do something to give my people a chance to escape. We can't outrun them on the sea, but I doubt they will launch a shore party to hunt for anyone who escapes ashore." She paused and shot

Chibs a hard look with her one good eye. "Someone has to stay and fight to give our people half a chance. She is my ship, Chibs. I won't just abandon her."

The knot that had formed in his stomach had worked its way up into his throat. Goosebumps rose on the flesh of his shoulders, arms and back while his vision began to go blurry as tears welled in his eyes. "You won't face them alone. I won't let you."

Lilith faced Chibs. Her glare softened. "Somehow, I knew you would say that."

"We'll need enough crew to work a few of the guns. Before we send the rest ashore, we should have them load both batteries and run them out, that way we can fire each one of the guns once without having to reload. Once we have fired, we will use the hands that remain behind to keep firing as many guns as we can. That should hold them off from approaching the shore until our folks have the time to escape." Chibs said as he fought away the tears that threatened to come streaming down his cheeks.

"Who will stay?" Lilith asked. Her grip tightened around the pommel of her sword.

Chibs shrugged. "I think, Cap'n. The easier question will be who will go. I can't imagine you will have a hard time finding volunteers to stay and fight. This crew would sail with you to the ends of the world and beyond. We will probably have to force some of them to go."

Lilith's lips spread into a half smile half grimace. "Omibwe."

"Aye, the young lad won't easily leave you to your

fate, Cap'n. I think he is still quite taken with you," Chibs said with a grin of his own. "But, I won't have it. He and his mother both need to go. They deserve a chance at a peaceful life somewhere."

"Jilhal won't be easy to part from you," Lilith said.

Chibs shook his head again. "No, but she will go if you tell her, Cap'n."

"Renly will stay. I doubt anyone could talk him into leaving, as will Hammer Hands, Crowley, and some of the others who have been with us for quite a while." Lilith looked over the deck and paced toward the helm. "But, I don't want any more hands than what we absolutely need to fire a few guns and keep our sails aloft."

"Three for each gun should do," Chibs replied while running his hand over his thick beard. "I imagine if we have a half dozen hands for the deck and another half dozen in the rigging, we could make a few sail adjustments if we needed to."

"Fifteen hands," Lilith stalked past the helm and braced herself against a section of rail that had escaped their last engagement unscathed. "The rest go ashore."

"They won't like it, Cap'n," Chibs growled.

"They don't have to," Lilith replied while looking out over the deck. "But, they will go."

Afternoon drummed on and the sun arced its way through the western skies. The winds held steady from the northwest and pressed the approaching ship closer with every passing hour. It took the better part of one of those hours for the crew to mount a pair of long nine pounder cannons on the Maiden's stern, and another hour after that the ship began to approach their cannon's range. Chibs ordered the elevation on both guns to be run all the way up and a pair of warning shots to be fired. The result was two plumes of seawater shooting high into the air.

"Keep an eye on them Renly," he told the Maiden's gunner, "once they get closer to range we will have to let them know we have some fight left in us."

"Aye, Chibs," he gestured over the deck of the ship, "not much, by the look of it."

Chibs nodded and chewed at the stem of his pipe. "Not as much as we would have, no, but still more than most. See if you can't plug a couple of holes into the bastards as they approach. That might give them a reason to hold back, which is all we need."

Renly stood from where he had been looking down the barrel of one of the nine pounders and gave Chibs a hard stare. "All we need for what?" He paused and furrowed his brows into a deep frown. "Does the captain have a scheme? Is there a plan to best these bastards?"

"In a way," Chibs replied while averting his eyes out to sea. Renly was an experienced man at sea. Chibs knew that if anyone understood the danger the Maiden was in, it was him.

"What is it?" Renly pressed.

Chibs chewed at his pipe and remained silent for a moment while scanning his eyes over the sea. He couldn't avoid the question for long. The approaching ship would be within range before the sun set. Darkness would be their only savior. Darkness, and cunning. But not all of them would be saved. "The captain has a plan. She will announce it to the crew when the time is right. That's all I can say for now."

"What is this?" Lilith voice cut through the gap of wind and waves that filled the awkward silence between Chibs and Renly.

Chibs gnawed at his pipe stem furiously, hoping to avoid a confrontation between them. He knew the plan wouldn't sit well with many aboard the Maiden, Renly being one of them. "Renly was asking what the plan is, Cap'n. I'm sure many of the crew want to know. It's no secret that we can't outrun them, and everyone knows that we are in no shape for a fight."

Lilith narrowed her glaring eye. Her hands trembled on the pommel of her cutlass. Chibs watched her as her gaze drifted from him and fell on the ship pursuing the Maiden. With a sudden turn, she looked over the deck of the ship she commanded and heaved herself up onto the fragments of intact quarterdeck railing.

"Crew of the Drowned Maiden!" Lilith shouted, "The Maiden's final hours are upon us! We are being pursued by a ship of unknown allegiances. She is faster than we are, we cannot run for long. Our ship is damaged, our crew is at half strength at best and we don't know how many more pirate hunters and navy ships there are out there." She paused and swayed as the breeze tugged the stay line in her grip. "This fine ship has liberated so many of us from the bondage we were trapped by. I won't stand idle and watch while chains are shackled to any of your wrists or ankles." The deck of the Maiden remained silent but for a few grunts of assent. "We are sailing for the South American coast and we should sight land with the moon's rising. When we get close enough to shore, I want you all to abandon ship. I will keep a small company here aboard the Maiden to fire her guns and fight off the enemy for as long as we can. We do this, so that you may have a chance at freedom and a better life somewhere in South America."

Chibs watched while the captain's words settled in with the crew. Wind whipped at his beard and tousled his stained linen shirt while the constant sound of water breaking along the Maiden's bow rippled through the air. A rush of heat beat into his face and he could feel his cheeks growing redder with every heartbeat. He pulled his pipe from the grip of his bite and raised his voice for all to hear, "I know what many of you are thinking. I know you don't want to abandon the ship, or the captain. But, this is what the Maiden set out to do. To free you. This is what Cap'n James would have wanted, and its what Cap'n Lilith has commanded. Now, load all the guns and run them out. We're going to make one hell of a racket when the rest of you are rowing to shore!"

'U.S.S United States'
10 June 1809
26 degrees 35' N, 76 Degrees 54' W

The shine and glare of sunrise sparkled against the sea. It made identifying the newly sighted vessel nearly impossible even as the ships closed with each other. To the naked eye, a silhouette could be seen, though it distinguished nothing more than the fact that a ship was indeed closing on them from the east while they were also sailing away from what Captain Woodhaven presumed was H.M.S Cutlass. He was in between a rock and a hard place. The Cutlass had the weather gauge on him and would be able to freely maneuver while firing her guns. The United States in turn had the advantage of being windward to the newly sighted vessel, but he could only press that advantage as long as he stayed out of Cutlass's range. He felt like he had been lowered from the edge of a sizzling skillet only to be dropped into the fiery tongues of a raging inferno. His plan to make turns with the wind at his beam and fire successive broadsides at the approaching warship had been thrown into upheaval as soon as the newly arrived ship had been sighted, just as his first lieutenant stated in his off hand comment. Their tactical situation had gone from slightly unfavorable to an impending disaster.

The captain squinted his eyes against the glaring sunlight. Whatever her nation of origin, the ship to the east was in, or near, United States' class. Even through the shine and glimmer of sunlight on the sea he counted three masts. The hull didn't seem to sit out of the water quite enough for a big ship of the line, but she was no sloop or brigantine either.

"Mr. Smith, our speed if you would," Captain Woodhaven said in a dead calm voice.

Lieutenant Smith turned to the quarterdeck where a

pair of midshipmen were just about to begin taking a reading. "Run your line."

"Aye, sir," one of the midshipmen replied before dropping the weighted line into the water. He let the fibrous threads drift through his fingers as the ship continued sailing while another midshipman watched as sand passed through the bottle neck of a small hourglass.

"Time!" The midshipman watching the glass called out. His seized the escaping line in his grip and began to haul it in hand over hand while counting knots.

"Twelve knots, sir," the midshipman hauling in the weighted line called out. "Near enough to thirteen to account for."

"Very well, thirteen knots," Lieutenant Smith recounted before turning toward his captain. "Twelve knots by reading, sir. Near enough thirteen to make out reckoning by."

"Thirteen knots it is then," Captain Woodhaven replied before gesturing out over the stern. "How far away would you put her then? Your best estimation, of course."

The lieutenant stared out over the stern and narrowed his eyes. He remained silent for a solid minute before turning to the captain with his reply. "I would say she is near enough to a mile, sir. Gaining to be sure, but still a mile off our stern."

"Right," Captain Woodhaven replied. "And the added elevation we will get from our natural list with the wind. How much would you say that will add to our range?"

"That is hard to say, sir," Lieutenant Smith said with a deepening frown. "I can't even fathom the equation we would need to start that figure."

"It's quite simple, lieutenant. We fire at elevation and determine the distance between impact and hull, then wait the requisite amount of time for our adversary to cross into range before firing an accurate volley." Captain Woodhaven said with a grin. "It's a bit like stabbing into the dark at first, but, when we successfully range her, when we do mass our fire it should prove to be effective."

"Stabbing into the dark," Lieutenant Smith repeated. "And what of the other ship? The one approaching from the east?"

Captain Woodhaven squinted against the morning sun and faced the easterly vessel. "She is beating close haul, not an ideal point of sail for an engagement, I'm sure you would agree. Judging by her size, I would say she is a threat to consider. But, while we are still upwind of her, we will carry out our planned maneuvers. If she is a neutral vessel, she will turn to and sail away. If she is hostile, I imagine she will make her intentions known once cannon fire begins to fly. Either way, the answer will present itself. If we are to be trapped by an enemy on both sides, lieutenant, its best we prepare to repel borders and defend the ship with everything we have." He paused and looked around the deck of the United States. Men were preparing for the next maneuver, climbing shrouds and ratlines with muskets over their shoulders and pistols tucked into their belts. The marines were crowded into the fighting tops and strung along the ship's railing amidships. He drew breath in through his nostrils and lowered his voice so the lieutenant would be the only man to hear him. "If it comes to it, lieutenant, we must deny them the prize. If we cannot hold the ship, she must go below the sea or up in flames. Is that understood?"

Lieutenant Smith's eyes widened. His skin seemed to go a translucent shade of pale and Captain Woodhaven thought he even caught the young officer's hands trembling. "Aye, sir. They will not have the ship."

"If it comes to that," the captain said with an encouraging nod. "But, we aren't there yet. Hell, for all we know the ship to the east could be a damned Frenchman. They would just as soon join our battery against a Brit."

"Yes, sir. I'm sure they would," Lieutenant Smith's expression of shock finally broke into a smile.

Captain Woodhaven paced from the starboard railing aft to the edge of the stern. He withdrew his collapsing brass telescope and extended the instrument to its full length before holding it up to one eye. Through the slight distortion of the glass he focused as best he could on the ship pursuing United States from the west. Her bow line was bluff, and the figure of a carved woman was proudly displayed beneath her bowsprit.

"A man of war indeed. If that isn't the Cutlass, I'll be a thrice damned fool. They were laying in wait for us, and I sailed us right into the teeth of their guns. They could have let fly with a broadside the moment they saw us."

"But, sir. They didn't," Lieutenant Smith offered with a frown. "Why do you suppose they didn't?"

Captain Woodhaven shrugged off the lieutenant's concern. "Who knows? My point is that they got the drop on us, again. It won't happen a third time." He pulled the telescope away from his eye and focused for a moment with his naked vision before replacing the instrument. "Come about, hard over larboard until our battery bears on them, lieutenant. Fire a ranging shot and let's see where we stand. Maybe the threat of accurate fire will dissuade them."

U.S.S United States' decks shifted as the helmsman put the wheel over for a hard turn to larboard. In the tops, sailors scrambled to make changes as the ship shifted in relation to the wind. Orders flew through the rigging and footfalls thundered over the deck. The ship wheeled with her larboard turn and came about with her larboard battery bearing down against the bow of the British pursuer.

"Fire when ready, lieutenant," Captain Woodhaven ordered.

"Aye, sir. Fire when ready," Lieutenant Smith repeated before relaying the order below to the gun deck.

Moments passed and Captain Woodhaven felt his heartbeat accelerating inside of his chest. The bow of the pursuing warship continued her onslaught against the sea in front of her, rolling white capped ridges of water away from the timbers of the ship. A single shot ruptured the calm of the morning air and sent a cloud of bluish white smoke into the breeze. The smoke disappeared as steady winds brushed it over the deck of the ship and out over the seas eastward. Every eye on the United States turned toward the western horizon as captain and crew alike waited with wide eyes and held breath. A plume of seawater shot skyward. It was in line with the British warship's hull and near enough that sailors on her bow would get a taste of the salty water if they happened to be looking forward. Captain Woodhaven smiled. He imagined the reaction of the British commander. Accurate fire at the very far edge of cannon range, the ultimate answer to the British doctrine of yardarm to yardarm slugfest combat. He would finesse his ship through her course and batter the Brits as they approached. United States was fast enough to keep them at bay for as long as he desired, and the damage he could inflict in only a few volleys of fire would almost certainly slow the Cutlass.

"Another three minutes and then fire each gun in turn," Captain Woodhaven said in a flat tone. "We will score some hits and then turn back with the wind. In this manner she will pay for every hour she pursues us."

A distant boom echoed over the sea. Several shouts from the men of United States warned the crew of incoming fire and sent men on deck diving for cover while Captain Woodhaven stood fast with his telescope in hand. A wisp of blue gray smoke drifted on the wind away from bow of the Cutlass. The shot whistled through the air, its sound grew in intensity until it reached an ear piercing crescendo before the cannon ball splashed into seawater just a few dozen yards aft of United States' stern.

"They'll need to do better than that, won't they boys?" Captain Woodhaven growled as his crew picked themselves up from the deck and resumed their tasks. He turned to Lieutenant Smith who was running his hands over his uniform coat and straightening his hat as he picked himself up from the deck. "Fire in turn, lieutenant. Let's see how our gunnery compares to theirs."

The order was relayed in turn and within moments a booming report sounded from United States' gun deck. Gun smoke cleared with the wind and Captain Woodhaven raised his telescope to focus on the Cutlass. Seconds passed. The captain drew a slow breath to steady his focus. His eye remained steady on the bow of the Cutlass as her hull broke through the sea and sent a steady ripple of white capped water away at an angle. Through the hazy focus of his telescope, Captain Woodhaven watched the starboard rail of Cutlass erupt with the shock of impact. Wood exploded and went flying and dozens of sailors on the deck of the Royal Navy ship dove for cover.

"A hit!" Lieutenant Smith shouted. A cheer arose from the United States' crew.

"Lieutenant Smith, fire in turn the rest of the battery," Captain Woodhaven ordered as the cheers and shouts carried on the wind. "Then bring us about hard over, I want to keep her at this range."

The lieutenant repeated his order down the weather hatch to the gun deck and a series of thundering reports issued forth from United States' larboard battery. Pluming clouds of gun smoke swept over the deck before being carried eastward over the sea and giving the climbing dawn sun an ethereal haze. As the last gun sounded, top men and helm acted in turn and the deck of United States began to shift into a hard starboard turn eastward. Captain Woodhaven kept his focus on the Cutlass as the last shots of his volley sliced through the air toward the pursuing warship. He switched between watching with his naked eye and peering through the brass telescope. A plume of seawater ruptured skyward off of the warship's bow and then another before the ship showed signs of an impact directly to her hull. One of her sails shuddered violently before a large tear revealed itself through the soft focus of the captain's telescope. A shockwave of splinters and broken timber revealed another direct hit on the hull before the bowsprit erupted into a mess of shattered wood and recoiling rope. Several more shots impacted the Brit's railing along her starboard bow and one snapped her forward mainsail spar. Each successful hit gave Captain Woodhaven a spark of hope.

"We will punish her for every hour of pursuit before turning to and taking the ship," he muttered to himself, knowing full well the odds were far heavier in the enemy's favor. "I have the advantage of gunnery, and the crew is ready. Today, I will have my revenge."

"Captain!" A voice cried down from the fighting tops. "The ship to the east! She's coming about!"

11

'Drowned Maiden'
22 May 1809
12 Degrees 45' N, 72 Degrees 32' W

The words echoed through her soul. They reached out through time and distance, creeping in from her subconscious like the shadow of a memory. "We have no choices here," the voice said before fading away and then returning to her thoughts with, "There is only one way that path ends." The voice was soft and caring but carried a biting edge of fear, fear that Lilith was only too familiar with. Lilith tried to shrug off the voice of her mother as it reached from beyond the grave. She had forged her own path, a path where she did have choices. Freedom. She had won herself freedom. She had torn away the shackles the world had tried to place her in. She had turned the tables on her enemies and in the process tore away the shackles from scores of others. But, the words kept haunting her. As the sun sank low, they came to haunt her again.

"There is only one way that path ends."

The spray of the sea seemed to lack its usual feeling of cool refreshment. The wind at her back seemed hotter than it ever had before. The Drowned Maiden's decks didn't hold the hope they once had, she was a dying ship on her final journey. Lilith looked aloft at the filled form of canvas sails that for the last few years had been a comfort to her. Those sails had carried her wherever she desired. They had kept her out of reach from the arms of those who would see her bound back into chains of torment and despair. Their promise seemed hollow now, as the ship they carried slogged through the sea toward her doom. The Drowned Maiden was a shell of her former self, an aged shadow of what she had been. The shadows of evening grew long, but despite the sun's retreat toward the horizon a muggy heat had set in. The breeze seemed to thicken as a bank of dark clouds formed in the northern skies and Lilith could almost feel the impending storm. A puff of smoke and the rich smell of pipe tobacco announced Chibs' arrival on the quarterdeck.

"A bit of nautical weather may work in our favor, Cap'n," He said through his bite, smoke trailing as his words spilled out. "Not that we could escape either way. She's taken on enough water, high seas are just as likely to sink us as anything. But, our new friends off the stern will have to take in sail. Could be they lose us."

Lilith looked north and west at the warship chasing after the Maiden. "She'll be on us before the storm hits, Chibs. The best we can hope for is that our crew manages to get to shore before it gets too rough for the small boats."

A pair of puffs in rapid succession indicated that Chibs was deep in thought. Lilith looked at him from the corner of her eye. His eyes were narrowed, and his jaw was set forward so that his graying beard rested against his chest. "I've turned it over in my mind, Cap'n. Over and over. And it doesn't sit right with me," Chibs drew in a breath of pipe smoke and exhaled through his nose. "Why don't you go with them? The crew going ashore. You could-"

"I will not," Lilith interrupted. "This is my ship. She went down once, and I was prepared to go with her. This time, there will be no escape, and I will go down with my ship while giving every chance I can to Jilhal and Omibwe and the rest of the crew." She drew in breath and savored the smell of Chibs' pipe smoke. "We sail to our fate, Chibs. There is no escaping it this time."

"She should last until we get close enough to the coast for the small boats, Cap'n. Last I checked, there was three feet of water in the hold. It's rising. We are taking on water somewhere. I can't find a breach in our hull, but that doesn't mean there isn't one somewhere." Chibs drew a few puffs from his pipe and shifted his elbow to lean against the shattered remains of Maiden's railing. "I figure if we can set the crew to rowing ashore, our guns should be able to keep our enemy at bay for a time."

"All we need is to buy time for our people to get ashore. After that is done, we will greet our fate with sword in hand and cannons roaring."

Chibs smile broke wide, revealing his smoke-stained teeth and a redness in his cheeks. "Aye, Cap'n! That we will, that we will."

The Maiden slogged along through the waning hours of evening as the sun finally dipped to the western horizon and sent a haze of varying shades of orange, red and violet in streaks that arced high over head and mingled with the first appearance of stars. The formation of clouds along the northern horizon crept on a southerly course and sent sporadic jags of lighting down toward the sea. Through the distance, they looked like a towering wall that hung over the sea. On deck, the crew was readying small boats and rigging the ship to be maneuvered by a skeleton crew.

"You can't mean it, captain," Omibwe said from his place behind the ship's wheel.

Lilith looked over and realized he had been in earshot of her entire conversation with Chibs. "I do, Omi. You go with your mother ashore. She will need you far more than the ship does, or me."

"You are just going to give up?" Omiwbe asked with his hands planted firm on the helm. "After all we have been through. After all of the people you have set free? I don't believe that there is no way out."

"Clever plans won't work this time, I'm afraid," Lilith replied with her hands resting on the hilt of her sword. "If we sail to the coast, some of you may be able to escape and make lives for yourselves. If we continue to sail in an effort to escape this pursuit, eventually, we will be outnumbered by ships. There are pirate hunters and navy ships out there searching for us. That path only ends with our entire crew in chains or dead. If I can buy you and your mother a chance at freedom, true freedom, then I will do whatever it takes to see that outcome."

A distant shot echoed through the evening's dying light. Lilith turned and found a trail of smoke rising from the bow of the warship pursuing her. Her heart fluttered and her hands went cold. A whistle rose in the air and Chibs shouted a warning for the crew to take whatever cover they could. Lilith, unconcerned with the consequences of a cannonball impact, remained on her feet. She paced to the stern railing as a burning ball of defiance rose within her. The whistle grew in intensity before suddenly fading away as a geyser of seawater erupted within fifty yards of the Maiden's stern. They were almost within the warship's range. But, that meant the warship would be near the range of their own stern guns.

"Chibs," Lilith called without moving her glare.

"Aye, Cap'n?" Chibs said as he pulled himself back to his feet.

"It's time to return fire," Lilith said. "Let them know they face a stout fight ahead if they continue their pursuit."

Chibs ambled his way to the nine pounder cannon that Captain Lilith had ordered mounted at the stern. With a grin he patted the iron cannon. "This old girl will show them a thing or two. I've got her rear wheels un-shipped and a brace plate beneath the front of her carriage." He looked back at Lilith with a devilish grin.

"We might just have a reach that they don't."

The salted old quartermaster leaned down over the cannon and laid his head along the barrel. A puff of smoke wisped into the air, followed shortly by another. Lilith watched as he stood up and shot a quick glance over his shoulder. "She'll do," he said through another cloud of smoke. He stepped to the side of the gun carriage and took hold of the braided lanyard attached to the flint firing mechanism and shouted, "Tally ho!" The cannon roared to life and bucked with the enormous force of recoil as it belched out a cloud of gray blue smoke and cinders. Chibs pulled his pipe from in between his clenched teeth and arched his back to shout, "Chew on those biscuits you sorry dog flogging bastards!"

Lilith focused on the bow of the warship in the failing light of sunset. She waited for the plume of seawater that she knew would be sent skyward by the shot as it fell short and dove into the sea. To her surprise, and delight, a distant crash reverberated through the breeze and the telltale shock-wave of shattered wood rippled across the front of the warship. A cheer rose from the decks and rigging of the Maiden. They had scored a hit even while their enemy had shown the failing reach of their cannons. Lightning struck in Lilith's blood. Could they survive this encounter? She dared not hope for victory, the odds were too far against her. Turning to face her adversary would be suicide. But, if she could score hits and run with everything the Maiden had in her, they may just escape with their lives.

"Chibs," Lilith snapped.

"Aye, Cap'n?" Chibs replied in a hearty voice.

"Keep firing, land as many as you can on her bow. Don't let up. We may just be able to convince them to heave to and turn off."

Chibs ambled to the side of the gun carriage while a pair of hands made it ready to fire again. "Aye, aye Cap'n. Fire away as she bears!"

For the briefest of moments, Lilith could see herself escaping the fate she had imagined. Light was failing, the shadows of night were stretching their inky fingers over the surface of the sea and would soon envelope both the Maiden and her foe in their dark clasp. Her ship was wounded, but she was still sailing. If she could keep on going just a little while longer, the night could cover their escape. Possibilities opened in her mind. A hard turn. Doused lights and quiet on deck. They could let their foe slip by them and beat a course northward toward Haiti. It could be done. They had been through tight scrapes before, they could wriggle their way out of this. It was only one ship.

The thought hit her as hard as if it had been a twelve pounder shot dropped from the highest yard in the rigging. It was only one ship that chased her now. But, according to the pirate hunter whose innards she had laid open for the sunshine and the world to see, there could be forty more ships prowling the seas in search of her and Batard De Mur. The wind had cooled as the sun slipped beneath the waves of the western horizon, total darkness would soon swallow everything. The kindling of hope that had awakened in her spirit died away like a spark that could not find its tinder. Her hand wrapped around the hilt of her cutlass and squeezed the leather wrapped handle so tight she could feel the blood leaving her fingertips.

"Land! Captain! Land off the starboard bow! Maybe three miles off!"

The cry came down from the forward top. Lilith pulled her blade from its scabbard and let the tip of the sword press into the worn timbers of the deck beneath her feet.

"This is it, then," she said into the wind as if her adversary could hear. "If this is to be my end, so be it."

'H.M.S Redemption'
22 May 1809
12 Degrees 45' N, 72 Degrees 32' W

"Fire!" The gun captain's command was cut off by the roaring blast of the bow cannon. A shockwave rippled through the air while gun smoke filtered away from H.M.S Redemption's bow and the gun captain shouted for his crew to make the cannon ready for another round. "Hurry, lads. Swab the bore and get her powder rammed!"

Captain Pike paid little mind to the flurry of action around his bow guns. His eyes remained locked on the Drowned Maiden. There was no denying it was her. The black flag that flapped in the breeze above her stern erased any doubt in his mind. The grotesque skull with twisted horns protruding from its brow, the canted trident and the length of broken chain that bordered the bottom of the black field. It was her. He was sure of it. He wondered what scheme Lilith and Chibs were hatching to escape him. Over the course of the last several hours, Redemption had slowly closed the gap with the pirate ship until Captain Pike judged that they were nearly within range of his long nine pounder bow guns. He ordered a ranging shot to be fired before fixing his stare on the stern of the ship that had at one point saved his life.

"Right before sending me ashore on a suicide mission and abandoning me to my fate," the captain muttered under his breath. He could still feel the searing hot pain of betrayal in his mind, the bite of razor-sharp barnacles, the crushing feeling of being surrounded by seawater and the hard grip of the shackles that had been on his wrists and ankles. Being keelhauled had been the most excruciating experience of his life. His face, arms, legs and back had been ripped into ribbons. His lungs had filled with seawater. He had literally drowned each time he had been run beneath the hull of North Wind. The practice of keelhauling had fallen to the wayside in the minds of many commanders in the Royal Navy. It was considered cruel, even by those captains who regularly ordered men to be flogged over minor infractions. Ordering a sailor to be hauled under the keel was tantamount to a death sentence. It was a punishment rarely used. Few sailors in the Royal Navy had witnessed a keelhauling, fewer still had survived such an ordeal.

As he studied the stern of the Maiden, the pain came

rushing back to his mind as fresh as if he were experiencing it again for the first time. Admiral Torren had ordered the punishment, but Lilith had set him on that course.

A geyser of seawater plumed up from the surface as the ranging shot fell short of its intended target. The captain narrowed his eyes. Another three hundred yard, slightly to the left, and they would be on target. Three hundred yards could be closed in half a turn, but the sun was setting.

"Mr. Jensen, un-ship the rear wheels and prop the front of those carriages up with a deck plate. I need more range," the captain said without averting his stare.

"Aye, sir," replied Redemption's gunner, Mr. Jensen. "That should give us more range, sir. But, we will be risking those carriages."

"Your concerns are noted, Mr. Jensen. But we are losing daylight and I do not want her to slip through our fingers. Give me the range we need to land hits," Captain Pike said.

"Aye, sir," Mr. Jensen said before turning to the captains of the bow gun crews. "You heard the captain! Un-ship those rear wheels and prop the front of those carriages up with a deck plate. Get to it, lads, we need the reach to get to her before the light gives out!"

Captain Pike pulled his telescope from inside of his uniform coat and extended the instrument to its full length. The Drowned Maiden appeared to be in sorry shape, worse even than when he had crossed paths with them last. He lifted the brass tube to his right eye and studied her in the waning light of evening. Her railing was freshly damaged. There were holes and tears in her sails, and it appeared that the fantail window array had been ravaged. Not a single pane of glass remained intact. His gaze wandered from the cabin area up to the stern railing where it landed on a pair of iron cannons. A burly man in a ragged shirt could barely be made out through the hazy focus, he was standing next to one of the gun carriages. A wisp of smoke rose from where the stout man was standing.

"Ah, Mr. Chibs," Captain Pike said aloud, "no doubt he is un-shipping his carriage wheels and bracing a deck plate as well." He smiled as he thought of it. It had been Chibs who had taught him the old gunner's trick in the first place. His smile faded quickly though, when a brilliant flash filled the view of his telescope and a cloud of cannon smoke erupted from one of the Maiden's stern guns. Chibs already had his gun set for the added elevation.

"Down! All hands, get down, take cover!" Captain Pike turned and shoved the sailor closest to him to the deck before grabbing the lapel of Mr. Jensen's uniform coat and pulling him to the deck. The whistle of an incoming shot pierced the air. Captain Pike could feel the impact coming in his bones even before it arrived, it made the scar tissue on his back burn with the hot pain of treachery. As his body sprawled onto the deck timbers, the shot found its mark high on Redemption's bow. Wood cracked and shattered. Men screamed in sudden agony as shards of the ship went flying and found flesh. She had scored the first hit.

"Lieutenant Thatcher, damage report if you please!" the voice of Lieutenant Dodran cut through the screams and patter of falling shards of wood. "Mr. Jensen, ready those guns and return fire as they bear!"

Captain Pike struggled to his feet. A pain shot through his brow and radiated along the side of his head. He reached his hand up and touched his fingers to the side of his forehead. Sticky warm blood oozed from a cut just a few inches from his right eye. His balance faltered for a heartbeat. The captain withdrew his hand and examined his fingers covered in his own bright red blood. "Well done, Lilith. But, it will take more than this to avert your undoing." He looked around his feet and found the collapsible telescope he had been using when the incoming fire had started. With unsteady knees, he bent down and retrieved the sectioned brass tube and paced to the base of the bowsprit while fighting through a wave of shock and nausea. The captain lifted his telescope up to his left eye and studied the ship. The sun had slipped completely beneath the western horizon and ambient light from the sun was fading fast. The Drowned Maiden had become a dark form in the late glow of evening. She was listing to one side, no doubt she had been damaged in some encounter, but deep in his bones Captain Pike knew that the salty old quartermaster, Chibs, would try to use that to his advantage.

"Three points over starboard and adjust those jibs, we'll gather some speed at a stronger point of sail and close this gap!" Mr. Bush, the sailing master shouted through his brass speaking trumpet.

"Belay that order," Captain Pike said over the sailing master's shoulder, "Bring her about larboard, three points should do. Keep her stern facing us, Mr. Bush and keep us on the same sailing point."

"But, captain, you said we need to close the gap-" Mr. Bush began to reply.

"Aye, I did," Captain Pike interrupted, "but she is listing to her larboard. They will try to use that added elevation on their starboard battery to land more hits against us, mark my words. Come about larboard and bend every sail we have. We will close the gap and bring our guns to bear right on her fantail. With any luck we can take out her rudder and then pummel her as she drifts."

"Land in sight! Three points from starboard!" The call echoed down from the forward lookout high in the rigging. "And it looks like the pirates are turning starboard, they are lowering their small boats off the larboard side!"

The captain managed a grin as Mr. Bush's eyes widened at the announcement. He handed over the telescope in his clasp and nodded to his sailing master. "Let's get to it Mr. Bush, we haven't any time to lose. It sounds to me like they are preparing to abandon ship. I would rather deal with them out on the open water than in the damned jungle."

"Aye, sir." Mr. Bush replied before repeating the captain's orders through his speaking trumpet. "As you were! Three over larboard and bring about that jib. Keep her tight at broad reach and let fly with those royals!"

Captain Pike walked aft along Redemption's starboard rail. All around him sailors were helping wounded men to their feet or carrying away those who could not stand. Orders flew across the deck like whizzing shots from muskets and the deck of the ship shifted onto her new course. Within minutes Redemption was clipping along under the power of every sail she could fly and rapidly closing the sea gap with her enemy. Her new course would bring the starboard battery to bear for a raking pass at the Drowned Maiden's stern while avoiding her starboard battery altogether. By the time Lilith and Chibs recognized what he had planned it would be too late. If they turned any further to their starboard, they would risk putting their sail in irons with the wind, stalling her speed and surrendering themselves to full broadside on their beam. The thought brought him satisfaction, but no joy.

"Mr. Jensen, have the starboard battery ready and run out," the captain shouted over his right shoulder.

"Aye, starboard battery ready and run out!" Mr. Jensen replied before echoing the order below to the gun deck.

A succession of wooden clunks rattled from the starboard side of Redemption's hull as her battery cannons were run out into their firing positions. Rumbling wheels and creaking ropes cried out as the gun crews labored to muscle their cannons into place.

"Gun one ready," the first gun captain shouted.

"Gun three ready," the next gun captain's voice

came right after the first.

"Gun five, ready!"

"Gun seven ready!"

Each gun crew ran their cannons out into position and their respective captains reported to the battery commander once they were ready and in position to fire. Captain Pike looked over the starboard railing and scanned along the hull as the cold iron snouts of his cannons protruded outward one by one. His gaze crossed to the Drowned Maiden. Her stern was exposed and Redemption was closing the gap even faster than before. Her dogged turn would fail to bring the pirate's cannons to bear in time to score any hits before Redemption's battery was able to rake her stern. With any luck, the captain thought, their first salvo would render the pirates unable to alter course, and thus unable to defend themselves.

"Lieutenant Dodran, have the starboard battery fire as their guns come to bear, and larboard battery run out and ready," Captain Pike said as he hurried toward the quarterdeck. "Mr. O'Malley, marines to the fighting tops, I want swivel gun and musket fire on their decks as soon as we come about."

"Aye, aye sir!" Mr. O'Malley replied.

"Mr. Bush, once the starboard battery has completed their volley, bring us hard over starboard and lay me alongside pistol shot on their starboard beam."

"Aye, sir. Hard over starboard once the volley is finished and alongside pistol shot of their starboard side."

"We will take some hits, for sure," Captain Pike said,

"but Redemption will carry the day."

Below deck a voice cried out. "Fire!" It was drowned by the thundering roar of a cannon firing. The smell of burned gunpowder wafted into the sea air as a brilliant flash erupted into the dark. Only a heartbeat elapsed before the next gun captain raised his command to fire and sent another roaring shot into the night air. One by one, the starboard battery fired their shots as their guns came to bear against the Drowned Maiden's stern. Captain Pike watched as the ship that had once saved him was hammered by accurate fire. Her stern exploded in blasts of shattered wood, her rudder ruptured into shards and her hull trembled with each successive impact. As the last gun's report sounded, Mr. Bush shouted commands through his brass speaking trumpet and Redemption's hull shifted its course through the sea.

Captain Pike crossed the quarterdeck and closed his right hand around the hilt of his sword. In the fighting tops, marines began firing their muskets in rapid succession. Swivel guns barked to life while musket fire tore into the Maiden's decks and rigging. Lines snapped and wood splintered as lead shot flew through the air. Redemption slowed as her hull passed close by the Maiden. Mr. Bush had taken the liberty of having sails reefed. The Maiden's stern was in shambles, and as her deck slowly came into view through the dark as Redemption pulled alongside, Captain Pike discovered that the damage his raking volley had caused extended well past the pirate ship's fantail. The deck was littered with sprawling bodies, dead and wounded pirates lay in various contortions of pain and panic. The helm was shattered, as were the aft castle stairs on both sides of the deck. A deep gouge showed where a shot had managed to nearly topple her aft mast. But, he saw no signs of Chibs, or Lilith.

"Fire the larboard battery and prepare to board," Captain Pike ordered without averting his stare from the carnage aboard the Maiden.

"Fire!" A vigorous shout echoed from down on the gun deck. The larboard battery erupted into a near simultaneous explosion of reports. The flashes of the cannons lit up the early night like salvos of lightning from a dark storm cloud. Acrid smoke choked the night air as cannon shot smashed into the Maiden from the close range volley. The sound of wood shattering into splinters filled the captain's ears. Spars crashed to the deck, lines snapped and recoiled through the night. Voices cried out in pain.

"Grapples!" The shout came from Mr. O'Malley, Redemption's master at arms. Lines with barbed iron hooks were thrown across and drawn tight as the crew began to draw the Maiden in for a boarding action.

'U.S.S United States'
11 June 1809
26 degrees 28' N, 76 Degrees 47' W

Every eye aboard the U.S.S United States fixated on the ship to the east of them. It was silhouetted by a blazing sunrise, her masts, lines and sails cast shadows ahead of her as her bluff lines tacked over the wind and slipped into a new course. For a moment, it appeared as though the shadowed ship was coming about to bear her guns against United States. Captain Woodhaven squeezed his fingers against the wooden rail of his ship so tight that the grain began to bite his skin.

"Starboard battery at the ready," he commanded over his shoulder. If this was to be a two on one fight, he would make it a memorable end.

A series of wooden thunks sounded as gun ports on the starboard battery were slammed open. Wooden wheels rumbled as gun crews strained to heave out their cannons. Captain Woodhaven strained his eyes against the glaring sunrise. Sunlight shimmered off of the sea and made it nearly impossible to ascertain any detail of the ship beating close haul to the east. Her course change would put her directly through United States' field of fire, but after passing they would have a clear line of fire against United States' stern. A chill formed in Captain Woodhaven's spine. If he turned to now, he would surrender the weather gauge to both vessels. It would not prohibit him from employing his planned tactic of running before the wind and turning to levy accurate fire at interval, but it complicated things. If both ships were in pursuit, he would be hard pressed to effectively hold them at distance. If they both managed to close with him, he would be in jeopardy of losing his ship to the enemy.

"Starboard battery is ready to fire, sir" a midshipman reported from just aft of where Captain Woodhaven stood.

The captain paused and drew a breath of morning air in through his nose. As he squinted against the intense sunrise. "On my order," he said while fighting to make out any detail he could of the ship closing on their position. The wind at his back felt cool and brisk. It carried with it the briny smell of the salty sea. His face was already beginning to feel the heat of the sun. Wind whipped at his ears with the familiar song of slipping waves and creaking lines. Another sound lingered just at the edge of hearing. It was faint at first, barely audible through the sound of United States' bluff bow breaking through the sea and the patter of footfalls on deck.

Captain Woodhaven held up one hand and bellowed a command over his shoulder, "Silence on deck. Still and silent!"

The footfalls ceased. Captain Woodhaven strained his hearing. Over the rush of the wind and the breaking of the sea he could hear a telltale rattle, the beat of a snare drum. Any commander worth his salt would have summoned his crew to quarters on first sighting. They weren't beating to quarters. The shrill whistle of a fife followed. It played a melodic series of notes that Captain Woodhaven recognized. He squinted hard through the glare until the ship's foremost sail occluded the sunrise. The captain felt his heart skip a beat. His mouth went dry while a chill ran up the back of his legs before gripping his spine and sending the hair on his arms to stand on end. Along the ship's rail stood a formation of officers in dark blue uniform coats. As the snare drum rattled its rhythm and the fife continued its melody the officers rendered a sharp salute in unison.

A voice from the forward fighting tops called down, "Captain! She's flying the stars and stripes! It must be the Constitution on her way back from the Barbary coasts!"

Captain Woodhaven lifted his right arm into a sharp salute. His eyes drifted to the stern of the vessel and found red and white stripes with a circle of white stars on a blue field fluttering in the wind as columns of sun broke through the sails and rigging. She was sleek lined and bluff of bow, her sails were pitched as she beat her way close haul past United States beam. He had never felt such relief in all of his days at sea.

"Signal flags, sir," a midshipman shouted from near the quarterdeck. "Make all haste in pursuit of hostile vessel."

Captain Woodhaven lowered his salute and turned inboard. "Bring her about, hard over starboard with the wind. We will beat close haul on Constitution's beam."

"Aye, sir!" the first lieutenant replied before turning and repeating the new orders.

Captain Woodhaven allowed himself a smile. It was a new day at sea, and the constitution was heralding a new age in the world.

12

'H.M.S Redemption'
22 May 1809
12 Degrees 45' N, 72 Degrees 32' W

A hurricane of noise flood Captain Pike's hearing. Pistols and muskets fired, wooden gangplanks were dropped between vessels and a flood of footfalls rumbled as sailors and marines crossed to the deck of the Drowned Maiden. Darkness was broken by muzzle flashes as swivel guns and small arms fire continued. Swords clattered together in a steel on steel death rattle that seemed to grow in intensity with every passing heartbeat. The captain held his saber in one hand and a pistol in the other. His eyes scanned the darkness that had swallowed both ships. He searched every flash of light for signs of Lilith, unsure of what he would do if he saw her. More swords clashed, another salvo of pistols and muskets fired. Flashes of light erupted all across the Maiden's deck. He listened with his hands clasped tight around his weapons, waiting for any sign of Chibs or Lilith, Renly, Omibwe, Jilhal, or the French Doctor LeMeux. Nothing. Just the noise of battle and the cries of the wounded.

"You won't take me alive you bastards!" A familiar voice shouted, "Tell your king he can sit on his damned crown!"

Captain Pike fought the urge to smile. Chibs had always held a deep seated hatred for the Monarch he had once served. He forced himself to take the first step up onto the gangplank. The last time he had been aboard the Drowned Maiden, she was off the coast of Nassau and he thought he had been tasked with presenting the Nassau governor with a forged letter of marque in order to gain a pardon for the Maiden's past crimes. He had been betrayed, abandoned and left to face the consequences for Lilith's treacherous plan. He had paid for it, dearly. With each step, he thought of the sea water invading his lungs as he was keelhauled. He thought of the searing pain across his back and his legs, how his belly and his arms had bled. The sting of the saltwater, the wretched coughing when he was finally hauled up onto North Wind's deck. He thought of the hopelessness he had felt when Admiral Torren had him hauled up on deck in the driving rain to watch while the ship that had saved him was pummeled by broadside after broadside. He thought of how she had faltered and succumbed to the water of that cove. And yet, here she was.

A swivel gun roared from the Maiden's quarterdeck, and Chibs' familiar voice roared, "It's going to take more than a crew of nancy navy boys to take me!" A handful of sailors fell to the shower of riffraff fired from the swivel gun's smoking barrel. Captain Pike flexed the hand he gripped his sword with and started his way across the Maiden's deck. All around him, men were locked into combat. Pirates and sailors fought with sabers and pistols, bludgeons, boarding axes and their bare hands. A crash of broken glass and a pistol shot sent a streak of fire across the Maiden's deck and suddenly Captain Pike could see with clarity what was unfolding across the ship. Chibs stood on the shattered remains of the ship's quarterdeck with a sword in his hand. He had a deep gash in his upper arm and one across his chest. The captain hesitated for a moment when he noticed that part of Chibs' left arm was missing. It hadn't slowed his fervor. He was holding off a pair of Redemption's sailors and at his feet lay the body of a Royal Marine with his throat opened from ear to ear. He slashed his sword at the sailors and caught one of them across the face with the edge of his blade while shouting, "I'll cut every one of you to ribbons before you take me alive!"

Through the glare of flames and the haze of smoke, Captain Pike could see that Chibs intended to make this his final stand. The weather hatch was sealed shut. There would be no access to the lower decks of the Maiden without someone on the inside to open it, or an ax and twenty minutes to force the hatch open. The captain cocked his pistol and raised the weapon to aim through the orange red haze. He looked down the muzzle at the burly, bearded pirate he had once regarded as a friend and pulled the trigger. A flash protruded from his pistol as the weapon recoiled with a snap. Captain Pike narrowed his eyes to see the effects as Chibs stutter stepped for a moment before collapsing his knees to the deck. The shot had caught him high in the chest, but the grizzly old pirate wouldn't surrender that easily. A grimace of pain and rage twisted Chibs' face and he twisted his sword point down to the deck in order to lift himself back onto his feet.

"Chibs!" Captain Pike shouted, "That is enough! Surrender and you will be treated gently."

The old pirate's eyes searched the deck of the ship, lost in the fore and smoke until they landed on the captain. A moment passed. Hatred and pain faded to disbelief and were quickly replaced by disdain.

"She should have left you to drown out there," Chibs growled from somewhere deep in his chest. His words came with much strain and a telltale red froth that stained his lips and teeth.

"She did leave me to die, when it was more convenient for her, but nonetheless," Captain Pike said.

"But here you are, living and breathing," Chibs forced his words. "Turn cloak, turn again. No true north for you boy, just go where the wind blows you."

"Not boy," Captain Pike corrected, "Captain."

"Not mine," Chibs growled before spitting out a glob of blood.

"Where is she?" Captain Pike asked.

Chibs smiled, his blood-stained teeth showing wide like something from the gates of hell itself. "You'll see, boy. You can kill us, but you will never take the ship!"

His words struck an icy pang of fear into the captain's blood. His eyes shifted again to the weather hatch and Chibs let loose with an uproar of gurgling laughter. "Where is she?" Captain Pike demanded.

Chibs lifted his sword and struck out at the nearest sailor while shouting, "You're about to find out!"

As Chibs' blade connected with another sailor from the Redemption's crew, Captain Pike froze with a deadly realization. His eyes drifted over the larboard quarter of the Maiden. Small boats were rowing into the darkness and toward shore. Lilith and the crew never meant to fight them off. The powder magazine.

"All hands! Back to Redemption! Hurry!" Captain Pike screamed, "Pull back to the ship!"

The deck of the Drowned Maiden seemed to go still for a moment as Captain Pike's command was lost in the commotion of battle. Pistols discharged, swords clattered together, some even fought with blunt objects or bare hands. The captain's desperate cry to evacuate the deck of the Maiden was lost in the pitch of fighting. He turned toward Chibs who remained defiantly on his feet with his sword in hand.

"Down to the depths for us, boy. And you're coming with!" Chibs said through a ragged cough.

Captain Pike lifted his sword and struck out at the burly, wounded pirate. His steel was met by Chibs' own. "All hands! Back to the Redemption! Now!" He cried out as loud as he could.

With an arcing faint, Chibs wheeled his sword in recoil from his parry before stabbing forward in a thrust of reckless abandon. His sword found Captain Pike's flesh just above his waist and the salted old pirate drove the blade hard until Captain Pike could feel the back of his uniform coat giving way to the sharp point. A rush of warm blood flooded out of his abdomen. He recoiled at first, but Chibs refused to relent his grip on the hilt of the weapon and pangs of pain radiated through his stomach and back. He wished for one more breath, just one last desperate scream to warn his crew of the impending doom they had all overlooked. Strength left his legs. His knees buckled beneath him before crashing down onto hard deck timbers.

It started as a rumble. The Maiden trembled and groaned; her decks seemed to heave. The weather hatch which had been tightly secured blew off and flew high into the air as a violent explosion ripped through the lower decks of the ship. Another wave of tremors shook timber, iron and canvas and sent deck boards flying into the air. She had done it. She had ignited the powder magazine and doomed everyone aboard to a violent fiery death. The next explosion ripped Captain Pike from his feet with a force that rendered him unconscious. His body flew overboard and slapped onto the sea surface before being dragged under by his own weight. His senses began to return to him as he felt the sea invade his mouth and nose. It pried its way into his eyes and ears before slipping its clasp around his throat to steal the last of his breath and dragging him down to the cold crushing deep.

Thank you for reading the final installment of
Treachery and Triumph
Be on the lookout for more sea stories and for my other series.

Find my other book series, sign up for newsletter announcements including special releases and giveaways. Just scan the QR code below.

Follow along on Facebook and Instagram for cover reveals and special announcements.

If you enjoyed this title, please be sure to leave a review on Amazon or Goodreads.